The PASSOVER COMMANDO

The PASSOVER COMMANDO

by IRVING R. COHEN

CROWN PUBLISHERS, INC., NEW YORK

Inquiries should be addressed to Crown Publishers, Inc., One Park Avenue, New York, N.Y. 10016
Printed in the United States of America
Published simultaneously in Canada by
General Publishing Company Limited

Library of Congress Cataloging in Publication Data

Cohen, Irving R
The Passover commando.

I. Title.
PZ4.C67698Pas 1979 [PS3553.0424]   813'.5'4   78-11442
ISBN 0-517-53631-5

To Marna, who never stopped believing

Force is as pitiless to the man who possesses it, or thinks he does, as it is to its victims; the second it crushes, the first it intoxicates.

Simone Weil, *The Iliad, or The Poem of Force*
(Trans. by Mary McCarthy)

Moses: "I have followed the light into darkness."

Christopher Fry, *The Firstborn*

The
PASSOVER
COMMANDO

Part I

Therefore they did set over them taskmasters to afflict them with their burdens.

Exodus 1:11

1

Power?"

"Power."

"A game?"

"For children?"

"Yes."

"Impossible. They couldn't handle it."

"Have you actually played it?"

Aryeh sat and listened, sipping his third hot Tuaca and water, giving only surface attention to the conversation. The words he heard were already sliding into each other, but he did not care; the evening promised a variety of pleasures, and intellectual stimulation was far down on the list.

The bar's background music had already shifted from the afternoon's folk rock and Bluegrass into the early evening's baroque; off in a corner of the room a flute made love to a harpsichord and was rewarded with murmured assurances of devotion.

He found a little more room under the small table and slid down into his movie-watching position so that he could feast his eyes on the woman's face.

Her hair and eyes were dark, and her face ivory; Ivanhoe's Rebecca must have looked like that, he thought. No, it would have been King Ahasuerus' Esther. But neither one would have spoken in public with such vivacity, or spread her net for so many men at once.

As she spoke, her eyes engaged each man in the circle in turn, as if she were interested in his response alone, as if her story were for his ears only.

"I've never done it myself," she said, "but it's really very simple. You put blue, yellow, and white chips into a bowl, as many chips as there are children in the class, and each child takes one without looking into the bowl. There are only a few blue chips, more of the yellow, but most of them are white.

"Those who pick a blue chip can give orders to those with yellow or white, the ones with the yellow chips can give orders only to the white, and the holders of the white chips have to take orders from the other two kinds."

"And then?"

"Then, some of the children find out what it's like to be under somebody's control all the time and take orders, like 'Pick up my pencil!' or 'Get me a drink!' And some of the orders go too far, like 'Give me your lunch!' and slowly the group begins to set its own limit on power."

Aryeh let the discussion wander away from him again, content with watching the play of expression on her face, the grace with which she involved her listeners (innocence? guile?). He looked past her at the long crowded bar, the weathered barn paneling on the walls, the asparagus fern and English ivy hanging in baskets suspended from the ceiling, and finally back to the group on whose perimeter he sat. The tables were small and crowded together, and strangers drifted in and out of each other's conversations.

A statement provoked a burst of laughter, and a voice replied, "Even for third graders, that'd be awfully precocious. Especially for third graders."

The first speaker said, "Remember what Kissinger claimed, that power was the ultimate aphrodisiac?"

"Now be serious," the woman said in mock severity.

"Serious, serious? How can we be serious in the face of such childish nonsense?"

4

Aryeh did not remember having heard the voice before. It was resonant, assured (actor? courtroom lawyer?), but overcontrolled, the voice of a man who had had too much to drink, knew it, and was trying to conceal the fact.

Beyond the precision with which the man spoke, there was a trace of accent, soft enough to be attractive, but not strong enough for easy identification, although he thought he caught an intonation he had once described as "Walter Slezak charming."

He leaned forward so that he could see the speaker. The man was middle-aged, in a range somewhere between the late forties and mid-fifties. Whatever color his hair had been, it was not yet either gray or silver, but was fading toward the buckwheat tone that aged unstained redwood ultimately reaches.

Aryeh could not see his eyes, but his profile was strong, and his face almost unlined. His clothes had the quality of hand-tailoring, and sat lightly on a frame that seemed younger than the face.

"Of course it's childish, or anyway, childlike," said the woman. "After all, we're talking about third graders. But what makes you say 'nonsense'?"

"Yes, Dieter," someone said, "speak up."

"Well," Dieter said, "you talk about Kissinger. Yes, he knows something of power. But ultimately, he does not know the essence of it, its very heart. And even if I underestimate him, and he does understand power, he has never truly experienced it."

When the woman made a sound, he held up his hand and said, "That surprises you? No, it is not surprising. Kissinger, you see, deals with all the trappings of power, the rituals, the symbols, the staged performances for the people to look at on television. But even in private, in all those rooms where they confer, sign treaties, agree on their pacts, they come no more to the core of power than your sweet little children and their colored chips."

He leaned forward and patted the woman on the thigh. It seemed to Aryeh that his hand lingered a moment longer than was necessary, or perhaps as long as he himself would have liked to rest his hand on that inviting terrain. The thought disappeared when Dieter began talking again, and to his surprise, he found himself listening intently.

"Instead of your little yellow, blue, and white chips, they have pieces of paper, of parchment, with many signatures and melted wax seals, but still they are all merely pieces of paper. The point is, they are all very far removed from the people those pieces of paper are supposed to affect.

"If anything happens to those people, Kissinger is not there; he reads about it in the newspapers, just like us. And perhaps by the time the people are supposed to be affected, another piece of paper has been signed, canceling the first. That may be power of a sort, but not real power."

He's wrong, Aryeh thought, he's merely juggling words. It's a shallow recitation, but phrased well, and his delivery makes it sound meaningful. He leaned forward and asked, "Given what you've been saying, how would you define what you call real power?"

The woman fed him a smile, turned back to Dieter, and demanded, "Yes, give us an example."

Dieter hesitated, but as others in the group joined in, he nodded. "I'll show you what I mean."

He picked up his margarita, flicked his tongue at the salted rim, took a sip, and leaned back. He closed his eyes and Aryeh thought for a moment that he had fallen asleep. When he opened them and began talking, his speech was slurred, but the words were clear.

"Let us think of a country road, in the very late winter or early spring. The sun is shining through the white birches, and there are pretty little flowers pushing up through the patches of snow.

"On this road, moving along it, there is a command car and a truck and behind them, a column of people marching. They come to an open spot in the woods, a kind of meadow, and everybody stops.

"The people, there are perhaps forty, fifty of them. They are, let us say, Russians, Poles . . ."

He stopped, as if an inner censor had issued a warning, but he paused so briefly that the interruption passed almost unnoticed.

6

"Anyway, an officer says to the sergeant, 'Pass out the shovels.' After the shovels are passed to the people, or most of them, the sergeant says 'Dig,' and the people dig.

"When the officer is satisfied, he says 'Collect the shovels.' After the shovels are collected, he says to the gunners, 'Shoot.' The gunners shoot and the people, the forty, fifty, they all fall into the grave they have just dug for themselves."

When he stopped speaking, there was a silence which seemed to Aryeh to drown out all the other sounds in the room. Then, suddenly, a number of voices all at once: words of disbelief, murmurs of horror, and someone saying, "You know, I saw Steve McQueen in a movie about something like that on TV the other night."

But for Aryeh the country road had taken on the feeling of a dimly remembered reality, of a place he had almost seen. It may have been because of the sureness of the voice, or the alcohol inside of him, or perhaps a draft from the front door, but he found himself shivering.

He leaned forward and, almost anticipating the answer, asked, "Did you ever actually see anything like that?"

Dieter looked around the circle of faces, hesitated, and then said, "No, not exactly. That is to say, a friend of mine, an acquaintance, was the one who gave the order."

One of the listeners said "Some friend!" and Dieter added quickly, "You asked me, and I told you. But do not judge him too quickly. It was a long, long time ago, and I know the man; he will continue to pay the price for that one single day until he is lowered into his own grave."

As he continued, Aryeh hastily erected a mental blackboard, quickly chalked on it the heading "Why I Should Be Forgiven," and stood in front of it with a pointer, projecting onto it Dieter's phrases, winking at one, smiling at another, nodding to still others, as one would in the company of old familiar friends with whom there is no need to use words of greeting.

It's such a familiar litany, Aryeh thought, I wonder if they were taught it in school: Nazi Germany, a boy educated without knowledge or memory of democracy, brainwashing through mass spectacles, the war, the slow realization of guilt, the burden carried, all that and more.

"You talk about Steve McQueen," Dieter said. "I saw an old film about the American war in the Pacific. The GI's are pinned down by Japanese machine-gun fire somewhere on Guadalcanal, and the sergeant, the tough but good-hearted kind, is killed. One of the men says, 'Let's get those slant-eyed yellow rats for the sergeant,' and they attack."

When one of the men in the group twisted his lips in disgust, Dieter stopped and pointed his finger at him in triumph and said. "You see! You are offended. That's just it. No one of us here today would think of using such language to describe people. But your parents, the people who saw that film during the war, they were not offended. That is the way they thought then.

"Believe me, I am not comparing the two things, but I ask you, if you judge him, remember the way people looked at things then, not the way we look at things now."

After a brief silence the conversation drifted away to other channels, but Dieter and the woman, now sitting next to each other, were deep in conversation, her dark eyes intent on his face.

I don't believe it, Aryeh said to himself. I don't believe it. What he talked about made no difference to anybody here. Their attention span must have lasted for all of five minutes.

An acquaintance came by carrying a chessboard and a box of chessmen. He pointed at Aryeh and motioned at an empty table, but Aryeh waved him away.

He was angry, knew he was angry, and briefly wallowed in his anger before he realized that it was not a single anger he felt, but multiple angers: anger at the way the shape of the evening had changed, at the woman for her growing involvement with the man named Dieter, at the group for its casual acceptance of the horror presented to them, and at Dieter himself for having presented it so vividly.

"White birches," he muttered, "pretty flowers." Who would remember details like that? No, he argued with himself, let's be fair, that's the kind of thing memory seizes upon to bring an incident alive; the "redemptive detail" is the term you use in class.

But you remember details like that when you experience them yourself, not once removed. He sat up as the implication of what he had been thinking exploded in him: Dieter had not been talking about a "friend"; he had been talking about himself. New anger boiled in him at Dieter for having been there, for having been the man in charge, for having given the orders, for having collected the shovels afterwards, for being alive, still.

Even as his anger grew, his mind fixed on something he had heard in Dieter's recital but could not force into consciousness. He tried to recall it, but it refused to step forward and identify itself. He gave up and tried to forget the whole episode and to recapture the feeling of well-being he had felt before the conversation. The warmth would not return, but his anger had largely subsided when suddenly it leaped out at him.

The pause. That pause, the tiny hesitation when Dieter had said "Forty, fifty of them. Perhaps Russians, Poles . . ." Or what? Lithuanians? Esthonians? Hungarians? Ruritanians? No. He knew the word that would have come next, but did not want to articulate it, not even in the dark, silent crevices of his brain.

And more than that. Dieter had been almost persuasive as he had pleaded his case. His argument that it was too easy and too simple to make judgments on one period from the knowledge and morality of another had more validity than Aryeh wanted to concede at that moment.

But attitudes were one thing, killing another. Killing . . . civilians, he thought firmly. And when Dieter spoke of self-punishment, repentance, guilt, as if he were a character out of Tolstoy, his voice had been calm, almost devoid of feeling. But earlier, when he had been speaking of the killings, even in the midst of what presumably had been a tortured recital, Aryeh thought he had heard a faint whisper of satisfaction and perhaps even pleasure.

Without volition, he made a sound which began as a sigh and ended more like a groan. The woman glanced at him. At the same moment Dieter excused himself, got to his feet, and walked toward the landing leading to the restroom, following a single floorboard with the deliberation of a tightrope walker going blindfolded over Niagara Falls.

"It must be brutal, living with feelings like that," the woman said to Aryeh.

He stared at her, astonished at her sensitivity. "It'll pass, I suppose," he said. "I'll survive."

"You?" she asked, not trying to conceal her scorn. "I was talking about Dieter."

We shall have to do something about Dieter, he told himself. He wrote a brief mental scenario: he would wait until Dieter returned and order another hot Tuaca. He would take a sip or two and then get up to leave. He would stand up clumsily, his sleeve brushing against the glass and knocking it over, the still-hot liquid shooting across the table and pouring directly into Dieter's lap. Nice, he thought, very nice indeed.

He saw it on film: tight shot of a hand placing a drink on the table. Medium shot, Aryeh picks up the glass and puts it to his lips. A 180° pan shot of the bar seen from Aryeh's point of view. Medium shot of Aryeh drinking. Full shot of Aryeh standing, the table, Dieter beyond him, the drink spilling over into Dieter's lap. Slow motion shot of drink going over the table, becoming normal motion as Dieter jumps to his feet.

Enough, he thought, enough. You're being childish. He remembered the final dedication of a strange film he had once shown his class: "To those who express their anger by smashing lettuce for a salad." That's Aryeh, he said to himself, and suddenly decided to leave.

The woman was laughing again and did not look at him as he left. Dieter was coming down the steps as he went up; he tried to think of something to say, something that would congeal the blood in Dieter's veins, but nothing came and Dieter paid no attention to him.

He shivered again as he walked out of the back door and into the rear parking lot. The bar had been warm; the night fog was cold and clammy. His body reacted to the change in temperature and informed him that he should have used the restroom before leaving. He stopped, decided he was in control, and moved toward his car.

As he approached it, he cursed softly. Someone with a car almost the same color as his own had slid dextrously into the narrow slot to the left of his, but so closely that he could not get into it from the driver's side.

As he walked behind the car next to his, his brain translated the message on the personalized license plate: DIETER. He nodded his head with the satisfaction that comes when prejudice begs for justification and is offered the appearance of proof.

As he stared at the plate with revulsion, his bladder once more signaled distress. Turning to go back to the bar, he thought of another solution.

Indeed, indeed, he thought, that would be a very nice touch. He nodded his head in agreement and walked to the driver's side of Dieter's car. The window was covered with moisture but had been left open an inch or so, and he peered inside.

Neat, he thought. Very neat. But it needs something. He hesitated, still looking into the car, knowing he was being foolish, then shrugged off his own warning. He put his hand on the door handle and sighed with relief when he found it locked; he was going to be saved from his own foolishness. "Aryeh, the self-inflicted idiot," he muttered. As he pulled his hand away from the door handle and began turning away, a bright light flooded him.

"This is the police," a voice behind him said. "Put your hands on the roof of the car where we can see them, slow and easy. Careful now."

Even in his slightly befuddled state, he knew enough to obey immediately. The top of the car was wet, and he had to force himself not to jerk his hands away when he touched it. Steps sounded behind him, and then hands patted him intimately and expertly.

"All right, now turn around. What were you doing with that car?"

"Nothing," said Aryeh, quickly. "Nothing at all. I was about to get in and then realized it wasn't my car, just before you called out."

"That's like maybe the hundredth time we've heard that one," said the policeman. "Wouldn't you say, Joe?"

Before the other officer could answer, Aryeh said, "Look, that's my car right next to this one. You can see from the back it's pretty much the same shape, and it's the same color and in the fog I didn't catch the difference.

"Anyway, if you saw me, you know I didn't reach for my keys to open the door, and that's because I knew my own car wasn't locked and this one is."

The policeman named Joe said, "Let's see your ID."

For a very brief moment Aryeh was tempted to tell them that the law required him merely to identify himself, not that he carry written ID, but he rejected the idea, thinking that he had already had his dose of stupids for the day, with perhaps enough left over for the next day.

He took his wallet out of his pocket, his fingers fumbling as he extracted his driver's license from the glassine compartment, and handed it to the policeman.

"You can check my registration, too," he said, "it's in the glove compartment."

One of the officers vanished briefly. He came back and said, "It checks out. And his door is unlocked, like he said."

The other officer examined the driver's license and said reflectively, "Aryeh. What kind of name is that?"

"It's Hebrew," Aryeh answered. "It means Lion of God."

"Does that mean you're somebody special, like a rabbi or something like that?"

Aryeh grinned tightly.

"No, it means I can be handed a shovel and told to dig." Then seeing the officer's face change, he added, "I'm sorry, that's a personal joke, at my expense, not yours. No, I'm nobody special and I'm sorry that I gave you the wrong impression about what was going on here."

The two officers looked at each other briefly. Aryeh saw no signal pass between them, but the policeman holding his license looked at it again, then returned it to Aryeh.

"OK. But next time when you're not sure, it's a good idea to look at your license plate first. That way, with all these foreign cars looking alike, you won't make a mistake."

"Right," said Aryeh, with the fervor of relief. He waited until the police car backed out of the parking lot, waved at its driver, and got into his own car, sliding across the passenger side and under the steering wheel. He sat for a full minute not moving; when he reached for his car keys, his hands were trembling slightly. Dammit, he thought, this has turned out to be a totally foolish evening, and he leaned his head back against the headrest and closed his eyes. His body was protesting against the damage done to it by his emotions, his mouth had a sour taste, and his veins had tiny bubbles racing through them.

Almost too late he realized that he no longer had a choice and slid out of the car, once more moving across the passenger seat, and went back to the bar. When he finished in the empty washroom, he washed his hands, staring at the pale stranger in the mirror. He barely noticed that Dieter and the woman were now sitting by themselves in a corner.

He got back into the car, started the engine, and carefully backed out of the slot, still thinking about the police, not Dieter. He despised himself for his unexpected servility to the police and cringed as he mentally replayed his babbling. At the same time he argued with himself that he could not have acted differently, and there was no reason for his trembling. If he had seen a policeman's hand rest on his holster, it had probably been more a protective reflex than a threat, and all in all he admitted to himself that the officers had acted with some degree of justification.

Yet he could not let go. He thought of finding another bar somewhere, a quiet neighborhood bar where the regulars tolerated but did not talk to strangers, and talked only about important inconsequentials, then rejected the idea. But he did not want to go back to his flat, not yet, and continued to drive aimlessly.

He drove down to the Marina, switched off his lights, and sat looking at the fog-shrouded lights marking the outlines of the Golden Gate Bridge. *Nuit et Brouillard, Night and Fog,* the Resnais film on the concentration camps—exactly right, Aryeh, he told himself.

With that thought he removed himself from what happened outside the bar, and other angers rushed in to fill the vacuum. Emotions triggered by the thought of Dieter continued to simmer just below the surface, and the experience with the police had somehow only raised them closer to the boiling point.

"Damn it!" he said aloud, pounding on the steering wheel, "Damn it! Damn it!"

How do I get this out of my system? he asked himself, and immediately decided that it was the wrong question. It's Who do I talk to? and knew the answer as he asked the question: Martine.

2

Her Wednesday evenings were more ritual than habit. Martine would buy one or two very small but very expensive lamb chops, a fresh vegetable or two, and whatever fruit was in season. Since San Francisco bakeries did not operate on Wednesdays, fresh bread was not available, but she always kept a half loaf of sourdough in her freezer.

When she got home that night, she took the bread out of the freezer, put the other food away, and made her preparations: a small tray of thin rye crackers, some Boursin, and a glass of wine from which she sipped as she moved around her apartment.

She started her bath water running, set the tray on the tub, found the Tey mystery she was rereading, and put it on the floor alongside the tub. In the living room she sat on the floor in front of her record cabinet, trying to decide which of her favorite composers best complemented her mood. She chose a Dvorak *Serenade,* then reluctantly put it aside because it occupied both sides of a record; she had no intention of being out of the tub in time to turn it over. Finally, she decided that classical was acceptable and put on her favorite Boccherini symphony, waiting until the last possible moment to place the needle on the record.

She sank gratefully into the steaming water, floated as well as she could, and then began to eat and read. She stopped when the second movement began, waiting for the special moment when the mark of Boccherini's temperament appeared: the controlled, elegant phrases, surrounded by silence, followed by a new logic and a beguiling, mysterious descent. I wish I could find a man like that, she thought wistfully, unexpected currents in a familiar flow.

After the bath she prepared her dinner, moving leisurely, pausing occasionally for a glance at the evening news on TV. She ate slowly and with pleasure, pushing thoughts away, and savoring the food she had prepared.

Having eaten, she washed the few pots and dishes, then consulted her TV program. She found an old Walter Huston film, turned the set on, and watched Daniel Webster almost lose his soul by using the Devil's own weapons.

When the film ended shortly before 9, she had achieved the relaxation she wanted and was ready for bed. Twenty minutes later she put the lights out and slid under the single blanket. Her last conscious thought, one minute later, was of the way her ability to fall asleep immediately had at first amused her ex-husband, then irritated him, and finally angered him. That was my marriage, she thought, and thought no more.

She dreamed of a misty morning; she stood on the valley floor in Yosemite, looking up at the mysterious face of Half-Dome. It blurred about the edges, then tautened and became a full circle. A bell began to ring deep within it; slowly, she translated the tolling into the sound of a telephone and realized with annoyance that it was hers and that she was awake.

She pulled the blanket from the bed, wrapped herself in it, and walked into the living room, muttering about invasions of privacy. A street light that she sometimes thought of as her private moon lit her way to the phone.

She looked at it with distaste, glanced at her watch, and picked up the phone.

"It's me. Who's this?"

"Aryeh. I have to talk to you."

"Aryeh, Oh God, it's Wednesday night and it's eleven-thirty and you have to talk to me?"

"I know, I know, and I'm sorry, but I have to talk to you. I really do. I need to talk to you."

"Aryeh. Listen to me. Are you on something?"

"No, dammit, I'm not on something, I'm not loaded, I'm not smashed, I'm not stoned. I have to talk to you."

Martine squeezed the muscles of her right shoulder, sighed, and said, "I'll never get back to sleep now, so I suppose. . . . Aryeh, I have to ask you a question before I agree."

"Martine, don't ask it. When I want to go to bed with you, I say so. You have to grant me that much grace, if not much else. I mean what I say; I need to talk to you. Please."

"Where?"

"That all-night restaurant near you, on California. I'll be waiting for you."

"Fifteen minutes," she said, and hung up.

She dressed quickly, choosing her clothes with care. She put on an old and especially shapeless full-length dress over a pair of boots, then threw a dark shawl over her shoulders. Her husband had despised the outfit, calling it a "turnoff." Aryeh had had the same reaction the first time she had worn it, but she found his objection more tolerable, "This year's look is the pregnant peasant?"

When she walked into the restaurant, she glanced into its one alcove and saw a hunched-over figure in a black coat, looking like a morose crow. When he turned and she saw his withdrawn smile, she regretted the mistrust implicit in her choice of costume. Whatever Aryeh wanted, lechery had no part in it.

She asked the waitress for a pot of tea, and slid into the booth across from Aryeh. He studied her face but said nothing; she touched his hand lightly and asked, "What is it?"

"Wait until you get your order. Once I start talking, I'm not likely to stop."

He waited until the waitress put a pot of tea in front of Martine, then described the scene in the bar and the episode in the parking lot, continually reverting to Dieter and his story.

"It's taken me a while to figure out what this is about, but I finally got there. For the first time in my life I've begun to understand how my parents felt about the Nazis."

He shook his head, and said, "No. That's not it. Maybe I've always understood; maybe it's in my bones, like strontium 90. The smoke from the ovens was still in the air when I was born. But I think, maybe for the first time in my life, I can feel my parents' feelings, not just understand and feel for them."

"Aryeh," she said gently, "that's impossible. You can't feel what they felt then; you were still in diapers. As bad as it was, it's a horror out of another time, not yours and mine."

"That's much like what Dieter was saying. But I do feel it. That's it exactly, I do. Tonight I talked to a man who killed Jews for the one and plain and simple reason that they were Jews. And he relished it! Goddamn it, he relished it, and I've got to do something about it!"

His voice had remained at the same level during most of his recitation, but now its fervor and emphasis carried beyond their booth. A man in a long shapeless coat, sitting at the counter in the room beyond, turned to look at him.

The movement caught Aryeh's attention, and he said abruptly, "Let's walk," and signaled the waitress, asking for the check without waiting for Martine's response.

Outside, he looked at her clothes for the first time. "Are you going to be cold?" he asked. "This fog is more miserable than usual."

She put her arm inside his and answered, "There's always body heat."

The few cars on the street drifted by making small whispering sounds, their headlamps projecting beaded sprays of light into the fog. The dark clothes worn by Martine and Aryeh transformed their figures into extensions of the night, shrouded and unreal even when they passed under the streetlamps. Aryeh's voice became quieter and more restrained, but retained its intensity.

"I'm not like my parents in one respect. They grew up, for a good part of their lives, using the word 'human' almost as if it were a synonym for 'good.' I know better. I've known better for a long time. And still, tonight was something very different. Tonight I talked to a man who killed calmly and, in spite of all he said, knowingly. Killed civilians, killed Jews."

Martine pulled her arm away and turned to face him. "Look," she said, "I have some small sense of what you feel, but you're making far too much of what to me is simply an ugly little incident."

"You weren't there, you didn't see him, you didn't hear him."

"Exactly. Your story is already at least one approximation away from what happened at that bar. And even from what you've told me, the word Jew never came into it. You're building from film images and expectations and maybe even your own nightmares, but that took place inside of you, not back there at the bar, and probably not back a third of a century ago."

"Damn it, Martine, I heard things that go beyond words. Maybe some of what you say is true, but if you'd been there, you'd understand that I have to do something."

"What? Make headlines? Become another Weisenthal? Tell the world that you've discovered a Nazi war criminal? If he's around fifty now, he was all of nineteen or twenty then. A nineteen-year-old war criminal? Aryeh, no."

Aryeh muttered to himself and turned his face away.

Martine stopped walking and pulled him around to face her, saying, "Look at me when I talk to you. I have another question. Why me?"

"I needed someone I could explain it to so I could get it out of my system, not someone who would understand instantly what I was going through."

"Dear God, you and your arrogance! How I hate it!" she said, curling her hands into fists and making fierce little punching motions at his chest, but barely touching him.

"Problems, lady?" a voice asked behind them.

A police car had crept up behind them, its motor still running. A man in civilian clothes sat at the lowered window on the passenger side, his elbow resting casually on the door, his hand out of sight.

"No," Martine said quickly. "No problems. It's just a lover's quarrel. This clunk wants to go to his place and I want to go to mine."

The man laughed, sighed dramatically and said, "The things some people find to fight about!" As the car moved off into the darkness, he gave Aryeh a mocking half salute.

"Now you see," said Aryeh, his voice carrying resignation rather than triumph.

She looked at him blankly. "See what?"

"Powerlessness. That's the other part of it, powerlessness, being subject to other people's power. You reacted the way they did. The point is you snapped right to when the policeman spoke. You didn't simply tell him there was no problem; you didn't tell him it wasn't any of his business.

"You accepted his power to do something to you, and you wanted out in a hurry. I did exactly the same thing with the police back at the parking lot. That's where it's gotten all mixed up with Dieter. All these years I've believed that if it had been me back then, I would have fought every single step of the way. But tonight I'm looking at that feeling of powerlessness from an angle that's new to me. Tonight, it's become immediate, personal. And Dieter is the center."

Martine shook her head. "What you mean is that Dieter is the focus. What's clear . . ."

He cut her off with "What's this arrogance bit?"

She said angrily, "Are you referring to the arrogance in the way you interrupt me when I talk, or what I said before? And I'd damn sight rather that you didn't say anything at all than give me one of your boyishly abashed looks."

He studied a bow window on a building they were passing as if he had never seen one before and said nothing. She let out her breath and said, "First tell me exactly what you meant when you said you had to explain it to somebody."

"It's very simple. If I'd talked to Selig, or my friend Simon, either of them would have understood what I was talking about before I'd spoken a dozen sentences about Dieter, saying 'I know, I know,' trying to soothe me. I didn't want to be soothed. I wanted to be able to spill out the whole nasty mess."

"And you still don't know what I mean by arrogance? Do you know what you just said, really? That only another Jew could understand how you feel, that nobody else could really feel the agony. Bull. Jews were the main victims, but there were others."

When Aryeh started to speak, she said calmly, "Shut up until I'm finished. I almost gave up on you the first time we met, when you said that inane thing about 'always liking French girls.' If you hadn't seen my face change and reacted with an apology, I would have walked away from you.

"I'm not French. I was named by my parents after a German minister, a Lutheran I think, who stood up to Hitler. Relatives of my own family died in the camps. And there isn't a single blond, blue-eyed monster among us."

"Martine, will you get it through your head that I'm not talking about any holy Crusade against Germans? I'm talking about one single man, one individual who admits doing what he did. And it didn't take any red-hot pincers to get the truth out of him. He boasted about it, I tell you!"

"Maybe he did, Aryeh, maybe he did. I don't know. Maybe tomorrow I'll care whether he did or not, but not tonight. I want to get back to my place, back where it's warm and familiar, and not listen to any more of this. Please?"

They walked back to their cars in silence, bodies not touching. Aryeh walked Martine to her car, abruptly said, "I'm sorry," and left. She watched him walking down the street, his tall body hunched over, his hands plunged deep into his pockets and felt a moment of pity.

She climbed into her VW camper-van and swung out into the street. When she passed Aryeh's car, she saw him sitting in it, motionless, looking straight ahead. She gave a small beep of her horn; he acknowledged it with a wave of his hand but did not turn his head.

When she got home, she undressed, wrapped her blanket around herself, poured a small glass of brandy, and sat in front of her TV set, watching a Western where good and evil all but wore signs, willing herself not to think of Aryeh or the man named Dieter.

When, finally, she began to yawn, she went to bed, promising herself on the way that the next Wednesday night she would either leave the phone off the hook or pull it out by its roots the first time it rang.

Aryeh's teaching schedule was heavy for the next two days, and his students made constant demands on his time. He pushed Dieter out of his thoughts, knowing that the memory of the evening might jump out at him at any time. His mood remained dark over the weekend, and he avoided going into the bar, immersing himself in reading and films, seeing three in two days.

His mood had lightened by the time he approached the new week's schedule. When Aryeh drove through the two stone pillars to the campus of San Tomas Community College, he made a mental note to use them in an article satirizing one of the troglodyte intellectuals (Buckley? Kristol? Kilpatrick?), perhaps for the next issue of the faculty magazine. The topic would be the death of modern education as exemplified by those pillars: iron gates hung from them, flanked by stone buttresses curving in downward arcs ending two feet above the ground, barely ten feet from the gates, and past them, the earth.

Thus, he would say, when the entrance to learning is made easily accessible to all those who would enter, there are no longer heights to climb, no walls to scale, no challenges. If he could get the right tone, his colleagues would be amused, and at the same time, his department chairman, thinking him to be serious, would congratulate him, but caution him to be cognizant of public opinion.

He played with the idea until class time. By the time the period was over, he had completely forgotten the idea and his pleasure in it. When the class began, he stood on the stage of a small lecture room in the Humanities building, looking at the two-dozen students scattered among the fifty seats in the room.

"The name of the film is *The Fifth Horseman Is Fear,* and it's a Czech film. That's all for now," he said and motioned the projectionist to begin. Putting his hand on the stage, he leaped lightly to the floor and made his way up the aisle to a seat almost precisely in line with the center of the screen.

The film was mainly about an elderly Jewish doctor in Nazi-occupied Prague who, although already stripped of his credentials and humiliated by the Germans, was asked by the underground to find morphine for one of their wounded members, at the risk of his life.

Aryeh had thought it a beautiful film the first time he had seen it but was totally unprepared for its impact on him during this showing. Three times during the course of the film he came close to tears; in a movie house he might have let himself weep, or left the theater, but here he fought for control and won.

When the film was over and the lights went on, he waited for a few moments, then walked down to the front of the auditorium, where he swung himself up on the stage and stood facing his students. Not good, he thought, watching their faces and listening to the small restless sounds, not good. They haven't reacted well.

"Anybody want to begin?" he asked.

"Well, it proves one thing," a young woman student said. "The Czechs are just as sexist as we are."

He looked at her in astonishment, mentally rerunning the film and unable to find the reference. "What convenient hat did you pluck that rabbit from?" he demanded.

"I know what she means," another woman student said, "that scene with all the girls taking showers."

"Women, not girls," the first speaker called out.

"They were closer to girls than women," said Aryeh, "and that was fundamental to the scene. But let that go for a minute. What makes you say it was sexist?"

"Well, there was no point to that scene except maybe the director's got a thing for young female flesh or maybe they read *Variety* too and wanted to hype up its prospects with an 'R' rating."

"I thought that scene was beautiful," said a male student.

When hissing began, Aryeh held up his hands. "Free speech, honest exchange of opinions and all that, yes? Now, why did you think it was beautiful?"

"The cinematographer or cameraman, or whoever it was that was responsible, got some beautiful textural contrasts and excellent detail during that scene, especially in the way the shower water rolled down the bodies of the women."

With anger clear in his voice, Aryeh asked, "Now that we've all seen exactly what was in front of our eyes, did anybody see beyond that?"

There was no answer except for the shifting of bodies and a whispered discussion between two students. Under other circumstances he would have picked up the variety of signals which indicated discomfort or boredom or rebellion, but his anger carried him on.

"I'll stop taking your intelligence for granted and carry on this discussion, if we can still call it that, as if you were a group of third graders. Would some daring soul like to tell me what the film was about, in one sentence, and if you tell me the plot, you're out of this class."

"You're never relieved of responsibility."

"Good. What else?"

There was more shifting and then silence.

"Does the title of the film give you a clue? *The Fifth Horseman?*"

Someone called out, "Hell, I don't even know who the other four were," and a few of the students applauded.

"Does anybody know who the Four Horsemen were?"

When there was no answer, he said, "War, Famine, Pestilence, Death. But this film is saying the Fifth Horseman threatens when people are too timid or cowed to do what they know they should do. It's an allegory. That's the meaning of those shots of contemporary Prague before the story itself starts. It's a way of saying that evil must be fought wherever we find it, whenever we find it.

"And that scene that none of you seem to be able to feel, the shower scene, was intercut with shots of Nazi officers downstairs in the same whorehouse, waiting for the girls, young girls, to come down to them. The scene in the shower celebrates life, and then shows the viewer that it is about to be pressed into the service of death. That's what the scene was about, for anybody with the eyes and the heart to understand."

Even in his anger, he noted that only a few of the students were looking at him. Silence followed his speech, until one of his favorite students spoke. "Sir, you're asking the impossible."

"Wait a minute. Wait a minute," said Aryeh. "What's this nonsense about 'sir'? I thought we were on a first-name basis."

"The teacher in a third grade class is an authority figure . . . sir," said the student, to applause.

Without waiting for Aryeh's reaction, he continued, "You're asking us to react to what you react to and that's impossible. The Nazis were part of your generation, at least in the sense that you were alive during the period. There's not a single person in this hall right now except you that was even alive then."

"That's right," another student said. "And it's time the whole thing got buried. It's ancient history. I saw a movie the other day with some old Nazis in it, and they were older than my own grandfather, even."

"Sure," another called out. "They're a vanishing breed."

"Maybe even an endangered species."

"Like the supply's running out, you know?"

"Get 'em while they're hot, folks!"

A black student in the back of the hall got to his feet and yelled out, "You're crazy! There are still Nazis around, and this time it's the blacks they're after!"

Suddenly the entire class was in an uproar. With one part of his mind Aryeh realized that he was the main focus of their resentment, that they were saying things to make him hurt, and that under other conditions they might have reacted differently. Another part of his mind was thinking about the phrases: "vanishing breed" and "endangered species." Dieter? Endangered?

He devoted his full attention to restoring calm in the classroom, apologizing in midstream for the third-grade reference, but it was clear to both him and the class that any further discussion of the film was futile.

When the day was finally over, he drove out of the stone gates without noticing them. Perhaps, he thought, what I really need is someone who will understand immediately. Selig? No, he would mother me. Simon.

He called Simon several times later that evening. He let the phone ring ten times on each call, but there was no answer.

At 3 A.M. Simon was led out of the holding cell. A guard brought him and eight others to an office where an assistant district attorney told them that all the charges against them had been dropped, and that they were free to go.

"Don't think, any of you, that this means you've got a false arrest suit on your hands," warned the assistant D.A. "The charges would hold up if we wanted to press them, but we don't."

His voice changed slightly, becoming more personal and its pitch lower. "There are a lot of people around who understand exactly how you feel, including some of the arresting officers, but you gave them no choice. And if anybody quotes me on that, I'll deny every word."

Simon's eyelids felt as if he had been swimming through sand, and his body felt sweaty and dirty. This, too, shall pass away, he told himself; a hot shower, perhaps a bite to eat, and some sleep, and he would be in good shape again. What would not pass, he realized, was the distasteful discovery of a deep pool of something close to hatred taking up space somewhere inside of him.

His original impulse to avoid the meeting had been strong, not because of any intuitive sense, but because he abominated any kind of meeting.

"Look, Kid," he had said to his brother when he had called, "it's not my contract, it's not my profession, and I hate meetings. If you like, call me when it's over, and I'll meet you someplace for a drink."

The Kid had pressed hard, arguing that they had not seen each other recently, that they would leave as soon as he had a sense of the way things were going, that no final action could possibly be taken that night and therefore the meeting would be short, that no matter what happened they would stay no longer than an hour, that he would take Simon out afterwards for food and drink at his expense, and that Simon could name the place.

Simon agreed. After dinner he drove down to the Civic Center Plaza and parked his car in its underground garage. He amused himself for a half hour in the library's music and art department, browsing through Grove's *Dictionary of Music,* and copied down a statement about Fibich to amuse the viola player of his quartet: "Some compositions are nothing but Schumann and water."

He left reluctantly and strolled across the deserted plaza to the building where the Kid's meeting was to take place, walking slowly, hoping that it would at least be under way by the time he arrived. As he crossed the street a small group of people scrambled out of a van and raced into the building ahead of him. As far as he could tell, he was the last to arrive.

The meeting was already in progress; he accepted his self-congratulations modestly and looked around. The Kid was sitting near the right-hand aisle of the center section, about halfway down the auditorium. Simon made his way there, excused himself as he pushed past three spectators, and sat down next to him, touching him on the shoulder to signal arrival.

The Kid grinned at him and said, "Marshmallow. I didn't expect you'd cave in so easily."

Simon made a small circular motion with his hand and said, *"Noblesse oblige,* duty to the next generation, passing the torch, and all that. What's happening?"

"They're having a preliminary discussion of the new budget. There's no way it's going to be any bigger, and there are going to be cuts, but the question is whether it's salaries or jobs. Pay attention and maybe you'll learn something about life. Even Mozart had to scramble for his guilders."

Simon nodded, and slid down in his seat, feeling around under it for mementos left by earlier generations of meeting-goers. He found several petrified wads of what had once been gum, deposited by spectators as bored as he. Looking around the hall and finding nothing to claim his attention, he pulled his feet up on the seat, clasped his arms around his knees, and rested his head on them.

He was mentally practicing his part of the opening section of the Mozart *E Minor Divertimento* when a sudden silence, followed by the creaking of ancient seats, brought him back into his surroundings. The speaker on the podium had stopped talking and was looking over the heads of the audience to the back of the auditorium. The Kid was half out of his seat, his body twisted in the same direction. Simon put his feet on the floor and forced himself upright, turning to look.

Eight people were filing quietly into the hall—seven men and one woman in their twenties and early thirties, clean, neat, and dressed in Nazi uniforms, complete with swastika armband on the left arm.

The first in line walked down the aisle looking straight ahead, carrying himself like an experienced squad leader sure of the training of his squad, who knows that those behind would follow wherever he led, without question or hesitation. Eight rows from the stage he stopped, excused himself politely to the man sitting on the aisle seat, and led the group into the center section of the row. When the squad took their seats, they sat calmly and quietly, palms on their knees, looking at the stage.

The brief silence was broken when the man who had been sitting on the aisle seat stood up, ostentatiously returned his seat to its upright position, walked up the aisle several rows, and took another seat. A smattering of applause followed and then an uneasy silence.

The speaker on the platform began talking into the microphone once more and completed his statement. The name of the next speaker was announced. As she walked up to the microphone several people began booing. She turned around angrily, but resumed walking when someone called out, "Not you, lady, them!"

"What's this all about?" asked Simon.

"The next point coming up on the agenda, after ours, is about a busing plan, and I guess they're here to demonstrate against it. They shouldn't have been allowed in. They're here to provoke a riot, that's for sure, and don't give me any First Amendment crap about their rights."

"Down, boy, down," said Simon. "Take it easy. They haven't done anything, anyway, not yet."

"No, just killed six million Jews."

"Not unless you believe in mass reincarnation."

The Kid turned angrily on Simon, but before he could say anything, someone to Simon's left yelled, "Throw them out! Throw them out!"

The cry was quickly picked up in several places in the auditorium. The Kid looked around, jumped to his feet, and began yelling with the others. Simon reached a hand out to pull him down and then withdrew it. His brother had long ago made his peace with being called "Kid," and Simon secretly believed he liked being known as "The Kid," as if "Billy" preceded it. But being treated paternally enraged him.

A woman sitting on the stage behind the podium walked over to the speaker and conferred with her briefly. The speaker nodded and moved away. The woman took the microphone and asked for quiet "so that the meeting can proceed in an orderly fashion." Then she added, "This is a democratic meeting, that is its purpose. All those who wish to speak will be given an opportunity to do so." She said something else, but Simon could not hear her over the growing noise.

The chant of "Throw them out! Throw them out!" started again, accompanied by a rhythmic drumming of feet and hands beating on seat arms. When the sound subsided, a woman with the sweet face of the motherly figures seen on TV giving advice to anxious young brides stood up on a seat and yelled, "Never again, you bastards, never again!" The echo of her words developed into a cry throughout the hall, and then died away.

The group in Nazi uniforms sat quietly throughout the shouting, showing no reaction to the yelling around them, nor speaking to each other, their eyes fixed on the podium.

A young man wearing a faded fatigue jacket with a XX Bomber Command insignia on the sleeve raced up to the stage, grabbed the microphone, and yelled, "If nobody else will do it, we will. Out! Out! Out!"

Simon was on his feet trying to see what was happening. All around him people were leaving their seats and running to where the Nazis continued to sit in disciplined silence. His view was blocked by clumps of people standing on their seats, but he could see tangled movement and caught sight of a bloodied face.

As the Kid pushed his way to the aisle, he turned and yelled at Simon, "Do you need any more proof?"; but Simon had turned to watch files of police running down the aisles from the back of the auditorium.

The loudspeakers continued to plead for order above the sound of boos and shouts. The yells died down momentarily, but as pairs of policemen began moving up the aisle dragging protestors the roar grew even louder.

The Kid was screaming at the first pair of policemen that passed, "Not them! Not them, the Nazis!" One of the policeman pushed the Kid as he passed, sending him falling back into the row of seats.

Simon suddenly heard a familiar voice yelling, "Cossacks! Cossacks!" as he tried to reach the Kid who had already recovered his balance and was now standing again. Simon pushed past him and again heard the voice yelling, "Cossacks! Cossacks!" only vaguely beginning to understand that it was his own.

A policeman confronted him and said, "Shut up, you, or I'll take you in for inciting to riot."

Simon stared at him, looked down to the center of the auditorium where the Nazis were now methodically hitting back at anyone within reach, felt fury choking him, and screamed again, directly in the policeman's face, "Cossack! Cossack!"

"That's it," the policeman said. "You're under arrest."

He took Simon's arm and began pulling him. Simon started to swing his free arm to strike the officer, but a small cool part of his brain took over. He gulped air and forced himself to go along quietly.

As the police pushed him and others up into a waiting wagon outside the building, Simon caught a glimpse of the Kid's face. He was shouting something at him, but the noise of the crowd absorbed whatever sounds he was making.

Later, in the holding cell, he kept muttering to himself in disbelief. Cossacks? Cossacks? My God, he thought, in my entire life, not once in my entire life have I ever said that word aloud, not once have I ever heard anyone speak it. Maybe there is a racial memory. Dear God, Cossacks! Stupid, stupid, stupid.

He was still trying to understand what had happened when he walked out of the Hall of Justice. The Kid was waiting for him, and Simon flinched when he saw the look of pride on his face. I'm a hero; he thinks I'm a hero. I'll bet even Jean-Pierre will finally approve of me. Damn.

Jean-Pierre removed his filter mask and snapped the off switch of his sander. He reached up and turned the floodlights on, then dropped to one knee and sighted along the slab of walnut carefully, tilting it to the right and then left, sighting down its entire length.

He moved to the opposite end of the trestles on which the walnut rested and repeated the process. Satisfied there were no scratches visible, he turned the floodlights off and started the vacuum cleaner. Working carefully, moving with the grain, he removed the sanding dust. When he was finished he put the vacuum cleaner down, switched the floodlights back on, and circled the table.

Whistling Schubert's "The Trout," he removed the 600-grit wet-and-dry paper, turned it over, and replaced it in the sander's spring clips. The walnut glowed with a soft patina that seemed to begin well below the wood's surface, but he was not yet satisfied; the burnishing with the smooth side of the paper was the necessary final step.

When he finished sanding, he brushed the surface with a soft-bristled blackboard brush, examined the walnut surface once again, and began his preparations for the final finishing. He opened a metal locker at the rear of the shop and took out a gallon can of an oil and wax finish he had learned to use in France.

He poured some of the mixture into a shallow plastic container, took a stick to which several wrappings of old sheeting had been tied, soaked it in the mixture and, using it as a swab, covered the entire slab with the liquid. When he had finished, he checked the surface and added more liquid to a few areas that looked dull.

He poured the excess liquid back into the container and put it back into the locker, then turned off the overhead fluorescent light and went outside, snapping the padlock behind him. He lit a cigarette, leaned against the building and stood looking out at Richardson Bay, his mind filtering out the tangle of weeds, bent pipes, and other industrial leavings that separated him from the water.

The cigarette still between his lips, he got into his pickup truck, turned, backed up, and drove down a dirt road to a coffee shop a mile away. A few mid-afternoon regulars were there; he chatted briefly with one, nodded to another, and sat down at a table with parts of several newspapers on it.

He thumbed through them and pulled out the first section of San Francisco's afternoon newspaper. A waitress approached him, put her hand on his shoulder and asked, "The usual, Jean-Pierre?"

He ignored her, his eyes fixed on a headline: "Nazis Riot At School Board Meeting," then caught himself, turned and smiled at her and said, "Yes, sure."

He ignored his usual technique of reading the paper straight through from front to back, but read the story from beginning to end, even reading the fine-print list of names of those arrested at the bottom of the last page. Halfway down the list he spotted a familiar name, looked at the accompanying address and grinned to himself, "The child is now a man," and shook his head at the man across the table when he realized that he had spoken the words aloud. He was still grinning when the waitress brought him a toasted sourdough muffin, a jar of jam, and coffee.

He read the story a second time, noting that the charges had been dismissed against all but one of those involved, and grimaced slightly when he realized that only two of the American Nazis had been booked, and that both of them had been released on light bail.

He looked at the date on the paper and nodded; it was not one of Simon's rehearsal days. He went to the pay phone near the coffee shop's entrance; when Simon answered the phone immediately after the first ring, he said, "Shalom, my friend. Welcome to the real world."

"Up yours," said Simon. "What's new with you?"

"I've been reading a very interesting newspaper story," he said. "It seems that some cool *dégagé* type got himself involved. I offer congratulations."

Simon said nothing for a moment. "Look. You've heard me speak of my friend Aryeh. He's here right now, and he's got an interesting story. I think it's especially for you. Come over."

Jean-Pierre looked at the wall clock. "I have a finishing job in the shop that requires a wipe down, but it won't take me long. Five o'clock, yes?"

"We'll be here," said Simon and hung up. He turned to Aryeh, "Jean-Pierre will be on the way soon. He wants to hear your story."

"I'll tell him," Aryeh said. "I'll tell anybody who'll stand still long enough, for that matter, but I'm not sure he'll be interested."

"Jean-Pierre? He'll be interested. Fascinated would be more like it. He probably would have creamed your friend Dieter if he'd been there, and he may not understand why you didn't."

"I should have," said Aryeh. "I think."

"No, you shouldn't have. But he'll think so. He showed me a snapshot once. His father, a couple of uncles, a couple of others, all on a picnic somewhere, mugging for the camera, one putting horns on another, that kind of stuff, bicycles in the background. Jean-Pierre pointed his finger at each one of them, one after another, saying, 'This one died in this camp, this one died in that camp, this one they led into a Gestapo HQ and nobody saw him again,' and so on, his voice absolutely flat."

Aryeh nodded somberly, then asked, "Jewish?"

"No. That's the unusual thing about him. Gypsy. French Gypsy. They were almost wiped out."

When Jean-Pierre rang the doorbell, the two men were sitting quietly, listening to a record. Simon opened the door for him, and they shook hands formally. Jean-Pierre put his arm around Simon's shoulder as they walked down the hall, listened a moment, and said, "Mozart. The *Adagio and Fugue.* Happy, happy."

Simon shrugged. "It fits my mood. Come in and meet Aryeh. He's got a very interesting story for you."

"And you do not have?"

Simon shrugged again. "Routine, all in a day's work. Nothing more than you read about in the paper. No, I'd rather forget about it, the whole thing was stupid."

He introduced the two, gave Jean-Pierre a drink, and said, "My Nazis were imitations. Aryeh met the real thing, and nothing in the world can keep him from telling you about what happened."

As he had done with Martine, Aryeh had omitted the young woman when he told the story to Simon. Now, facing an unknown, he said nothing about Dieter's car and the episode with the police in the parking lot.

During the first portion of the story, as Aryeh set the scene, Jean-Pierre leaned back in his chair, one leg hooked over its side, sipping at his glass of wine. When Dieter entered the story, he pulled his leg back, sat up, and remained erect, his drink forgotten. By the time the recital was over, the drink was on the floor and Jean-Pierre was leaning forward, arms hanging between his knees, his eyes fixed on Aryeh's face.

When Aryeh finished, Jean-Pierre stood up and said, "I will tell you something. If it had been me, and I had been there, I would have done a thing to him."

"Aryeh would have liked to do a thing to him then," said Simon, "and I have a feeling he would still like it."

"What?"

Aryeh shook his head. "I don't know what I want to do. This is the third time I've told the story, in addition to all the times I've gone over it mentally, and the story itself is beginning to supplant what actually happened. Sometimes I think I'm reacting childishly."

"No. No," said Jean-Pierre. "It would be childish to say that your Dieter does not really exist, to forget him, to declare his past is already history, that forgiveness is nobility. No. They spawn, these Dieters. They make new generations, right, Simon? And we sit and listen to Mozart. No. Trust your feelings, Aryeh. It is right to want to do something to him."

"He may be much less than he sounds," said Simon. "How do we know?"

"And he may be much more," answered Jean-Pierre. "How do we know? You ask the wrong questions, Simon. A man who wishes to escape his past or forget it, that is perhaps one kind of thing. To redeem himself, that is another. But the question is this. What kind of animal is it who recalls such a past only to take pleasure in it?

"The existence of such a man is offensive. I tell you, Aryeh, I say it to you very seriously, you should indeed do something to him."

"I don't see how we can," said Simon. "We're rational human beings. This isn't an opera, with the commandant dragging Don Juan down to hell in retribution.

"Look, he must feel secure to be able to tell that story, even with all his protestations. He's no war criminal hiding under a false identity who somebody recognizes on the street and screams at. He's real, he's been legitimized, and there's nothing to be done."

When Jean-Pierre made a sound in his throat, Simon added, "If it makes you feel any better, I don't think I'm arguing with you, Jean-Pierre. If I am, my heart isn't in it. I'm arguing against my instincts. Once, just once, it would be . . . ," and his voice trailed off.

Aryeh stood up abruptly. "I seem to be back where I started, and I don't know where that is. I'll be in touch."

He shook hands with both men and left. As he waited for the elevator he could hear faint strains of Mozart from behind Simon's door. Yes, he thought, Dieter tells his story and we listen to Mozart.

Did they play Mozart over the loudspeakers?

He erected his mental blackboard and chalked on it: stupid, morbid, self-pitying—check one box. He checked all three.

6

His mother called him two nights later. "Aryeh," she said gently, "I especially want you to come this year. Zayde is getting frailer all the time, and while I am not saying that this will be the last Seder over which your grandfather will preside, I have had to admit to myself that it is possible. It would please both of us if you would come. This year, will you come?"

"This year, I will come," said Aryeh, and hung up.

For a moment he had an impulse to call back and invent an excuse (an out-of-town seminar that he forgotten momentarily?), then rejected the thought. He could not turn his back on his mother's request but something more than that had made him accept, perhaps a sense that he had rejected too much of his own past. No, he thought, not rejected, ignored.

Warmth washed over him as he entered his grandfather's house, and he understood immediately why he had come. The territory was familiar, no longer home, but a land to which he was native.

When he was seven, the spring his parents had gone to Europe, he had lived in this house with his grandfather and grandmother. She was long since dead. His principal memory of her was that of a short, silent, plump woman with an inexhaustible supply of cake for a hungry boy. There was another memory, brief and vivid: he had walked by an open door and seen her in a rocking chair, faded brown photographs spread out on her lap, crying.

That spring he had been in the house and watched the preparations for Passover: the daily dishes locked away and the Passover dishes, the ones with ths gold stripe around their edges, carefully brought out. When all the preparations had been made, his grandfather walked around the house, one hand holding Aryeh's, the other holding a burning candle, looking for crumbs of leavened bread. When he found a small pile in the last closet he searched, carefully left there by Aryeh's grandmother, he swept them into a small cloth sack and burned it.

It had been ritual and tradition, Aryeh knew now. Symbolically they were in Egypt, the household preparing for the flight from Pharaoh's soldiers. As there was not time for the bread to rise, it had been baked without yeast into flat cakes. For this reason his grandfather's house had been purified by fire of all leavened bread. But at seven he had understood none of that. The circuit through the house had been all magic and marvel, and he had clapped his hands in victory when his grandfather had found the pile of crumbs.

Everything was familiar, the smells of food cooking, the ceremonial settings on the table, and all the remembered faces. A room full of innocent Dorian Grays, he thought. They've aged but they remain unchanged.

His mother came over to kiss him and said, "Say hello to Zayde."

"Mother," he said, "I'm a growing boy and may even achieve puberty soon."

She laughed, kissed him again, and murmured, "Such a clever one. Now go. And keep your hands off your girl cousins."

He understood his mother's anxiety when he saw his grandfather standing near the head of the table. The biblical prophet of his childhood, the man who could change from playmate down on all fours into the Avenging Angel existed no longer.

Over and over, Aryeh had heard the story about the day that one of his uncles, returning from a new public school, had reported that they had recited the Lord's Prayer, and that he had bowed his head with the others. Zayde had left his chair at the head of the table, walked over to the unfortunate, and knocked him out of his chair with one majestic sweep of his hand, thundering, "You will bow your head to no God but your own!" Then he picked the boy up, put him back on his chair, and returned to his place.

He had become a frail old man. His hair and beard were as full as ever, but in combination with the flowing white robe he wore, they accented the wrinkled and almost translucent quality of his face. The Angel of Death is near, he thought, and felt pity. Then said to himself, no, pity would anger him.

He searched his memory for an ancient Armenian saying. Yes. "To the son, thou shalt revere thy father because he is your closest link to the beginning of time; to the father, thou shalt revere thy son, for he is your closest link to the Day of Judgment."

This room is full of reverence, and he stands at its center, Aryeh thought. But if I ever dared say such a thing to him, he'd roar with laughter and look at me with affectionate contempt.

When his grandfather saw Aryeh, he threw his arms wide and embraced him, kissing him on each cheek as Aryeh leaned down, and then on the lips.

"Now there are two reasons for the lamb," he said, "if I am willing to concede the validity of the New Testament. You have come back."

"Yes, I am back," said Aryeh.

His grandfather stopped smiling and examined Aryeh's face. "Double meanings? I think perhaps it is for your sake," he said, "and not mine and not . . ." but was kept from going further by a young child tugging at his robe and calling, "Zayde, Zayde!"

He beamed at the boy and said proudly, "The firstborn of the fifth generation!" and walked off hand in hand with the child, listening gravely to an incomprehensible babble and nodding his head occasionally.

When there was a pause in the greetings and embraces, Aryeh studied the long table covered with an enormous white linen tablecloth. Each place setting included a ceremonial wine goblet, which tradition demanded must be filled and drunk four times. The ritual dishes were already on the table, near where his grandfather would sit: a plate of matzohs covered by a gold-fringed embroidered cloth, the roast lamb bone, a dish of bitter herbs, and all the rest.

His grandfather had now taken leave of the child, seated himself in an armchair at the head of the table, and leaned back, propped against several white pillows. His mother walked about the room telling everyone within reach that the Passover service was about to begin. The room separated itself into tribes, families, and subfamilies: wives, husbands, daughters, cousins, nieces, in-laws; and all sat.

Some followed intently as his grandfather began the ceremony, chanting the Hebrew phrases; others continued whispering quietly or sometimes laughing softly; children crawled under the table; and there was a steady flow of ritual dishes. He noted with pleasure that the ceremony had become more relaxed, had become more of a celebration than he had remembered. There had been a time when his grandfather would have demanded absolute silence and absolute attention, and received them.

The room quieted when the time came for the youngest who could do so to ask the four questions that are a springboard for explaining the history of Passover; there was applause when they were concluded successfully, and the ceremony continued.

Tension began to build in the room when a chased-silver goblet was placed in front of his grandfather and filled with wine so that it almost overflowed; this was the only time that wine was not provided for all, and it reminded Aryeh that the moment was coming that as a child had filled him with an incomprehensible terror.

The talking stopped, children were pulled onto laps or placed into chairs and quieted, and his mother came from the kitchen and sat next to him.

His grandfather had been reading quietly from the *Haggadah,* the special prayer book for the ceremony commemorating the Exodus, the flight, and deliverance from Egypt. As the room quieted he turned the *Haggadah* over and placed it face down on the table. When he closed his eyes, the silence in the room deepened and became total; when he opened them again, he had somehow once again become the grandfather of Aryeh's youth.

His grandfather looked around the table, put the first joint of the forefinger of his right hand into the silver goblet, uttered a single short word whose ending hung in the air like a muffled funeral bell, and flicked a few drops of wine onto the white tablecloth.

He said another word and another and another, each time flicking wine on the table. He did this ten times in all: the ceremonial recitation of the ten plagues sent down by Jehovah on the Pharaoh to force him to allow all the children of Israel to leave Egypt. The pause before he uttered the last phrase, the only one with more than one word, was longer than those that had separated the others, and his tone became even more somber.

When he was finished, Aryeh's mother left her seat, reached across the table, and picked up a small cut-glass container of salt. Using the tiny spoon resting in it, she carefully covered the wine stain with salt until the tablecloth once again seemed unblemished.

Aryeh sat staring at the silver goblet, seeing that implacable finger dipping into it, thinking of the wonder of the ritual, of the millions of fingers repeating that gesture over the tens of centuries.

Our traditions go back a long way, he thought. Even then, in Egypt, we already had traditions, while Dieter's people were living in caves and grubbing for roots.

He had not thought of Dieter before that moment, and his skin crawled as he realized that these could have been Dieter's "forty, fifty." He could not tolerate the thought, but it would not leave. He knew he was being morbid, and in an effort to separate thought from feeling, he transformed it into a scene in a film.

He blocked out the scene: one camera set up on the road as the caravan approached; another across the road from the "open spot"; and later, another behind the open grave to frame the shovels being picked up and the command car in the background. Grainy black and white, perhaps sepia. In any event, not color. And then what do we do about Dieter? Suddenly, in that moment, he knew the "thing" he would do to Dieter.

When he looked up from the tablecloth, he saw his mother looking at him with concern. He shook his head, smiled at her, and lifted his glass in salute, watching her relax.

Later, she came and stood behind his chair, one hand on his shoulder, the other stroking his head. "It's gotten to you, Aryeh, hasn't it? Your face is more alive than when you came in. I'm glad."

"Yes," he said, "it's gotten to me."

7

In the long drive through the dark countryside and in the days following, he went about his duties with the air of a man at peace with himself and the world. He played games between himself and Dieter: he was Moses, he was the Avenging Angel, he was all Four Horsemen, he was the Lord of Hosts, buffeting a tiny Dieter with the storms he unleashed, not letting him know from what direction the next howling wind would roar.

His film class noted his good humor and ascribed it to penitence for his childish outburst earlier; his English Lit class found the demands of a required essay more palatable than they had anticipated and assumed it was because the moon was in Leo; and his colleagues, finding his wit less astringent, decided that he had found a new passion and observed him carefully when they saw him talking to a woman student.

Near the end of the discussion in his film class, he announced the next week's film, urging them to be present for a special treat.

"It's a Japanese film, *Ikiru,* by Kurosawa. It's not a Samurai film, it's set in postwar Japan. Among its many themes is one that has been the binding glue in this term's sequence, that is, the dual concerns of personal responsibility and that to do is to live. The film is explicit on the latter; its title translates *To Live*. You'll find a special treat in this one. The principal character of the film is played magnificently by Takashi Shimura."

He waited for a reaction, then realized that the class was waiting for him to say something more. "No recognition factor? Well, how many of you remember *The Seven Samurai?*"

Most of the students raised their hands, and a few applauded happily.

"Now do you remember Takashi Shimura?"

When there was no response, he gave them what he considered a sweet, benevolent smile, slowly rubbing the top of his head in a small circle, and said, "This would work better if I had a brush cut or were bald."

One of the students called out, "Hey, the leader of the seven. The one the villagers approached first to save them from the bandits—the one who went around convincing the others to join. He was great!"

"He was one of the ones who survived the battle," said another.

"That's the part Yul Brynner took in the American version," said another.

"Right," said Aryeh, "and while I didn't think of it before, his actions also fall into what we've been talking about—he, too, accepted responsibility."

He paused and suddenly thought, yes, yes, that's it, and looked with such intensity at a woman student that she waited after class to see what he had in mind, but he left without the usual postclass discussion with his more ardent students.

Why should I be selfish? he asked himself. And besides, I can't take on the whole job myself. And even more important, in the original version it took four: Moses, his brother Aaron, the Angel of Darkness, and Jehovah himself. It would be presumptuous of me to take the entire burden on my shoulders, wouldn't it, Dieter?

Yes, he thought with growing excitement, I'll be adapting the story into a script, and producing and directing. Why not be casting director as well? Satyajit Ray writes his own music, but there's only one of him. No, Chaplin. Were there others as well?

Enough, Aryeh, he cautioned himself. One thing at a time. The question before us is, Who?

Jean-Pierre. Without question. He would be as eager as I am myself, if Simon's portrait of him was accurate. Perhaps even more so.

Simon. Yes, with a small question mark. He would do it, not without questions, not without hesitation, but he would do it, partly because of what had happened with the neo-Nazis, partly because the idea would interest him. "I will join you, because your character interests me," one of the seven samurai had said to Takashi Shimura.

The Kid. Certainly, even if Simon doesn't join in. He's a displaced person politically. He wouldn't go within ten miles of a terrorist group; there's no political group to whom he'd consider allegiance, but he wants something. A target of opportunity? That he wouldn't be able to resist. Besides, although he doesn't know it, he's not very far removed from the orthodox who wear a beard and attend synagogue every Saturday.

Martine. Question mark, question mark, question mark. She'll be both revolted and amused by the idea. But will there be anything more than that? She's nonpolitical, but so is this. Maybe she does understand about the horror? The problem is that she doesn't look at causes, but at individuals. Still.

That's five of us, with luck. Not bad, but the number five is mostly angles and sharp corners; this needs more rounding. Six, a sweetly curved figure.

Selig. Quiet, sweet, devoted Selig. Of all of us, he's the only orthodox one. No, not orthodox any more; but there's something else. He's of the tribe of High Priests, even though he doesn't work at it. And what a beautiful link, literally and symbolically: all the High Priests are descendants of Aaron, brother of Moses. Very nice indeed. Everything is linked if you look closely enough. I will spin a very interesting web for you, Dieter.

8

Aryeh had never understood why envy was a sin, but if it were, he was committing one as he sat in Selig's outer office, waiting for him to finish a phone conversation.

The secretary had watched him carefully when he had examined the rosewood paneling on the walls, then satisfied that he was not contemplating either theft or arson, had turned her attention elsewhere.

The rosewood veneers, like everything else in the room, were genuine, not formica or some other substance treated to resemble wood. The small table on which magazines and a lamp rested was a Saarinen, not an imitation, and the abstraction hanging on the wall was attractive, costly, and original.

If there were such an aptitude as attraction for money, he thought, Selig had been blessed by it, and deservedly. Good old Selig, a really good man, in the sense of the word that had gone out of fashion.

When a light on her telephone console went out, the secretary spoke into her phone, then said to Aryeh, "I told him you're here and he said to come in. He's about to make another phone call, but you're to go in anyway."

The inner office contained furnishings a century behind those in the outer. Selig's desk was a softly glowing walnut table with Queen Anne legs, and he sat in a mahogany and cane revolving chair. The only incongruous note was Selig himself; he wore a blue denim suit with pronounced white stitching that made him look like a plump blueprint.

"My advice," he was saying, "is to put the club's money into CDs. TBs are no longer attractive for short-term funds, and they could be something of a bother, considering your situation." He listened a moment and said, "Don't be ridiculous; I was happy to offer the advice," and hung up.

He beamed at Aryeh, said "Shalom," and came around the desk and hugged him.

"Hungry?"

"Starving."

"Good. We'll eat upstairs. They serve a beautiful veal Mornay. I guarantee it."

As the captain led them through the restaurant to their table, Aryeh examined his surroundings, thinking, the American Dream given physical redemption, in the sounds if not the sights of heavy dinnerware, glasses clinking, quiet assured laughter. A home for Dieter, probably.

"You're writing again," observed Selig. "That glazed, remote look is the sure sign."

"Only on the inside of my head. It sifts down through my mouth sometimes, but rarely reaches paper. Anyway, this is exotic terrain for me."

"Much less than you think. If you could open all these skulls you'd probably find more insecurities and anxieties than in your entire faculty. They have better tailors and better barbers and better Scotch, that's all."

Halfway through the veal, Aryeh suddenly shifted the conversation from a college classmate whose face had appeared on the front page of local newspapers and began talking about the conversation in the bar.

"I can't leave it alone, Selig. I have to do something. I have to introduce some symmetry into the universe."

"Aryeh," said Selig, "you have no idea of what I would give to hear phrases like that coming out of my mouth. It fills me with admiration, even though I haven't the faintest idea of what it means."

"I mean I want to do something about that man Dieter. No, I mean I want to to do something to him. Something that will put him on the other side of power. Something that will make him a shoveler. Something that will make him feel what it's like to try to make sense of a world where somebody says 'dig' and you dig, trying to prevent yourself from thinking about why you and the others are digging, knowing all the time that you can't do anything about it.

"Selig, you know that stick they use in shuffleboard, the one with the curved end? No, better yet, that little rake that croupiers use in roulette and banco. Yes. What I want is for me to be the rake and make Dieter into a chip, a white one."

"Yes, now I understand," said Selig. "I understand when you put it that way. I understood the feeling while you were talking. And you want something from me."

"Your reaction to all this."

Selig smiled gently.

"No, I suspect that it's something much more important to you than that. People like to have my opinion on financial matters, they value that, but not on other things."

He smiled and held up a hand as Aryeh started to say something.

"No, don't interrupt. I don't talk this way often, so bear with me. Aryeh, we're fond of each other, truly fond, and for a great many years, I've known that if I could be somebody else, I'd choose to be you, all the way back to high school when you were dating the Deirdres and Deborahs and the girls with two first names and mine were always named Rebecca and Helen.

"You've never referred to me that way, but I suspect I've always been 'naive little Selig' to you, right?"

Aryeh looking down at the scrap of food on his plate, said in a voice clearly intended to soften the answer, "Yes. Sometimes, but not always."

Selig patted his arm. "It's all right. My problem is that I think of myself the same way. I'm very good at making money in ways that other people seem to think are difficult, but I don't understand your kind of mind, the way it works, the way you put words together and make them mean something they never meant separately."

"It's more show than substance, Selig. I play games with words. I talk. I plan things, but I don't do them. I play the game of being a writer. But what I want to do with Dieter is beyond a game."

Selig said, "This is all a game," and waved his hand at the room around them. He examined the palm of his right hand and spoke softly, so that Aryeh had to lean forward to hear him.

"But sometimes, I sit across the table from a man from Germany. I talk with him, small talk usually, sometimes business matters.

"And while I talk to him, there's another me at the table, the one that never in all his life has been able to comprehend what happened there, and never will. The Angel of Darkness comes into that other me and crouches over the man I'm talking to and asks, 'What did you do during the war? Which division of the SS? Which lover of poetry, which delicate sensibility conceived of *Nacht und Nebel,* "Night and Fog," as a euphemism for the camps? Of Return Not Required in place of Death Is Ordered? How did you carry out the orders? How did it feel? Tell me!'

"Every time it happens, thank God not often, I go home with a headache and tell Sylvia it's a migraine, and she hovers over me all evening. The problem, you see, is that part of me is convinced that I'm making it all up, that nothing ever happened over there, that I'm being morbid."

Aryeh stared at Selig, looking at a man whose existence he had never suspected, but seeing nothing in his outward appearance that was new to him.

"And still another part of me, Aryeh, another part of me says, Selig, you poor dumb stupid bastard, you haven't the faintest idea of what this man did, or even if he was there, and are you really going to tar them with the same brush? That's what they've always done with you and yours.

"But still, Aryeh, there's an imbalance, right? You want your Dieter to squirm? It's a very appealing idea."

Their waiter had cleared the table as Selig began to talk, but noting the absorption of the two men, he had retreated to a neutral corner. Both men were silent now, and he returned with the menu.

Selig looked inquiringly at Aryeh, who shook his head. Selig waved the menu away but pointed to the coffee cups. After they were refilled, he said, "I like that term symmetry. The balance of things. Six months ago I felt the same way, but I wouldn't have talked about it. Aryeh, you don't go to synagogue any more, do you? No. What about Passover? Did you go to a Seder??"

"I went this year," said Aryeh, "and it pushed me closer to doing something."

"I know. If it weren't for last year's Yom Kippur, I wouldn't be here discussing what part of me tells me is madness and another part of me says, I know, shut up. I'll tell you about it."

Selig had gone East with his family to visit his father and mother. Almost as soon as he arrived, his father had said to him, "I have a very important favor that I want to ask of you, Selig. Bless the congregation with me on the Day of Atonement," and Selig had agreed.

Even in the early days, when his father's town had been smaller, the synagogue stood at its edge, at the top of a slope descending to the Hudson River. The town had grown farther and farther in the opposite direction; the synagogue had remained, even when a more modern and more progressive one had been built on a sunny knoll at the other end of town.

"I am the only Kahen left in the congregation, the only High Priest; and when they learned you would be here, they asked me to ask you to give them the honor of joining me."

Walking to the synagogue, Selig's son asked, "How do you know you're High Priests?"

"Because I'm my father's son," Selig's father had answered. "It passed from generation to generation from Aaron, Moses' brother; and when we're called to read the Torah, we're identified that way.

"We can identify six generations in the family by that alone. I heard my grandfather called 'Jacob, son of Moses, the High Priest.' From him to you it goes, 'Israel, son of Jacob, the High Priest; Abraham, son of Israel, the High Priest; Selig, son of Abraham, the High Priest,' and when you become a man, you will be 'David, son of Selig, the High Priest.' "

There are other things passed from generation to generation, Selig told Aryeh. After the feeding of his initial curiosity in the strange synagogue, David was clearly bored, and he expressed his boredom the way Selig had at his age, looking through the prayer book for pictures, counting the people present, and practicing sleeping with his eyes open.

When the time came, Selig whispered to David, "I have to go now. Just watch the others and do what everyone else does," and stood up with his father.

They walked with stately deliberation to the transverse connection between the two side sections of the synagogue, facing the three steps leading up to the platform at whose rear was the Ark of the Covenant, which housed the congregation's Torahs.

His father stood at the base of the steps, and leaning on the wooden rail that separated the center section from the transverse aisle removed his shoes. After his father had walked up the steps, Selig removed his and followed him.

Both men stood on the platform with their backs to the congregation. They removed the prayer shawls from their shoulders and read the Hebrew inscription embroidered on them. As they did so, the entire congregation rose, turned their backs on the two men, and stood facing the rear of the synagogue.

When Selig and his father finished reading the inscription, they touched the shawls to their lips. Then each covered his head and extended arms with the shawl, so that it fell to the front and sides in flat planes.

Under the shawl, Selig touched his thumbs together. Then, keeping the first and second fingers pressed closely against each other, he extended the third and fourth outward as far as they would go, pressing them together too, leaving a gap between the two groups of fingers on each hand.

As his father began singing the ancient song that blessed the congregation, Selig followed his lead. The simple melody consisted largely of one syllable, repeated over and over. At it~ conclusion both men intoned in Hebrew, "May you be blessed."

When they were finished, they removed the prayer shawls, kissed the inscription once more, and returned the shawls to the position in which they had been worn earlier in the service. As they walked down the steps, the entire congregation queued up and began filing by, shaking their hands and thanking them for the blessing.

"It was after that, that it happened," Selig said. "At the first possible chance, I took David outside. He had seen the blessing before but never with me as High Priest, and I wanted to give him some sense, some real sense, of what had been going on: that we took off our shoes because the platform became consecrated ground the moment we stood on it; that we covered our faces because at the moment of blessing each of our faces became the face of God, too awful to look upon, according to the original meaning of the word; that our hands spelled out the initials of God's name and that the congregation had turned its backs for the same reason we covered our faces.

"I had started to do the impossible, to describe the first time I had done it, when I was thirteen, and had been in a state of frozen panic, overwhelmed by it all, by men five times my age, and more, shaking my hand, thanking me.

"A blue pickup truck up on those obscene mag wheels came roaring down the street. I guess it was the fact that David and I were still wearing our skullcaps that caught their attention. Anyway, they slowed down as they passed, and one of the kids in the front seat leaned out and yelled, 'Let's hear it for the oy-yoy-yoy boys!' and drove off. They were well down the block, with me watching them, before I realized that David was saying, 'Dad! Dad! You're hurting me!'

"You know what I was doing, Aryeh? I had my hand on his shoulder and I was squeezing it. Hard."

"I would have thought that stuff was as obsolete as corsets and hand-cranked telephones."

"I know. It's the kind of thing my grandfather was familiar with, and maybe even my father for part of his life. But that's not what affected me. The kids were no more than thoughtless or perhaps stupid. They probably forgot it a block later, and any other time I would have shrugged it off. But this time . . ."

Selig leaned forward and asked, "Did you see *Fiddler On The Roof?* There is a marvelous moment when Tevye stops singing 'Tradition' and advances toward the audience and says 'You want to know what tradition is? I'll tell you. I don't know.' "

He laughed with pleasure, then his face became intense and his voice deepened, becoming almost hoarse, as if he were pushing it against an obstruction, propelling it by forces he no longer controlled.

"I'll tell you what tradition is, Aryeh. It's men singing a chant thousands of years old, passed along by mouth to ear, father to son, generation to generation. Not only the melody but the syllables as well. The chant itself uses mostly one sound, repeated over and over," and he began singing softly, "Oy yoy yoy yoy, oy yoy yoy yoy yoy yoy yoy yoy yoy oy . . .

"When those kids came by, I made a connection I'd never before made in my entire life. That parody of Jews was taking five thousand years of tradition and dragging it into the mud. And just for a moment, a tiny, tiny moment, I wanted to hurt and maim."

He stared fiercely at Aryeh for a moment, then his face changed so swiftly that Aryeh thought of a fast film "wipe." Once again, it became the smiling, forever plump face of Aryeh's memory.

"Aryeh, they have a great strawberry mousse here. Join me," and he signaled the waiter without waiting for an answer. "Now tell me, what do you want of me? No, don't sigh and look like a stricken sheep."

"Yes," said Aryeh. "First, I've pretty well formulated what I'd like to do, and I think it may be very, very appealing to you. Will you join me and some others, some of them people you know, to discuss doing something to Dieter?"

"Second?"

"I've got his license number. It's simply a personalized plate. I've heard that you can get the name of the person holding a registration from the DMV. Can you get that and whatever information we can get about him from a full credit check?"

"And?"

"I'd like to know how he got into the country, and what his background is from whatever government papers exist on and about him."

"The answer is yes on the first and consider it done on the others. The credit check is simple, and I know a couple of people in Washington."

"When we have it, we'll meet. You should know that I'm going to do something even if it's only me, Selig."

"There are already two of us, Aryeh."

As Selig signed the check, Aryeh looked at him with a sense of loss, knowing that he would never look at him the way he had seen him before the lunch, never again, and felt a moment of regret for the way life had been before he had met Dieter. He added this feeling to the statement of charges against Dieter as he followed Selig out of the restaurant.

"Two of us," Selig had said. But their roles had reversed. He had walked into the restaurant expecting Selig to play Aaron to his Moses, and left cast as Aaron. At least it was good type-casting; DeMille might have cast him for the role instead of John Carradine. Aryeh smiled at the thought, and then began contemplating Dieter, about to undergo a strange new experience.

9

Aryeh decided that he would bat at least .800, and perhaps even 1.000, but that he would settle for .600, any three out of the five.

He had spent a considerable portion of the previous week talking to all of them, smoothing out conflicting schedules and responsibilities. Now he wandered around his living room, arranging chairs and trying to remember whether there were any smokers besides Martine and her little brown cigars, finally deciding to set out three ashtrays. He put ice cubes into a bucket and refilled the ice trays, then stood looking at his liquor supply and wondering whether he had time enough to run to the corner store for a bottle of bourbon. He had not yet decided when the doorbell rang.

He went to answer it, taking a last look around the room, saying to himself with disgust, whatever this is, it isn't a party, and stop worrying about it. By the time he reached the front door he had decided that perhaps it was a coming-out party for shovelers, and immediately realized that he was thinking like an adolescent romantic.

He relaxed when he opened the door and saw Simon and the Kid. Nice, it's bound to be .800, he reflected. When he opened the door for Selig ten minutes later, he had forgotten the bet.

Only Jean-Pierre accepted a drink, but Selig lit a cigar and the Kid a cigarette almost as soon as they entered the living room. The permutations of introductions caused a latticework of handshakes and mumbled acknowledgments, after which the group settled into a loose semicircle.

Simon sat at one end of the couch, with his spine almost on the seat itself, head propped against the back of the couch. The Kid sat on the floor near him, and Selig sat on the couch on the other side of the Kid. Jean-Pierre sat stiffly in a leather-slung director's chair to one side of the couch, and Aryeh sat loosely in an armchair, a coffee table between him and the others, his feet resting on it.

"Martine's usually quite punctual, so I guess she's not coming. Otherwise, we're all here."

"Martine? A Française? Who is she?" asked Jean-Pierre. He listened carefully as Aryeh described her background briefly, his facing slowly draining of interest.

"Now," said Aryeh, "individually you all know what this is about. I've spent a lot of time, too damn much, probably, deciding how best to sum it up, and it comes out like this: I want to make Dieter understand what it's like to be a victim by making him feel like one.

"I'm tempted to say it's as simple as that, but when any of my students use that phrase, I redline it and make nasty little comments in the margin. But you know what I mean."

"What are we to do to him?" asked Jean-Pierre.

"I know what I want to do, but that's getting into the mechanics of the script, and I think it should be reserved for later. Right now it's important for us all to be clear about our participation and to face the general limits of what we're prepared to do."

As Simon started to speak the doorbell rang, and he shifted ground. "I'll get it," he said.

Aryeh could hear Martine's voice, and smiled—an omen of success. He waved at her when she came in, but said nothing. She draped her coat over a chair next to Aryeh and put the paper bag she was carrying on the floor.

Aryeh introduced Martine, summarized what he had been saying, ending with, "I think Simon has the floor."

"It's not very much. It's just that I'm a little edgy about this, and it wouldn't take much for me to walk out of the door. I have a sense that we're about to act like a bunch of macho sixteen-year-olds—latest company excepted."

Martine nodded and said, "Latest company is close to feeling the same way."

"Oh? And what decided you to join us?" asked Jean-Pierre.

"Two hours ago, I wouldn't have," answered Martine. "I tend to operate on the principle that if I can't make up my mind about doing something, that something in me knows that I shouldn't be doing it and is holding me back.

"But on my way home I passed a store selling antique English postal scales. I looked at a beautiful little one that was in exquisite balance and thought to myself that it pointed to exactly where I was on all this.

"Next door was a toy shop, and I saw something that pushed me over the line. I'm slightly disgusted with myself for having bought it, but I did and brought it along. I think it speaks for itself."

She opened the paper bag, reached in and pulled out a cardboard box, holding it by its corners as if she were afraid of soiling her hands, and placed it on the coffee table so that the printing on the cover could be read from the couch. Aryeh and Jean-Pierre moved around to look at it.

The cover picture displayed a German World War II tank, the "Sturmpanzer 43," the Grizzly Bear tank. German text described it as "Furcht erregender Brumbär der deutsche Wermacht." The box contained parts for a 1/32 scale model.

"I might have passed it by except for what's on the sides," she said and turned the box ninety degrees. There were two pictures of the tank crashing through an already bombed-out building, each bearing the statement that the kit contained instructions for making a diorama of the scene.

"I looked at that and I thought about that man sitting in a bar somewhere, talking about that time, and his being able to offer it as an example of power and. . . . Well, I'm here."

Jean-Pierre shook his head. "I do not need such things to convince me. I think I am a balance to you, Simon, and to her," nodding at Martine. "I have a feeling that whatever we do to Dieter, it is not enough."

"I think perhaps we should talk about Dieter a little more before we go on," said Aryeh. "I want to read you something."

He walked to a glass and chrome table placed at the end of the couch where Selig sat. On it was a block of wood into which had been mounted scores of fine brass wires. When he picked up an envelope from the table, his hand brushed the wires, and they began quivering in all directions, making a whispering sound that lingered in the air.

Aryeh pulled two sheets of paper from the envelope, saying, "I asked Selig to get me some information on Dieter's status in this country, and he called a friend in Washington and told him the main things we wanted to know, that is, whether he is a citizen and whether his Nazi background is part of the official record."

"I'd like to add something," Selig said. "I don't know whether the information he sent is part of the public record, but he got it from the Immigration and Naturalization Service, and I didn't ask how."

"I'll read you part of it," said Aryeh. "It's a letter of recommendation from the owner of a wholesale hardware business in the mid-West: 'On March 23, 1945, I was in command of a battalion in bivouac three miles to the northeast of Aachen, after three weeks of continuous action.

'At 1100 hours of that day, the Officer of the Day reported that a perimeter guard had received a message from a soldier advancing under white flag, from a Lieutenant Dieter Holzer, in command of a small detachment that included himself and twenty men, a weapons carrier, a command car, and miscellaneous small armament.

'After I issued instructions to accept the offer, and the unit had been disarmed, Lieutenant Holzer was brought to my tent. In fair English he indicated that he considered that Germany had already lost the war, that he had done his full duty to his country, and that it would be wrong for brave men, on both sides, to die needlessly.

'Before he was removed for processing to a POW camp, we had several long conversations, during which he expressed his belief that the Germans and Americans had more in common than the Russians and the Americans, and that he was willing to offer whatever services were useful to us.'

"There's more," Aryeh said, "but I won't bore you with the reading of it. But Dieter worked for our good Lieutenant Colonel after he got out of either prison or prison camp, it's unclear which, and the Colonel found him loyal, courageous, true, and all the good things of life."

"I heard nothing remarkable in all that," said Simon. "Distasteful, but nothing more."

"I hear two things," Aryeh said. "One is that he wasn't consumed with patriotism or devotion to a lost cause. If he'd been briefed as to what to say, he couldn't have done it better. The more important thing is the time he spent in some kind of detention, seven months. Taking his own figure about the people he ordered killed, and he probably laundered the list before he washed it in public, it works out to approximately four days and five hours imprisonment per death."

"I don't think there's anyway of getting his case reopened without an impossible investigation first," said Selig.

"I'm not interested in the legal situation or in seeing that he gets properly punished. I'll repeat what I said before, I want one of them, him, to be pushed around by forces beyond his comprehension. Nothing more than that. All of that."

"Perhaps we should start discussing what it is we want to do," said Selig.

"We talk around and around," said Jean-Pierre. "Merde! Let's get on with it!"

"Yes," said Simon. "The game is all trussed and seasoned and waiting. But where is the pot to put it in?"

"That's the kind of statement that leaves me feeling that perhaps I should be someplace else," said Martine.

"It wasn't meant to be literal," Simon said. "It's called failed irony. I'm still feeling a little edgy."

"Don't start again, Simon," Jean-Pierre said. "We have been through that once. We all belong here, I think." He looked directly at Martine, who said nothing and after a moment turned her face away.

"Knowing something about Dieter as he is now might help," Selig said, taking a small notebook out of an inner pocket. "The full report is at the office, but I jotted down some points.

"He's five feet eleven inches tall, and his weight hasn't varied more than a pound in six years. His blood pressure is in the high end of the desirable range for his age, and he has one two-tooth bridge.

"He's a broker in the international used machinery market, which is in no way to be confused with scrap metal. He makes a great deal of money, and his credit and business reputation are both excellent.

"He has a small ski lodge on this side of the Donner Pass in the Sierras, and a rustic cabin in Inverness, where he cultivates exotic succulents.

"He contributes liberally to charity. He is a patron of the San Francisco Opera and has season box seats. He is an avid Mozart opera fan and has a large collection of records.

"He has no political affiliations and contributes to both major parties. He drinks and smokes moderately, exercises, and an acquaintance describes him as a womanizer. He has been married and divorced twice."

"In other words," said Simon, "a graduate of the Harvard School of Business Administration, class of '52."

"Or a man with a flair for burying himself in his surroundings," said Jean-Pierre.

Aryeh took advantage of the brief silence which followed to say, "Passover."

"Passover," said Jean-Pierre almost to himself. He repeated the word, pronouncing it as if it were two and accenting the second. "What does it mean?"

"It's the Jewish holiday which celebrates the deliverance of the Jews from Egypt," said the Kid. "Jehovah sent . . ." His voice trailed away, and he stared at Aryeh.

"Is that what you meant?" Aryeh nodded.

"The Plagues," said the Kid. "The Plagues."

Simon turned to Martine. "When Pharaoh refused to allow the children of Israel to leave Egypt, Jehovah sent down ten plagues on the people of Egypt to force the Pharaoh to reconsider."

"I know the general story," Martine said. "Moses and the bullrushes, the Last Supper, and all that. But what were the plagues?"

"Darkness, pestilence, locusts . . . things like that," said Selig.

"We can work out the specifics as we go along," said Aryeh. Obviously our powers are somewhat more limited than Jehovah's. We can do them literally or symbolically as we choose, to whatever degree we choose. The impact on Dieter is what will concern us."

He looked around the room, meeting each pair of eyes in turn, and took a deep breath. "Are we agreed?" He waited; when no one spoke, he said, "I think we ought to give this group a name."

"Like one of those World War II films with Errol Flynn?" asked the Kid. "You know, *Operation Burma.* How about Operation Dieter?"

"The Six Horsemen?"

"The Six Samurai?"

"Retribution, Inc.?"

"The Power Elite?"

"The Conscience Collective?"

"None of those," said Aryeh. " 'The Passover Commando.' Passover for obvious reasons; commando because we will function like one of the World War II military groups that would go out on a mission, return, go out on another, and so forth."

The Kid, Selig, and Jean-Pierre nodded approval.

"It's nice, very nice," said Simon. "But there's one small problem, the origin of the term *Commando.* It's a Boer word. It was used for the groups who hunted down runaway blacks."

Jean-Pierre said, "Simon, you think too much."

"As long as you know," Simon said.

"Do we tell him before we start?" asked Selig. "Jehovah warned the Pharaoh in advance as to what he was going to do."

"We're not trying to get him to do anything," said Aryeh, "so no warning is necessary.

"All we want is for him to feel. We'll make him feel as if he's walking around wearing a yellow Star of David, not knowing what's going to happen to him when he turns the next corner but understanding that something is going to happen."

"And what is going to happen to him first?" asked Jean-Pierre. "What is the first plague?"

"Blood? How?"

" 'And the rivers flowed red and the wells poured blood and the animals would not drink and there was terror and anguish and great moanings throughout the land,' " said Simon, then smiled at Martine and added, "I just invented that. But it's got the right tone and rhythm, and the basic idea is there. Water throughout Egpyt turned into blood. Actually, if you don't take the plagues literally, it wasn't blood. Some authorities interpret them as a series of natural disasters."

"The only disaster will be if we stand here forever, talking," said Jean-Pierre. He walked to the liquor cabinet, poured a little Burgundy into a glass, held it up to the light, and took a sip. "The question is, what water of his do we change into blood?"

"It seems to me," observed Martine, "that if we already possess the secret of turning water into blood, the choice is merely a small detail."

"Hardly," said Jean-Pierre. He turned to Aryeh. "Well?"

"I have an idea," he answered, "a very nice idea, but I'd like to ride with it a bit. Besides, it'll take some investigation and planning, and more technical ability than any of us have, with the exception of Jean-Pierre."

Jean-Pierre nodded, and murmured, "Blood. Cool." His face brightened and he said to Aryeh, "I have something for you. You are a man who likes wordplay. . . ."

The rising inflection in his voice had not yet begun to descend when Martine observed mildly, " . . . even more than foreplay," heard herself, and hastily added "probably," but it was too late. Her face had already risen ten degrees in temperature, Aryeh had found something

60

between his shoes of very great interest, and Simon was exhibiting signs of advanced cardiac arrest.

Jean-Pierre showed no change of expression. He waited until the others had recovered and said, "There is a French term *sangfroid*. It means to be self-possessed or, as we say today, to be cool. The words themselves, actually mean 'cold blood.' I would be pleased to assist you, Aryeh."

Selig said abruptly, "It's time to go," and got to his feet. The others followed his example. Aryeh made no attempt to delay the departures; instead he stood at the door shaking hands with each as they left.

Martine moved slowly, but put on her coat and buttoned it. She gave Aryeh a small sisterly hug. As she started out he asked, "What do you think, Martine?"

"Of the others?"

"All right. Of the others."

"Well," she said, drawing designs on the hall door with her finger, "Selig is a real dear. I've told you that before, except tonight I saw more iron in him than I'd suspected. The Kid—he's very young and knows exactly where white stops and black begins. And I'm troubled by your friend Jean-Pierre."

"He's Simon's friend," Aryeh said.

"I wouldn't have thought . . . no matter, he makes me uncomfortable. He's a hunter."

"If he is, he's not the kind that worries his game. He's attractive and he knows it, and doesn't have to press."

"It's not sexuality I'm talking about, and he's not my cup of tea nor am I his. I mean hunter, literally. Did you see the look on his face when somebody said 'blood?' You're absorbed with the idea; he relishes it."

"He's European, and his background . . . some of his family were Nazi victims."

"Whatever the reason, he seems to me to be a man born out of phase. We're caught between two times, but I feel that he would have liked with all his heart and soul to have been a grown man living in that time, with a moral license to kill." She regarded Aryeh solemnly, with a touch of sadness, and added, "We have to keep reminding ourselves that we don't have one, either. You do understand that, Aryeh, don't you?"

"Yes," he said, and watched her walk down the hall.

He closed the door and walked back into the living room slowly, stood for a moment behind the chair in which he had been sitting, then prowled around the room, picking up glasses and putting them down, sometimes removing them to the kitchen.

Once again, he stood behind his chair. In his mind, they were all back in the room, at the moment when it was his turn to say yea or nay. He thought back to the night in the bar, trying to recapture his feelings before Dieter had spoken. For a moment he wished fiercely that he had gone to a film that night, then shook his head vigorously several times and said aloud, "Let it begin."

Part II
דצבא

1

At 7:29 the hour hand of Dieter's radio alarm moved infinitesimally, causing a small tab of metal to touch another in the internal mechanism. At this same moment the minute hand completed the circuit, catching a violin and viola in mid-phrase of a Stamitz *concertante* and waking Dieter.

He was fully awake a few seconds after he opened his eyes. He turned his head to look at the crack between the heavy drapes to see if the foghorns of the night before had been accurate prophets. They had. A heavy gray dispiriting mist hung outside of the window.

In one easy motion he threw the covers back and swung his legs over the side of the bed. Sitting on its edge, he looked down at his stomach. With his thumb and forefinger he pinched together as much skin as he could, and nodded in satisfaction when it measured less than an inch.

He went into the bathroom and brushed his teeth, then went into the kitchen and drank a glass of fresh orange juice poured from a pitcher in the refrigerator. Back in the bedroom, he did ten minutes of Royal Canadian Air Corps exercises followed by twenty sit-ups performed with his hands clasped behind his head and his feet hooked underneath the bed.

After completing this ritual he showered luxuriously, shaved, and dressed carefully, but without his tie and jacket. He put on a three-quarter length Japanese *happi* robe with wide sleeves and a sash of the same material as the robe and went to the kitchen. He started water for coffee, put two eggs and three strips of bacon on the counter, and put two sourdough muffins into the electric toaster oven.

Before beginning to cook, he went to the front door and looked for his morning newspaper. It had been thrown against the edge of the plastic sheeting that covered his car. He brought it back into the house and continued making his breakfast.

When the bacon and eggs were ready, he slid them onto a plate which had been warming in the oven, split the muffins, spread them generously with lingonberry preserves, and began eating. Forty minutes later he had finished both breakfast and paper.

He poured a final cup of coffee, lit a cigarette, and sat thinking about the woman he had met two nights before at a minor consulate dinner. Mrs. Zorn was above-average height, elegant, and clearly knowledgeable. When she noted his glances at her, she had neither turned away nor lowered her eyes and lifted them again to look at him. She had, instead, returned the glance, with the slightest upward curve to her lips. There had been other signs of interest, equally unmistakable, but even another interested observer would have had a hard time deciphering them.

He had made quiet inquiries. She had been married and divorced three times, was wealthy and cultured. He had found her interesting — she would be unbearable as a wife, but as a partner for an affair she seemed near perfect.

He continued to think about the women in his life. He had all he wanted, but it had been too long since he had met one who intrigued him. Bed companions had always been plentiful, but several years earlier he had become aware that young, very young, women found him attractive. He recognized the implications and briefly felt panic, followed by depression. However, he no longer cared. If they were looking for a father and found one in his bed, he had no objections. They were everywhere. When he started going to the bar, it had been because of the complex cultural mix of its patrons; but now he used it largely for sexual forays.

He considered briefly whether to wait another day before calling Mrs. Zorn and suggesting a lunch date, then put her out of his mind and channeled his thoughts to the consideration of the key elements of the day's business schedule: first, the very important phone call to Toronto, the conference with his lawyer, and a business lunch which promised to be both boring and useful.

He brushed his teeth once more, carefully selected a tie and jacket, put them on, and double-locked the front door after writing a brief note to his part-time housekeeper.

The fog had deposited a film of moisture on the car's plastic covering. Carefully standing away from it, he folded it from front to back and put it into a small compartment cut between two studs in the siding, then wiped his hands on a small towel stored inside the enclosure.

He inserted the car key, turning it counterclockwise with his right hand, pulling upward and outward on the door latch with his left. The door resisted his pull for a moment. As it gave way, a torrent of blood burst out at him, splashing on his trousers and shoes and flowing into the alley.

His body reacted instinctively, even before his brain began its interpretation, and he jerked backward awkwardly as the blood spurted out. When the liquid hit him, he made a sound that might have been a scream if he had allowed it to emerge unhampered, but self-discipline and long-discarded training took over and stifled it, so that his cry resembled a strangled croak.

After the first spurt, the blood spilled out in pulsing bursts, as if a huge artery had been severed. Part of the plastic bag from which the liquid had erupted hung in a fold over the edge of the seat. As the blood poured from the main portion of the bag, some of it spilled into the fold, distending it into an obscene bladder. Slowly, the flow became a small stream which trickled into the tiny channels between the alley's cobblestones.

Dieter, staring without comprehension, suddenly felt a sticky wetness on his lower thigh where the blood had soaked through his trouser leg and shivered in disgust. He turned to go back to the house but instead shifted and turned back to the car. Trying to avoid the pool of blood on the cobblestones, he reached out and grasped a fold of the plastic bag, letting the sack drop to the ground when it was entirely free of the car. A few drops splattered against his hand. He grimaced, wiped it against his trousers, and went to the entrance door, where he took off his shoes before unlocking it and entering the house.

He hesitated in the entryway, then pulled his trousers off. Holding them bunched into a loose bundle with the soiled part uppermost, he ran to the bathroom. He quickly removed his alligator belt from the trouser loops, threw the trousers into the bathtub, and examined his legs and thighs.

The blood-soaked trousers had left a light pink sheen on the hairs of his left thigh. He soaked a washcloth and scrubbed his leg, cursing steadily the whole time, then dried himself carefully. He called the police only after examining himself once more, painstakingly, and putting on another pair of slacks.

When he heard the sound of voices in the alleyway, he was sitting in a cane rocker, his legs crossed, his hands on the rocker arms, breathing deeply but regularly, attempting to examine what had happened, refusing to allow confusion and anger to master him.

He pushed himself out of the chair and looked out the window. A police car sat at the entrance to the alleyway, blocking exit from it, and two uniformed patrolmen stood alongside his car, carefully avoiding the drying blood. One of them squatted, wiped a finger in the liquid, then rubbed his finger against his thumb. Dieter wrinkled his nose when the policeman sniffed at the thumb.

As Dieter opened the front door the second policeman was reaching for the brass knocker. His hand was still moving as the door swung open, and Dieter took an involuntary step backward. His face flushed as he almost lost his balance. He started to speak sharply, but recovered and said, "You see why I called you. The blood."

The policeman who had squatted down turned from his examination of the car and said, "It's not blood."

"But of course it's blood," said Dieter. "What else could it be? Why do you say it is not blood?"

"Because it's too thin for blood and it doesn't smell like it. Here," and he held out his hand to Dieter.

Dieter waved the hand away and shook his head. "I really don't give a damn in hell what it is," he said. "It's pure vandalism."

"Well, sir," the patrolman said, "if it's only vandalism, it's pretty sophisticated, that is, if your car was locked all night."

"It was locked," said Dieter. "Anyone who leaves a car unlocked in San Francisco, day or night, should be committed."

"I'm afraid I'd have to agree with that," said the patrolman. "But anyway, that plastic bag was inside your car when you opened and unlocked it, right?"

Dieter nodded.

"It's an odd kind of bag, and I figure it could've been made just for this purpose. So you see, the whole thing had to be planned in advance.

"That's what I meant when I said 'sophisticated.' Your typical vandal, now, he'll take a can of paint and throw it against a building or a car, or maybe he'll use a spray can and run, but he won't waste time on something like this. It's what they call 'undifferentiated anger' in criminal psychology. Here, it's like somebody doesn't like you, specifically, and wanted to get your goat."

"Doesn't like me?" repeated Dieter, and laughed with genuine amusement. "Of course there are people who don't like me, just as there are people who do not like you, and people each of us doesn't like. But I don't know anyone who is such a barbaric simpleton as to do something like this to my car."

"Barbaric, that's a good word for it. But I wouldn't say simpleton. It's kind of clever, they really figured out what they were doing. Look."

He reached for the car door and pulled it open as far as it would go. A piece of coat-hanger wire was wrapped around the window armrest. One end stretched out from the door for about a foot and was intertwined with a rusty piece of barbed wire that extended several inches farther.

"What I figure is that they put the bag right up against the door, then they attached this rig and set the barbed wire on the bag, so it'd snag and rip when you opened the car door. I figure that plastic is no more than 2 mil."

"But the car was locked," said Dieter. "I always make sure of that, and besides, when I opened it this morning, I clearly heard the lock click."

"That's simple enough," said the patrolman. "Any interested ten-year-old knows all about pin-pry bars and how to use them." When Dieter looked at him blankly, he said, "I'll show you," and went to the patrol car. He brought back a piece of metal about fifteen inches long, about an inch wide, and curved gently at its lower portion. Near the end of the curved portion, an elongated notch about a quarter-inch deep had been cut away.

"We carry it to help people who've locked themselves out of their cars," he said. "You just take this bar and slip it down between the door and the window; then you kind of feel around until you catch the lockpin in this notch, push against it, and bingo!

"This took planning, but it also took someone who wanted to do it enough to take a chance on being caught. But the thing that bothers me is, What's the point? It didn't do much damage to your car that I can see. I'd make a bet right now that it's a water-soluble dye with some kind of thickener in it, like cornstarch."

"It looks like some kind of warning to me," said the other officer.

"Warning? Of what?" asked Dieter. "I'm an ordinary citizen, and I'm not involved in anything that I should be warned about."

"You said earlier 'of course it's blood.' I'm just wondering out loud, did you mean anything special or did you say that simply because it looked like blood?"

"Anyone would think it is blood," said Dieter. "How can you be sure it is not?"

"I'm sure. I've seen enough of the stuff to last me the rest of my life, but we'll have the lab check it anyway, and we'll let you know what we come up with, if you want. About fingerprints—I don't expect there'll be much luck with them. That wax job of yours looks untouched."

Dieter nodded and said, "Thank you for coming," in the tone of a host politely wishing guests godspeed, and started to turn away when the other patrolmen said, "Excuse me, sir, but just one more thought."

When he had Dieter's attention, he looked somewhere past him and asked, "Can you think of any association between you and blood?"

"You just explained to me that you do not believe it to be blood," said Dieter, and his voice became momentarily sharp.

"What I meant is, Have you ever hit somebody with your car, and maybe hard enough to make them bleed?"

"Never," said Dieter. "In my entire life I have never had an accident or injured someone, and only once was there even a moving violation. You have my permission to check the records if you like."

"We'll take your word for it, sir, and if anything comes up, we'll be in touch with you. And if you think of anything that might lead to the perpetrators, we'd appreciate a call from you."

"When we patrol the neighborhood," said the other policeman, "we'll keep a special eye on your place. But if you don't mind my saying so, if it was my car, I'd think about a garage."

Dieter sighed and shook his head, "In a world where things like this can happen, having to adapt to them is almost as bad as the things themselves."

He shook hands with both patrolmen, said "Thank you for coming," and went back into the house. The patrolmen had not yet gone back to their car when he came out again, picked up his soiled shoes, and holding them away from his body reentered the house.

Inside, Dieter stripped and showered and changed all his underclothes, then called his office to say he would be late. Before leaving, he notified his garage to come and pick up his car and have it cleaned, called a taxi service, and added several lines to the housekeeper's note.

As he walked to the curb to wait for the cab, he stepped on a small patch of the liquid that had trickled its way down to the sidewalk. Scraping the sole of his shoe on the curb several times, he muttered, "Filth."

He sat stiffly in the cab, brooding over the morning's events. The police knew what they were talking about, he decided. It had not been simple vandalism, but an act of nastiness.

He sighed. Life had a way of lying in wait to upset the balances he had so carefully created for himself. This, and only last week he had found himself again telling the story of the shootings. Each time he told it, he resolved never to tell it again; and each time he told it, the numbers increased. Those of his acquaintances who had never recovered from the Freudian virus could offer simplistic explanations, but life was more complex than they dreamed.

2

"I drove by a little before ten, and there was a police car up on the sidewalk behind his car and two patrolmen were talking to him," said Simon. "At least, I assume it was Dieter."

"They were still there about a quarter after ten," said Martine.

"There was a man scrubbing the cobblestones with a long-handled brush about 10:45, and his car was gone. Except for that, there was no sign that anything had happened," said Selig.

The Kid said, "The problem with it, as far as I'm concerned, was that we didn't all get to see it happen, let alone the aftermath. It must have worked, from what you saw, and we can guess what he felt when all that red goo came tumbling out at him, but it's only a guess. None of us were there when it actually happened."

Aryeh nodded. "We'll have to remedy that when we do the next plague," he said.

"Les grenouilles," said Jean-Pierre. " *'Les grenouilles couvrirent le pays d'Egypte.'* Frogs. That is a most admirable god you have there. Admirable. Frogs, imagine!"

"He also imagined the existence of men like Dieter," said Aryeh.

"As they say, 'Ours not to reason why, ours but to. . . .' Anyway, we're back at the principal issue," said the Kid.

"Yes," said Jean-Pierre. "How. We cannot cover the land, but since we have affected his car, perhaps now we should affect his house?"

"Nice," said Aryeh. "I can see the scene: the man comes home from a hard day's work at the ovens, walks into his house, and everywhere there are frogs hopping about. I think you used the word displacement, Simon. That would indeed displace him."

"It might even send him running into the street, screaming," suggested the Kid.

"No, not yet," said Jean-Pierre.

"I have an idea," offered Selig, in a soft, tentative voice, like a man who expected the conversation to continue to flow around his voice, in the fashion of a strong current encountering a hidden snag.

"Tell us," said Martine. She had been listening to the talk intently, shifting her attention away only once, when Simon had stirred, as if about to say something.

"Well," Selig said, "I think the Kid's point is important, about not doing it in the abstract, so to speak, but doing it so that we can all see how he reacts. And more than that, my idea would give him a very large audience."

He repeated "a very large audience," looking like a man who had just had his first mouthful of a promising new wine bottling, and continued, "About a month ago, we had tickets for the San Francisco

Symphony, orchestra seats, and we sat in the row just under the box seats in the grand tier. Somebody above us had left a pair of gloves on the rail, and they must have brushed against them, and they came floating down. One of them landed in my wife's lap."

He stopped talking and smiled to himself. Jean-Pierre waved his hand impatiently and said, "Continue."

"That's all that happened," said Selig, "but that's all it took to set the whole place off. First there was a little flurry in the seats around us, and then it spread like the ripple effect when you toss a pebble in a pond. There were people looking at the gloves floating down, and people looking at those people, and others who couldn't see what was happening but knew there was something going on, and eventually I could see some of the players in the orchestra trying to peer in our direction.

"I've been thinking about Dieter having box seats at the opera. Suppose, some night when he was going to be at the opera, and we knew about it, we could release frogs from his box—no, into it. If a pair of gloves could cause that ripple effect, think of frogs hopping all over the opera house, and Dieter . . ."

He stopped and began laughing. Even before the final words had left Selig's mouth, Aryeh had slipped off his chair onto the floor, and sat there, pounding the rug with his fist. Simon's hands were clasped behind his head, and he was grinning with the look of someone whose cherished fantasy has come to life. The Kid had both hands raised, fists clenched, and was shaking them in a victory salute at Selig. Jean-Pierre's face was expressionless, but his eyes moved from one to another, narrowing slightly as he looked at Martine.

She sat shaking her head, almost in disbelief, but her lips were touched with a small smile, like that worn by a young mother telling a child it has been naughty but secretly admiring its audacity. When Simon caught her eyes, she shook her head again, then burst out laughing, and said, "We can't!"

Aryeh turned to her. "We can't? Of course we can. It would be a crime against humanity not to."

74

"No, wait," said Simon. "I admit it's a beautiful idea, almost a piece of conceptual art, but we can't do it. If it could be limited to Dieter somehow, if we could figure out a way to keep the frogs confined to his box, that would be lovely. But if we actually carry it off, a lot of people who have nothing to do with us are going to have their evening interrupted and perhaps ruined."

"Simon, my friend," said Jean-Pierre, leaning closer to him. "Let me tell you a little story. After the war, when I was growing up near the docks in Le Havre, I would sit in a café with a group of friends, sailors and stevedores and men like that, and I was quiet, and fetched them cigarettes, and they would let me listen.

"They all had been in the Resistance, and sometimes they would talk about the different types in the underground, like the men who would kill calmly and then soil their pants later. There was one man who was as good with a gun or the garrote or plastique as anybody, but all the same, before a mission he would always insist on talking about morality and justice and what he called 'the innocents.' You know what code name they gave him? Hamlet. *'L'homme s'étiole l'ombre pale de la pensée.'*

"Simon, you are a good man, but if the Resistance had been full of people like you, it would have accomplished very little. This idea is little more than what you call a practical joke, but the point is to judge it on its merits, not because of how it will affect the 'innocents.'"

The Kid, who had been listening eagerly and nodding in agreement, turned to Simon and said, "You're all wet on this one. It's not going to ruin anybody's evening, that's for sure. There'll be a lot of excitement, which is what we want, but that will pass and the opera will go on. Besides, it'll add to their evening because everybody will have something to talk about—you know, 'only in San Francisco,' stuff like that."

"Simon," Aryeh said, "the main argument for doing this lies in the way we execute it. The more confusion we create around Dieter, the more we can intensify his feeling of powerlessness. We can make certain it gets known that the whole thing started in his box and is directly connected with him, and there's our Dieter, trying to explain away the unexplainable."

"I think I go along," said Martine. "I'm still a little troubled by it, Simon, on your grounds, but it's too appealing to let go."

He studied her for a moment, then held his hand above his head, palms outward. "I surrender," he said. "But I hope your Hamlet survived to ask more questions, Jean-Pierre. Did he?"

"I did not think to ask," answered Jean-Pierre, not looking at Simon.

"Frogs in the opera house," said Aryeh. "Operation Frogs. Onward and upward. I can think of three things we're going to have to work on: we need information about frogs, information about the opera house, and we need to plan the mechanics of the operation."

"About the opera house, there is sometimes a guided tour. If someone goes on it, that would be useful," said Jean-Pierre. "And as far as things and the way they operate there, I have a friend. . . ."

". . . She," said Simon. "If anyone else says 'I have a friend,' it could be either sex; but in his case, there's not a waitress or female usher or ticket-taker in the entire Bay area whom Jean-Pierre doesn't know."

"A magnet is not responsible for the iron filings it attracts," said Jean-Pierre. "I have a friend who is an usher at the opera house, and I will talk to her."

"I will venture into frogs," said Simon.

"And I will take the guided tour," said Aryeh.

3

He stood on Van Ness, across from the opera house, and looked up at it, wondering about the architect who had designed the building as if he were in Italy, and the city fathers who had agreed upon the design. No, don't blame him or them, he thought; they wanted the legitimacy of Europe for the still raw West. When he saw the date carved into the cornerstone, MCMXXXI, he made a mental list headed "Interesting Thoughts Shot Down" and added an item.

The tour was scheduled to start in a few minutes; about thirty people were waiting for it to begin, standing on the steps or peering into the lobby's locked doors. He assessed the crowd, found no one of interest, and leaned against the building until the doors opened.

The tour started within a minute of schedule. The guide welcomed them, led them into the lobby, and issued a stream of facts about the history of the building, the people who had built it, the nature of opera in San Francisco in earlier eras, and other information, all of which the group absorbed with an air of interest. Aryeh listened attentively at first, waiting for a useful piece of information to emerge. Nothing came, and he let his attention wander away until the guide said, "The opera house sits on a river," waiting with obvious relish for an outpouring of disbelief.

My God, thought Aryeh, it's like *The Phantom of the Opera,* secret basements and passages, and searched for a way to link the creek that flowed beneath the subbasement with the frogs, but inspiration eluded him.

When they stood in front of the first row of orchestra seats, their backs to the stage, he paid careful attention as the guide pointed above their heads.

"The chandelier," she said, "is twenty-seven feet across, and has over seven hundred bulbs in it, and there's actually a kind of room inside of it so that the maintenance crew can change bulbs."

"How do they get into it?" asked Aryeh.

"I believe there's some kind of trapdoor in the ceiling, but I'm afraid that it's not included in the tour. The room, I mean."

"Of course not," said Aryeh, and drifted back into the shelter of the group.

He looked up again and mentally estimated the distance from the chandelier to the row of boxes. He envisioned little green bodies hurtling from the chandelier down to Dieter's box and felt momentary revulsion, then reminded himself that even it could be accomplished without harm to the frogs or the people below, these were not real plagues and he was not Jehovah. Besides, the frogs were not to be directed at Dieter; they must surround him, envelop him, or perhaps best of all, appear to come from him.

"There are twenty-five boxes," said the guide, "each with its own anteroom. Most of the seats, if not all, tend to be taken for the entire opera season."

Aryeh decided that still another question was safe, and asked, "You mean they're not available to the general public, like orchestra seats?"

"Sometimes there are a few, mostly at concerts, however; but they are available for the public to subscribe to. And, of course, we have a group of people who support the opera financially, and there are special arrangements for them."

When the group moved upstairs, Aryeh drifted to its rear and then followed the corridor leading to the grand tier. The use of a box next to Dieter's did not seem feasible; the anterooms were tempting, but only if they were cut off from the boxes by a door or curtain, so that the box occupants would be unaware of activity behind them during the performance.

He tried the first door he came to; it was unlocked; he opened it and glanced about swiftly. A curtain hung at the entrance to the box; a door would have been better, but the curtain filled the entire opening. Of course, he thought, it would have to, otherwise the light from the corridor would shine through.

He rejoined the tour group when they went downstairs and the guide led them up on the stage. Aryeh stood at the front of the apron, looking up at the boxes, trying to visualize the scene as it might take place, then corrected himself—as it will take place.

One of the group stood alongside of him and said, "It's fun to imagine being a singer or performer standing here, but I would guess that it's a lot different when there's an audience out there."

Aryeh nodded agreement. "Do you remember what Orson Welles did in the opera scene of *Citizen Kane?*" he asked. "Instead of hiring extras for an audience, he shot the scene from the back of the stage, into the footlights, so there never was an audience. It not only saved money but it gave more of an impression of the real thing than if he'd staged it. Brilliant."

The man considered him a moment and left. Aryeh, caught by his own story, tried to imagine himself as the young Orson Welles, working out the way in which he would direct that scene. Young, only twenty-five years old when he did it, and already making film history. That was a different generation, he told himself, with greater possibilities.

A rising feeling of self-contempt was dispelled when he heard the tour guide say, "Look up there, up above the side boxes," and turned to look in the direction she was pointing. "Those plaster friezes above the boxes on each side conceal sounding chambers. They were intended to house pipes for the opera house organ, but it was never installed."

"Are they used for anything now?" asked Aryeh with growing interest.

"No, nothing. Several years ago Ozawa put trumpeters inside, and it was really marvelous according to people who were here. I think they were playing Berlioz."

"Sounds more like Bruckner to me," someone muttered.

Choices, thought Aryeh, all kinds of choices. Dieter, we will do our best to make this a memorable season.

Back in the lobby he studied the list of programs for the coming season. These presented too many alternatives; the range was a large one, and it was impossible to assume that Dieter would go to all of them. Besides, most, if not all, of the operas were presented several times. How to determine which performance Dieter would attend? Student matinees and Saturday matinees were easy enough to strike off the list, but that still left too many other possibilities.

Perhaps the operation could be set up in such a way that they could react on a moment's notice; perhaps with the help of an inside accomplice. Jean-Pierre's "friend"?

He was halfway across the Bay Bridge on the way to his afternoon class when he recalled that there would be a Mozart opera, *Idomeneo,* rarely performed anywhere, and not in San Francisco for many years. Dieter would be sure to attend.

Although there would be several performances, Dieter was most likely to choose opening night; at least that narrowed the range. He was pleased with himself for a moment, then suddenly realized why he had chosen to forget that the opera was being given. The Passion According to St. Freud, he thought; it's always there. Damn it, why does Dieter have to like Mozart? he demanded of the car ahead of him.

4

People don't really understand frogs," the young woman told Simon. "I mean, a frog to them is either frogs legs meunière or a bullfrog sitting on a lily pad."

"There's Calaveras County, too," said Simon.

"That's up north, isn't it? Gold country? Do they have a lot of frogs there?"

"One day a year," Simon said, and she looked at him, puzzled.

The world's mad, he said to himself. Here she is, this shining young creature, living the simple life, working in a country store, dressed in what amounts to homespun, fighting to be in tune with the universe, and yet she knows about frogs legs meunière.

Still, she was engaging, with coloring that reminded him of Martine. But compared to her, this girl was nothing more than a rainbow soap bubble. He tried to visualize Martine, using her lips as a starting point to reconstruct her face.

"How many frogs are you interested in buying?" the young woman asked.

"I think perhaps two dozen," said Simon. "I mean, of course, if that doesn't break up too many families."

"Oh, they don't come in families," she said. "But there are many more varieties of frogs than most people realize. There's the small kind we have, you know? like three to five inches across, and there are frogs with hair, and there are even frogs that climb trees.

"And do you know what kind of frogs they have in Australia?" she asked. Her face carried the kind of happy smile worn by people about to fling open a door and yell "Surprise! Surprise!" Simon suspected what was coming but could not deny pleasure to that beaming face.

"No, I don't know," he said politely.

"None!"

He allowed himself to look surprised, nodded in appreciation, then decided he had had enough of real communication.

"I need to know something about frogs before I make up my mind. Do they travel well?"

"Like wine, you mean?"

"No, I mean if I put them into a container, with air of course, and drove overnight with them, say to Los Angeles, how would they do?"

"Oh, you'd have no problems. They would just sleep, they get very sleepy in dark places."

"And when I open the container?"

"They'll perk right up," she said, and looked at him suspiciously. "You're not planning vivisection, are you? Because if you are, I couldn't sell them to you. All life is valuable, you know."

"I agree," said Simon. "No, I won't vivisect them or harm them in any way. Actually, I'd be giving them their freedom, after a little bit."

5

Damn it, Jean-Pierre," Aryeh said, "we're not stalling. For me, this is like being at a banquet. Every course should be savored, each for its special quality, and each for the way it blends into the whole."

"Besides," said Simon, "Jehovah himself set the ground rules. According to some calculations, it took even him an entire year to carry out all the plagues. It would be presumptuous of us to do it more quickly."

"Make jokes, if it pleases you, Simon. Another time, I will laugh. For now, I take little satisfaction in what you are planning, but in any event, I am in favor of movement."

"And if it pleases you, Jean-Pierre," said Simon, "I can arrange for the frogs anytime we are ready."

"Whatever arrangements we make, we have to be sure he's going to be there for opening night," said Selig.

"We can be sure," said Martine. Her voice became precise, assured, and demanding, each word overarticulated, as if she were a tourist speaking to natives. "Hello? This is Mr. Dieter Holzer's private secretary calling. Mr. Holzer is on another line, calling from New York. He will have an important guest in his box for the opening night performance of *Idomeneo,* but he can't recall his box number and the tickets are locked in his desk at home. Would you be so kind as to check for him? He's waiting. Yes. Yes. Yes. Thank you so much."

She studied the fingernails on her left hand, burnished them against the sleeve of her dress, studied them again and said, "Box 23."

"So now we know. Let us congratulate each other. Can we now proceed?" asked Jean-Pierre. "My friend says there are usually two ushers on the grand tier, but it depends on who's on duty as to what it is they do during the performance.

"If they're opera or music students working to make money, they find a place to listen to the opera. If they're professionals, and the tier is considered the top of the ladder, they may sit somewhere reading or knitting or talking."

"In either case, they probably wouldn't pay too much attention to some sort of delivery," said Martine. "We could use my van, attach a magnetized sign with plastic lettering: The Flower House, Wholesale and Retail, that sort of thing, and we'd be taken for granted."

"Are you offering us an example, or do you actually mean that you would allow your van to be used?" asked Jean-Pierre, staring at Martine.

"Of course she means it," said Selig. "But who will make the actual delivery? It will require no more than two or perhaps only one. The rest of us will want to be there, to experience it."

Almost in chorus, Aryeh, Simon, and the Kid said, "Me."

"Let's not argue," said Simon. "Aryeh did the groundwork at the opera house, and he deserves to be a spectator. Besides, Aryeh, you and Jean-Pierre had the privilege of performing the first plague. Martine would call too much attention to herself, and besides we'll be using her van. As for Selig, he's the 'grand architect' of all this, and he deserves to be there to see his master plan unfold.

"That leaves the Kid and me. Any dissent? Good."

"I'll take care of getting orchestra seats for the rest of us, preferably down front and on the opposite side from Dieter's box, so we won't twist our necks watching the performance," Selig said.

Jean-Pierre stood up. "No, thank you. If I go, I will look down upon him from the balcony, and will make my own arrangements. If there is nothing further?"

"Just waiting," said Aryeh.

6

Martine, Selig, and Aryeh sat in a Japanese restaurant less than a mile from the opera house.

"I feel suspended in space," Martine said, "as if I were leading a life other than my own. I haven't the faintest idea of how I feel, or should feel. There's no frame of reference."

"I think I know how Selig is feeling," said Aryeh. "Guilty."

Selig nodded. "Sylvia was very happy to go South to see her sister, but something about the way she said goodbye made me feel that she knew I hadn't suggested the trip entirely for her sake. Sometimes I wonder whether she thinks I'm having an affair."

"It would have been very difficult if she were sitting with us tonight. We would have had to explain everything," Aryeh said.

"I have a feeling I would have enjoyed listening to the two of you trying to explain this madness to her," said Martine, "or to anybody. Including me."

"Second thoughts?"

"No, I'm looking forward to this with as much anticipation as the rest of you, with the possible exception of Jean-Pierre. It's just that I don't recognize myself in all this."

"Don't worry," Aryeh said. "Revelation will come."

"Revelation," Martine repeated. "That's where you find the description of the Apocalypse in the Bible."

When they drove into the Civic Center garage in Selig's Mercedes, Aryeh sighed. "This is wrong. No style. There should be a uniformed White Russian general to help Martine out of the car and a guards colonel to drive the car away."

Martine shook her head. "You're a half century late."

Selig and Aryeh wore evening clothes, although Aryeh at dinner had called attention to the white socks he was wearing. Martine had put her hair up and wore a velvet opera cape over a deep maroon full-length evening gown. As they walked across the Civic Center plaza, Martine in the center, they held hands like children on their way to a playground.

The small traffic circle in the front of the opera house was full of cars, with others double-parked on Van Ness, waiting to discharge their passengers. A steady stream of operagoers strolled from both corners to the entrance.

Selig looked at the scene. "The feeling that we know what's going to happen and they don't is surprisingly pleasant."

Aryeh nodded and said, "The two of you go on ahead. I'll wait here and call Simon as soon as Dieter arrives."

Dieter and Mrs. Zorn sat in a taxi at Van Ness and Clay. A dusty car with Tennessee license plates and a water bag tied to its radiator had tried to make too quick a turn and had stalled in the intersection, causing traffic in both directions to come to a halt.

"If I could have anticipated," Dieter said, "we would have taken my car."

"No matter," Mrs. Zorn said. "You can tell me more about the opera."

He had had lunch with her twice. Both times it had been pleasant; they had acted like racing drivers, watching a competitor take a practice lap, assessing strengths and weaknesses. What turns the campaign would take during the evening were still unknown and unplanned, but he relished both her company and the inherent challenge of the contest.

"It's an interesting opera," said Dieter. "Among other things, Mozart wrote a major role with a friend in mind, a *castrato*. You know the term?"

"The young boys who were castrated in order to keep their voices at adolescent purity? Yes. Really, I can still shudder at the thought. How barbaric!"

"Yes, that is so, but you must always remember that their attitudes were very different from ours, and we must take great care in judging them. Besides, the *castrati* often became wealthy and famous."

"Enough, Dieter, enough. Tell me the story."

"Let me tell you the legend on which it is based instead. Idomeneus, King of Crete, had been in the Trojan wars and had courted Helen of Troy. He was at sea when a great storm threatened, and he promised Poseidon, the god of the sea, that he would make a sacrifice to him of the first human being he met on shore if Poseidon brought him to shore safely. The first such that he met was his son. He kept his promise, but the gods were so outraged by his act that they sent a plague on the land."

"And this is the pleasant evening you promised? Castrati, human sacrifices, plagues?"

Dieter laughed. "Hardly. Mozart's music is always lovely, and the librettist lightened the story by adding a happy ending. In any event, it is fascinating. One wonders about the Greeks, you know, and why they understood as much about human beings as they did. Consider what can be read into this legend, for example, almost the reverse of Oedipus, that is, the father's unconscious wish to kill his son. Of course, that is . . ."

"Was the kid his only one?" asked the cab driver.

"Excuse me?" asked Dieter, turning away from Mrs. Zorn and looking at the driver's reflection in the rearview mirror.

"What I asked was, the king's son, was he an only child?"

"What difference does that make?" asked Dieter.

"Well, the thing is, is if he was, I mean the only one or the first one, it reminded me of the plagues on Pharaoh . . ."

"Yes," said Dieter. "The traffic seems to be unsnarled now, and we'll be there soon, yes?" and turned back to Mrs. Zorn.

Simon sat in the driver's seat and the Kid in the passenger seat of Martine's van, pointed in the direction of the opera house located three blocks away. Simon had parked the car near a telephone booth; the Kid checked that it was in working order and climbed back into the car.

A cardboard box with rope handles rested on the cover of the transmission housing between them, air holes neatly punched into its sides and top. The Kid was still muttering about Simon's declaration that their assignment was a composition for "piano, two hands" and not for a duet, or "piano, four hands," and that in any event, it would have to be carried out "piano" and not "forte."

"No way," argued the Kid. "The box is too heavy and too bulky for one man. One man carrying it won't have the right body look, not to mention that you're no Marlon Brando."

"Not that heavy," mumbled Simon.

"And besides, another pair of hands and eyes could prove to be handy, opening doors and such. Maybe even an extra mouth, if one of us has to do a snake-oil routine on one of the ushers. The trouble with you is that you're playing the protective older brother role."

"Reuben, you wouldn't be in this if it weren't for me."

"Reuben," mimicked the Kid. "Reuben. Q.E.D. You never call me Reuben unless you're being really serious and concerned. The last time was . . ."

He stopped talking and sat up in his seat. Simon was already watching a car with a revolving light fixture on its roof; it had been moving slowly toward them, stopping twenty feet away.

The car's headlights went to dim for a moment, almost immediately shifting to bright, the light shining directly into their faces. Both of them instinctively put their hands to their faces, but the car was already moving away from them. Across the street a garage door slid silently upward, exposing a dimly lit cavernous space. The car completed its turn and the garage door closed again. As the car disappeared into the darkness, Simon was able to make out the lettering on its side: "Protective Patrols, Inc."

"You know something?" asked the Kid. "I was as jumpy as if . . ."

". . . as if we'd been doing something really illegal," said Simon. "I know."

Jean-Pierre lay on his bunk in the houseboat, chewing on a vitamin C capsule and sipping occasionally from a large glass of orange juice. Twice he got up to adjust his stereo receiver, although a dial pointer informed him both times that it had been as finely tuned as possible.

He had no clocks on his boat, and he had given up wearing a

wristwatch when his had slipped into the mud at low tide and disappeared. He got up again, switched to a station that alternated tiny snippets of news with extended time and weather announcements, and hastily switched back to his FM station. Nothing had happened in the twenty-second interval.

He took another sip of the orange juice and lay back on the bunk, resting on his back, his arms folded behind his head, his left leg resting on the ankle of his right.

Merde, he thought. Once again he informed himself that this was all a childish game and not the meaningful thing he had expected. He envisioned himself back in Le Havre, telling the group about what had happened, and being patted on the head and told to go sit in the corner and play with himself. Meet your Dieter in an alley somewhere and rearrange the features on his face permanently; do that, at the least, they would have told him.

But this, *grenouilles?* Still, his own small additions, to come later that night, would be an improvement. He looked at his radio again, then stared at the planking above him, thinking of what was to happen to Dieter that night, and other nights and days to come.

The orchestra section was barely half full when Selig and Martine entered. As the usher led them to their seats, they both turned to look up at the boxes.

"We're going to have to be careful," said Selig. "If we turn to look too often, people near us will be turning to look as well. I think I understand now why Jean-Pierre decided on a balcony seat. He can look at Dieter as much as he wants without being noticed."

"No," Martine said, "I don't think that's the reason he didn't join us." But she merely shook her head when Selig looked inquiringly at her.

Simon sat quietly, wondering what the others were doing, how Martine looked in an evening gown, and speculating on the nature and depth of Aryeh's relationship to her. He loved Aryeh almost as much as he loved the Kid, but, he decided, Martine was too good for him. He had begun to wander off into a small beguiling fantasy when the phone in the outdoor booth began to ring.

The Kid opened his door, hopped down to the curb, and ran to answer it, coming back almost immediately. "The Clantons just got into the OK Corral," he said, "and they're waitin' on us."

"OK, Doc," said Simon. "We'll give 'em a little time to get nice and settled in."

Dieter remarked to Mrs. Zorn, "Our timing is almost too close to perfection. We'll have just about enough time to settle ourselves and look at the libretto."

As they approached the box, an usher said, "Good evening, Mr. Holzer. I gave my husband three to one odds you would be here tonight. A Mozart opening without Mr. Holzer would be unthinkable, I told him." She took Mrs. Zorn's wrap, hung it up, and murmured thanks when Dieter put a bill into her hand.

They made their way to the front row of the box, apologized to the other occupants, sat down, and looked out over the orchestra to the stage.

"I think Dieter has finally arrived," Martine said to Selig. "And if I'm right, he favors elegant women."

A moment later Aryeh joined them, whispering to Martine, "He's here." Both nodded; he leaned over so that they could hear him and said, "Do you know how I feel? It's as if we were in a Hitchcock movie, *The Man Who Knew Too Much,* the thirties English version, not that abomination with Doris Day. The editing and tension is tremendous: he keeps cutting from Edna Best in the orchestra, to the box where the potential victim of an assassin will sit, to an empty box, to Peter Lorre listening to the radio to see whether the plot will succeed, to the orchestra conductor, to Edna Best, to the chorus, with the beat picking up as the orchestral crescendo begins. It's all here, except the gun. I tell you, there's no reality, it's all been done on film."

"You're wrong," Selig said. "This is better than film. We have no surrogates. It's us."

The houselights began to dim, last minute rustlings sounded as final bits of conversation were completed, and the audience settled themselves in their seats. Aryeh slid down in his seat until his knees were almost parallel to his chin, leaning them against the seat in front of him. Its occupant felt the pressure and turned around to look at him; Aryeh mumbled "sorry" and pulled himself higher.

The audience applauded when the orchestra finished playing the overture, and they applauded again when the curtains swung away to display a room in the royal palace in Crete.

Dieter took a slim pair of folding opera glasses from an inside pocket, adjusted them, and offered them to Mrs. Zorn. She shook her head, and took a pair out of her beaded bag. On stage, Ilia, a Trojan princess, daughter of Priam, was singing of her misfortune as a captive of Idomeneo and asking, "For what harsher fate have the gods preserved me?" As she finished the aria following her recitation of her woes, Dieter whispered to Mrs. Zorn, "The first aria in the next scene is the one Mozart wrote for the friend whose problem I will not mention."

She smiled at him, allowed the glance to linger a moment longer than necessary, and turned her attention to the stage.

The tenor singing the role of Idamante, son of Idomeneo, waited for the recitative that concluded the first scene to finish, counted the duration of the applause, took his cue, and made his entrance, followed by his retinue.

The doorkeeper made no protest when Simon and the Kid informed him they had a delivery, glanced at the invoice, and waved them in. They parked, took the carton out of the van, and entered the opera house as if to go to the bar, but once out of his sight moved quickly up the stairs leading to the grand tier and the boxes. Two ushers were chatting idly near a window; Simon smiled at them, they nodded back and returned to their conversation.

"Here," said Simon in a low voice as they came to box 23.

He opened the door with his left hand, leaving it slightly ajar so he could see into the antechamber. "All right, children," he whispered, "everybody up."

He removed the cover and placed the carton on the floor, tilting it back against the wall so that it faced the curtain. The Kid, who had been standing just outside the door, motioned to him, and Simon left the anteroom quickly. He took a last look back as he closed the door; one of the frogs took a tiny leap forward as he did so. Beyond, he could hear enthusiastic applause as the tenor completed his first aria, "Di dolce speme."

The tenor was answered by Ilia, sang another aria, and she sang to him. As he was singing of Venus, "still not content with such massacre," he became aware of a slight disturbance in the black space beyond the footlights. He noted it in a small section of his brain, analyzed it as a latecomer stumbling into his seat, and put it aside; but instead of quieting, the disturbance seemed to be spreading and intensifying. Beyond the sound of the orchestra, he thought he could hear a tiny shriek and then the beginning of laughter.

Bufo B. Halophilus, a salt-marsh frog, pushed his olive head through the curtain, let his eyes adjust to the new light level, gave a short leap, and hit something hard. When he jumped away, he brushed against Dieter's right trouser leg.

Dieter's attention was on the singer. When he felt something touch him, he thought for a moment it was Mrs. Zorn, then dismissed the notion as being too gross for her style, deciding that a portion of her dress had brushed him.

Something hard plummeted against his left leg and moved away. As he was reaching for his pencil flashlight to investigate the annoyance, the woman behind him gave a small shriek, and a man said, "What the hell?"

A small, resilient object bounded into Dieter's lap. He recoiled, rising and pushing his chair back. His hand flicked the object; it immediately leaped away, but he felt a rough-textured surface clearly animal in nature. Others in the box were standing, and several were bent over, brushing vigorously at their feet and ankles.

"Frogs!" a voice screamed. "The place is full of frogs!" A man in the next box, peering over to see what was going on, suddenly staggered slightly, as if a child's fist had unexpectedly caught him off balance, straightened, and brushed furiously at his shirt front.

Behind him there was another small scream, and a voice urging, "Put on the lights! Put on the lights so we can see what's happening here!"

Below them, in the orchestra, several people were standing and peering through the darkness; others, still sitting, were saying "Sh!" and "Quiet!" Another cry of "Lights!" came from the grand tier, echoed in the orchestra seats to a background of laughter, and moved up into the balconies. A rhythmic clapping began in the second balcony, but faded away quickly for lack of support.

The stage manager looked out into the house, listened to the growing volume of sound, and motioned to the orchestra leader, who hesitated, then rapped with his baton on the music stand. The music died away raggedly, the last sound a doleful groan from a bassoon.

When the house lights came on, they revealed a man in full evening dress standing in a center box, arm outstretched, his hand holding a small wriggling creature. He called out, almost exultantly, "It's a frog! It's a frog!" Next to him, a woman stood holding the lower folds of her gown tightly wrapped around her legs. Beyond them, flurries of movement had extended to almost all of the boxes.

Some of those standing were applauding and laughing. A man who had stood up on his seat for a better look suddenly collapsed into it, briefly diverting attention in his direction.

"Look at the ripples! Look at the ripples!" Selig said in exultation, collapsing with laughter against Martine, who put her arms around him, and the two fell against Aryeh who embraced them both, all three laughing.

On stage, a chorus of Trojan prisoners and men and women of Crete had been about to sing *Godiam la pace,* "let us have peace," when the order to stop had come. Most of them stood in a professional "at-ease" stance, ready to resume singing at an instant's notice, but several had advanced to the footlights, enjoying the reversal of roles, themselves as audience, the audience as entertainers.

When the first faint background noises began, Jean-Pierre sat up in his bunk and moved himself closer to one of his speakers.

He smiled faintly as the tenor's voice and the orchestral sound began to be overlaid by other, unidentifiable noises. When the music faded away completely, he was sitting motionless, his nostrils slightly flared, eyes narrowed, like a mountain lion looking down on a grassy hollow that held his grazing prey.

He smiled again when the announcer assured his audience that the opera would resume its course, following a brief return to the studio.

Simon and the Kid moved quickly as they left the opera house, but not at a pace that might have called attention to themselves. A few blocks away they pulled into an empty lot and sat listening to the radio. When the opera house announcer informed the audience that there would be a slight delay in the performance, the Kid gave a yell of satisfaction and pounded Simon on the back.

As the house lights dimmed and flared and dimmed again, the audience in the opera house began its settling-down process for the second time. On stage, the chorus and the principals waited for the conductor to raise his baton.

A few rows up from the orchestra pit, Selig leaned over to Aryeh and said, "If we stay, I'm going to be making offensive gurgling noises the rest of the evening."

Martine and Aryeh nodded in agreement, but Martine asked, "Aren't we going to look suspicious if we leave?"

"No," said Aryeh. "Just indignant."

"I'd give a hundred dollars right now for just one look at Dieter's face," said Selig.

Dieter stood in the hallway behind the boxes, Mrs. Zorn beside him, talking to the assistant house manager.

"I cannot understand how something like this could happen here," he said to the manager.

"Nothing like this has ever happened before," said the manager, "and we will of course investigate fully. Meanwhile, you have our sincere apologies. We will refund your money, if you like, but may I suggest that you enjoy the rest of the opera as our guest?"

"That is very generous of you," said Mrs. Zorn. She took Dieter's arm and said to him, "Dieter, everyone else has returned. Shall we join them? I think I hear the music beginning."

"Of course everyone else has gone back," Dieter said bitterly. "This—this—occurrence has nothing to do with them."

The manager looked interested. "Are you suggesting that this has something to do with you?"

"Unfortunately, I can do more than suggest. Everyone else seems to have looked at it. You might as well, also. Look!"

He threw open the door of the anteroom so hard that it made a sound as it hit the wall behind it. The light from the hallway illuminated the cover of the box in which the frogs had made their journey. On the cover of the box were stenciled the words, "Dieter's Spirits—The Best In The West," followed by an address. "That is my address," said Dieter. "Now do you understand my comment?"

A voice from beyond the curtain called, "Quiet, please!"

The assistant manager closed the door. In a voice no longer dispensing oil for troubled waters, he said to Dieter, "Are you saying that someone in your establishment is responsible for this?"

"No, I am not," said Dieter. "I have no establishment. I am not a purveyor of liquor or spirits. Now or ever. Furthermore, that is my home address."

"Sir, we will launch a full investigation, I assure you, but at the moment . . ."

"Yes," said Dieter. "I know. 'For the moment there is nothing anyone can do. We will look into it. We will be glad to report to you if we find something out. But meanwhile . . .' Yes."

Mrs. Zorn removed her arm from his. "I should like to hear the rest of the opera, Dieter. And it does seem that this affair, whatever it means, is more related to you than to them. Are you coming?"

Dieter turned to respond to her, but she had already walked through the door. He looked at the assistant manager, who seemed vaguely amused at something and avoided meeting Dieter's eyes. Dieter took a deep breath, turned, and followed Mrs. Zorn into the box.

Down in the lobby of the opera house, Aryeh, Martine, and Selig had retrieved their coats. Aryeh and Martine were dancing a slow waltz to the music of an unseen orchestra, and Selig, his white scarf flung around his neck in schoolboy fashion, leaned against a pillar, smiling dreamily, and nodding in time to their movements. Thirty-five feet above them, under an unused radiator enclosure, a cousin of Bufo B. said softly to itself, *"R-i-b-b-i-d. R-i-b-b-i-d. R-i-b-b-i-d."*

"It's time," Jean-Pierre said aloud. He walked to the small refrigerator and took out a plastic bag, its top tightly knotted. He turned the light off, stood in the darkness for a few moments, then put the light on again.

He put the plastic bag on a counter, unlocked the only locked drawer on the boat, took out a faded blue velvet bag, untied its draw string, and took out a Luger, oiled and in working condition. He put the gun on the counter, reached into the bag again and took out a piece of parchmentlike paper rolled into a spill, and spread it out.

The paper said, in French: "This gun was used to kill the Boche who owned it. Dec. 17, 1943, Le Havre." He looked at the writing, then at the gun, sighed, and then, very slowly, returned them both to the bag and put it away.

He put the light out again and walked to his truck. After starting the engine and turning the headlights on, he flipped the switch that activated the heavy-duty floodlight mounted on the cab of the truck. He could hear a roar of protest from a nearby boat, even over the sound of the engine. He switched the light off, called out an apology, and drove away. A quarter of a mile down the road he made a right-angle turn so that he was directly facing the closed door of an automotive repair shop, flipped the switch once more, then climbed out, and adjusted the floodlight's swivel a few degrees downward.

He drove into the city wishing he could continue listening to the opera; perhaps an FM unit or even a tape deck would be worth the cost. One of the few pleasures for which technology could claim credit was that of driving through the darkness surrounded by the motion of music.

He drove to Dieter's house, parked in its alleyway, got out, and fumbled briefly at Dieter's door. The next part of the operation would require waiting, but he was prepared to invest as much time as necessary.

Dieter sat in the darkness of the box, unable to concentrate on either the music or the action of the opera. Years before, when dignitaries entering a film festival opening night had been bombarded with custard pies, the part of him that was forever the son of a rural tavernkeeper had been amused at the public humiliation of what he had then thought of as the elite. This was not much different, hardly more than a silly prank, but it had been aimed directly at him with malice and a touch of something sinister. Like the blood, he thought.

Mrs. Zorn refused the offer of a drink during intermission and stood quietly in the hallway. Two men walked by, and one of them said, "I hear they traced it to somebody with a German name."

The other said, "I was willing to toughen myself by standing in brine so I could suffer through six hours of *Parsifal,* but German humor? Spare us!"

Dieter turned to Mrs. Zorn, a comment about Mozart's Salzburg and its nearness to the German border working its way to his tongue, but when he saw the small amused smile on her face he said nothing.

After the opera she politely declined the suggestion of a bite to eat and asked to be taken home. He understood that the evening was over. When they arrived at her apartment house, he said goodnight, then waited for the doorman to bring him his car from the basement garage.

Jean-Pierre was parked in a driveway across from Dieter's house, facing the street. When Dieter turned in, Jean-Pierre started the truck without turning on his headlights. He waited until Dieter got out of his car, fed the truck just enough gas to give it some momentum, then cut the engine; the truck continued to roll silently and slowly across the street. When Dieter reached his front door, Jean-Pierre flicked the floodlight switch.

The powerful beam, slanting slightly downward, trapped Dieter in its arc, as if he were a prisoner caught attempting escape. He turned and faced it for a moment, rigid with shock, before throwing up an arm to protect himself against the light. Jean-Pierre stared at the frozen figure, then started the motor and drove away, simultaneously turning on his headlights and shutting off the floodlight.

Dieter heard the truck start and stared in its direction when the beam shifted away from him, but all he could see was a slowly fading corona. He turned back to the door, adrenalin still shooting needles of sensation into his bloodstream, and grasped the doorknob, then jumped back in revulsion as he touched something cold, moist, and yielding. When his eyes had adjusted to the dim light, he forced himself to look; hanging from the knob were several small, raw frog's legs.

7

Vermin. I feel like scratching," said Selig.

"The scale seems to be getting smaller rather than larger," observed Martine. "I don't understand the pattern."

Aryeh shook his head. "That's besides the point, and in any event, we shouldn't stray from the sequence because it makes us feel queasy. He's the one supposed to feel queasy."

"The pattern makes sense," said Simon, "if you take the naturalistic interpretation of the plagues. Think of a drought in Egypt; the blood is the resulting pollution of the waters. After that, the frogs go looking for a new resting place. Then, decay and vermin."

"You do not see what is in front of your eyes," objected Jean-Pierre. "The pattern is clear: the plagues build up and with growing force. That is the road for us to follow."

The Kid nodded his head. "Exactly."

"Let's get back to the problem," said Simon. "We're thinking of it as if it were going to happen to one of us, and we visualize a parade of ants or lice or bedbugs marching around and over us. If we look at it from his point of view, we can develop a whole new theme, perhaps an entire composition."

He stood up and began walking about the room, varying his path with each circuit, occasionally glancing at Martine as if he were testing an audience reaction.

"I have an idea for a kind of late nineteenth-century tone poem, a portrait in music called 'Dieter.' No, make that 'Dieter, Thirty Years Later.'

"We know some important things about him as a person. He has expensive tastes; more important, he has cultivated tastes, like his clothes, his seat at the opera, his look of a man who goes to a barber often enough to avoid giving the impression he has just come from having his hair cut.

"That can be one theme of our composition—all clean sounds, uncomplicated bowing, no slurring, controlled spaces à la Boccherini, that sort of thing.

"Now we develop a second theme in the brasses and horns, representing training, discipline, a belief in a regular and ordered existence, respect for the rules of society, and so on. Perhaps a troubled note here and there, but in general, the second theme is an ordered progression, like a Beethoven scale sequence, but without the dramatic shifts.

"The rhythms are clear, uncluttered, perhaps a touch of the snare drums here and there. All in all, we've got nothing that would sound strange to a late nineteenth-century ear, perhaps even a trifle old-fashioned. But we throw something else into it and everything changes.

"What? Dissonance? Syncopation? No, they're not all that new. A heavy rock beat. Amplified. That upsets everything that's part of the portrait."

He looked at the others. "You see? Translate that composition into people and what do you get—rock musicians, hippies, beggars, prostitutes, all the sorts that would be vermin to the man the composition describes."

He put one hand behind his back, the other across his chest, and bowed, the perfect conservatory student at the annual recital, then asked, "No applause?"

Jean-Pierre nodded. "I have long suspected that underneath your exterior lies a truly evil man. Congratulations."

"Do you realize what you've just described?" demanded Aryeh. "You've just laid out the closing scene of the German film version of *The Threepenny Opera*. All those thieves and cripples and pickpockets and beggars filling the streets of London, converging on Queen Victoria.

"I can see it . . . lines of people streaming up Polk and Larkin streets, along Clay and Pacific, crossing Van Ness, all converging on Dieter's house."

"And we in costume amid the mob?" asked Selig. "Aryeh, I'd like to take the idea seriously, but you're just playing with it. My God, the organization problems even if you could find the people. It's a dream, nothing more."

"It does not have to be a dream," said Jean-Pierre. "I know a way it can be accomplished with very little trouble for us, and much for him. I, myself, would prefer the real thing, however."

"Me, too," said the Kid.

"Let's hear it," said Simon.

"I have a friend—he, Simon, he—who makes porno flicks on a houseboat. When he's ready for one, and he's got his principals, he puts in a couple of small ads for extras. The number of people who show up for an easy day's work is incredible."

"I'm not too happy with my role here," said Martine. "I seem to be cast as the group prig. Nevertheless, someone has to point out that what we're talking about isn't really fair.

"I'm assuming that you'd use a newspaper ad to get a lot of people to Dieter's office or whatever. I have some personal feelings about the kind of people who lend themselves to that kind of thing, but it's simply not right to exploit them for our purposes. I have to admit, I loved the frogs, and I did accept the audience inconvenience, but that was small compared to what Simon's proposing."

Simon, once again making circuits of the room, stopped for a moment behind Martine, resting his hand on the couch a few inches from her hair, then reversed direction. "Simon hasn't made a proposal yet," he said. "Mine was a concept, nothing more, no specifics. But between Jean-Pierre and Martine, I do see something that is thoroughly satisfying, and perhaps even better than the physical scenario.

"The disembodied is more suggestive than the physical, especially for us. So far he hasn't been able to confront anybody and this is no time to start. We do it on the phone."

"You mean obscene phone calls?" asked Selig.

"No, we use the ad idea Jean-Pierre mentioned, but we ask people to call to make appointments for a casting interview for a film."

"Yes," said Aryeh. "Yes, indeed. We tell them in the ad, maybe in the *Barb* or some of the college newspapers, that the phone call is itself the preliminary interview, that the way they talk is the critical part, and the follow-up will depend on that call."

"How do you sound for a porno film? Heavy breathing? That puts us right back to obscene calls."

"No," said Simon. "That's not it. We advertise we're making a film about hippies. You don't have to specify anything more. It's like obscenity, nobody can define exactly what a hippie is, but everybody knows one when they see one. That would certainly be true of Dieter."

"It's not heavy enough," objected the Kid. "It's like that gag we did in high school. You know the one: you call a teacher at 1 A.M. and ask for David. He says there's nobody with that name there, and you say, 'Well, if he comes in, tell him Steve called.' You keep that up all night, with different names, until the teacher is off his rocker. Then at seven o'clock, somebody calls and says 'This is David, any messages?'

"We don't want to do something that easy. If we use the phone idea we've got to stretch it out, keep hammering at him until he goes bananas. The thing to do is to stretch it out. We put in one ad in one paper for people to call early in the morning two days running. Then we wait a few days, put an ad in another paper, and repeat the sequence at his office."

Jean-Pierre patted the Kid on the shoulder. "I can see you and Simon come from a common source."

"Well, Martine?" asked Simon. "It doesn't cost anyone more than one phone call that way. Would that satisfy you?"

"It sounds like the moral equivalent of being a little bit pregnant. But what's that line about being hung for a kid as well as for a goat, or is it a sheep and a lamb? We've come this far, and I won't say no. As a matter of fact, if I'm going to be honest with myself . . ."

". . . That would be valuable," said Jean-Pierre.

Martine, mouth open to speak, stiffened, and turned to look at Jean-Pierre.

"What would be valuable," she said, "is for you to explain whatever it is you feel about me. I've had a strong feeling from the very beginning that you don't want me included in this. I share some of that feeling, but for my own reasons. What are yours?"

Without looking at her, Jean-Pierre said, "It is just that I wonder a little whether your . . . sensitivity . . . to moral questions is perhaps something else, even perhaps something that you yourself do not recognize."

He looked first at Aryeh and Simon, then turned to Martine. "I have no desire to offend you, but there is, after all, a link between you and Dieter, and it cannot help but occur to me that perhaps your concern arises as much from that as from the questions you continue to raise."

"What kind of link?" asked Selig. "You're not saying that they know each other?"

"No," said Simon, and sighed. "I think he's saying that both Martine and Dieter are German, and that a German is a German is a German, if you don't mind the bromide."

"A bromide is something I could use right now," said Martine. She stood up and walked over to Jean-Pierre. "What do you see when you look at me? The SS? The Gestapo? I'm none of those things. My parents never were either. And even if that were the case, would you really punish the child for the parent? Do you think there's such a thing as inherited guilt?"

She turned away and whirled around again. "Where do you get your holiness? Because you're French? Tell me about Laval and Petain.

Tell me about the French policemen who rounded up Jews! Tell me about the Charlemagne Division of the SS! Go ahead, tell me!"

Aryeh started to move toward them, but Simon put a hand on his arm.

Jean-Pierre stood up, looking at Martine's furious face. He took a breath, but before he could speak, she said, "And on top of everything else, I absolutely, totally, unequivocally despise being interrupted when I speak." Her voice had been steadily becoming deeper, but it returned almost to its normal timbre as she added, "Your turn."

Jean-Pierre's face had tautened during her outburst, and spots of red appeared on his cheeks. He stared back at her and finally spoke. "I think perhaps I have been wrong. I apologize."

"Only perhaps?" she asked.

"It was you who spoke of honesty," he said.

She nodded and sat down. "What I was about to say was I would endorse the Kid's suggestion, but that it doesn't go far enough. What we've done so far doesn't add up to much more than a series of petty annoyances. But if after the first series of ads we wait two weeks and then put in another series, it will reinforce the idea that he doesn't control his world any more. That's what happens to victims."

She paused and added, "I suppose the suggestion qualifies me to be Simon's s-s-sister, according to Jean-Pierre."

"How about this?" asked Aryeh. " 'Wanted: Actors and Actresses for roles in film about a hippie commune. Authentic speech more important than acting ability. Call ------- for appointment between 7 A.M. and 9 A.M. Interview to be granted based on way applicants sound on phone.' That would be the ad for his home, to run two days."

"No, one ad listing two successive days," said Jean-Pierre. The first day have them call at his home phone, then three days later, at his office phone, the same thing."

"Depending on deadlines, it is so ordained," said Aryeh. With luck, in about a week from now, the 'movie of the day' will be *Dieter Meets the Vermin People.*"

8

Dieter was near wakefulness when the phone rang, and reached for it at the beginning of the fourth ring.

"Holzer here," he said, and listened to the outpouring of language first in perplexity, then disbelief, and finally in anger.

"You have the wrong number," he said and hung up.

He turned to go back to bed, disgusted at the break in routine, as well as at the call itself, saw that it was less than fifteen minutes before his normal rising time and decided it was pointless to return to bed. He was on his way to the bathroom when the phone rang again.

The same idiot calling again, he thought, but answered the phone. "What number are you calling, may I ask?"

When the mumbling voice at the other end of the line gave Dieter's number, he asked, "Who is this, please?"

"Who are you?" asked the voice.

"Why are you calling me if you do not know who I am?" asked Dieter.

"Oh," said the voice. "You're testing me. Well, that's cool," and launched into a flow of language remarkably similar to that of the first phone call.

Dieter broke in almost immediately. "What are you talking about? Is this some kind of practical joke? Get off the line or I'll have you arrested!" he shouted, slamming the receiver down.

He walked furiously to the bedroom door, then paused as he realized that he did not know why he had gone in that direction. He fought for control, telling himself that he must not react to annoyances in this fashion. This was the price of living in his times, the mark of a collapsing world. These were merely pinpricks compared to the madnesses that had been occurring about him.

Even as he reassured himself that these were purely accidental phone calls, he recognized a kind of anxiety building in him. He spun around awkwardly when the phone rang again, then stood still for a moment, breathing deeply, willing himself not to answer.

The ringing died away; when it began again several moments later, he was in full command of himself. He picked up the receiver and spoke his phone number into it. He allowed the caller to speak for five seconds and then broke in, his voice expressing nothing more than polite interest.

"Excuse me, please, but would you tell me why you are calling this particular number?"

He listened to the answer, and asked, "Do you have the advertisement before you? Yes? Would you be so kind as to read it to me?"

When the caller finished, Dieter asked in the same tone, "What is the date of the paper? You have only the clipping? It's the one they're selling now? I see. Just a moment, please."

He stood considering a moment, then said, "Thank you for calling. All the positions have been filled by now. You might tell your friends," and broke the connection.

Still holding the receiver to his ear, he waited for the resumption of the dial tone, then carefully placed the receiver alongside the phone base. He looked at it, then took two cushions from the couch and carefully placed the receiver on one and put the other on top.

No, not pinpricks. This was part of the same series of events having no individual meaning or discernible pattern, but clearly aimed at making a shambles of his existence. The quiver of anxiety he had felt earlier reappeared, only to vanish at a new, triumphant thought: they, whoever they were, had made a mistake; there was now a trail for him to follow.

He called the *Berkeley Barb* later that morning and spoke to several people, all of whom reacted without interest to his threat of a lawsuit, pointing out that the ad had been paid for by a money order with his name on it, that it had been accepted and published in good faith, and that no law required newspapers to check the authenticity of phone numbers inserted in advertisements.

When he finally talked to the clerk who had taken the ad, she remembered the circumstances of the placement.

"The man called in, and he dictated the ad and he asked how much it would be and I told him; he said he would send the money in right away and he did and we printed it."

"And you did not ask him for a name and address?" demanded Dieter.

"I did, and he said that if he gave it to me, somebody in the office could tip off their friends and all kinds of kooks would be showing up for jobs and anyway he wasn't into the person-to-person trip, and I said I could relate to that and he hung up."

"I see," said Dieter. "But if it happens again, any ad like this with my number, would you please call me first?"

At least, he thought, that will put a stop to it, assuming that the idiot clerk can carry out simple instructions. But even though he assured himself that he had circumvented their plans for further harassment, he could not relax. Several times during the morning his thoughts drifted away from his dictation, and his secretary had to clear her throat to get his attention.

The phone was ringing inside the house when he returned home. He resisted an impulse to wait outside until the ringing ceased and moved at a normal pace. He held his breath as he picked up the receiver, but the caller was a friend inviting him to stop by for a drink.

He took the phone off the hook when he returned home from dinner. He looked at it again just before getting into bed, thinking that he would not hang up the receiver until leaving for his office in the morning.

He had trouble falling asleep, and when he did, slept fitfully. When the alarm rang the next morning, he came back to consciousness slowly. His first thought was of the phone, and he got out of bed to look at it. He washed and dressed as usual, but decided to eat breakfast in a hotel restaurant downtown. Just before he left the house, he removed the top cushion from the phone and replaced the receiver.

The phone rang immediately; he nodded to himself, broke the connection without listening, and replaced the cushion.

The following morning he put the receiver back on the base after he had finished dressing, but before making breakfast for himself. The phone rang only once. When he answered, a male voice asked whether there were still any job openings. Dieter gave him an obscene answer and hung up.

He got into his car and backed out of the alleyway cautiously; as the rear of his car moved past a vehicle parked at the curb, he heard a furious honking and braked immediately. A three-quarter ton pickup with a shingled cabin on its bed shot by, with a bearded man yelling at him, "Pig! Pig! Pig!"

He pulled his window down to answer, but the truck was already out of hearing range. He muttered to himself and pulled out into the traffic lane.

After parking in the garage next to his office building, he cranked the car window almost to a fully closed position, then closed it all the way. He got out of the car, locked the door, took a few steps and stopped, turning to look at the car again. He stood indecisively for a moment, then returned to the car, unlocked it, lowered the window so as to leave a one inch gap, and locked it again.

He looked suspiciously at a man who entered the elevator immediately behind him; he wore a fringed leather jacket, and his long hair was twisted into little braids at the sides. Dieter watched him until the man got off two floors below his own.

Shortly after ten o'clock, his secretary knocked on his door and entered. "Mr. Holzer, there's something very odd going on with the phone this morning. I've received three very peculiar calls about a movie audition from some very odd-sounding people, and I've got one on hold right now. I thought of calling the phone company, but it's clearly our number they're calling. What do you want me to do?"

"Go to your desk and let me have that call," Dieter said, "and if he has hung up by the time you get back, let me have the next call. After that, unless I tell you otherwise, as soon as you determine it is that kind of call, you are to break in and say, 'All positions have been filled,' and hang up immediately."

"What is this all about?" she asked.

"Do as I say. That is all," he said and watched her leave the room.

The caller was still on the line. Dieter, in his politest fashion, interrogated him until he received the information he wanted. After calling a Marin County newspaper and giving the same instructions he had given the *Barb,* he spoke to his secretary, "Do with any future calls of that nature exactly as I instructed you earlier. They will come in only between 10 and 12 today and tomorrow."

He took the final draft of a contract proposal out of its binder and began studying it, but could not concentrate on its details. He slammed it back on the desk in disgust and stood at a window, staring at the traffic below.

Whoever it was who was intent on wrecking his life could be passing the building at this very moment, gloating and rubbing his hands with self-satisfaction.

No. Not one man; there were at least three of them. The police had said that the plastic container of liquid could not have been handled easily by one man, and the opera house had reported that two men had appeared with the carton of "wine" for him. And the paper in Marin had said that the call had been placed by a woman. Three, unless there were two different sets of two men; in that case, five.

So many unanswered questions, he thought wearily. What they were doing was the largest puzzle of all. But also, who were they? Why were they doing these things to him? For money? A new kind of blackmail?

No, he thought, not that. For money, they would have been doing more dangerous things. In that light the occurrences, taken individually, had been hardly more than petty annoyances. And if it proved that they had cost him Mrs. Zorn because of the way he had acted at the opera, that they could not have foreseen. Besides, that he would repair; it would take time, but he would repair the relationship.

This is the worst part of it, he told himself. My life has no coherence any more. I waste it away going over and over and over what has happened. Then disgusted at the tone of self-pity, he sat at the desk again, forcing himself to study the contract.

The calls to his office stopped exactly as he had told his secretary, and no more early morning calls came to his home. Nevertheless, he continued to sleep fitfully.

Two weeks after the first phone calls, when his phone rang shortly after 7 A.M., he leaped out of bed immediately, as if it were a call he had been anticipating, and almost as if a tiny part of him were welcoming it. When a voice began mumbling the now-familiar jargon, he smashed the receiver down on the base, then knocked the phone off its table with a sweep of his hand. If an iron bar had been handy, he would have smashed it, but nothing caught his eye as a potential weapon. Instead, he stood there, listening to the dial tone until it changed into a high-pitched whine.

His anger was followed immediately by a sense of helplessness. No, not that, he assured himself; one must do what is rational, that is all. He called the business office number of the phone company and asked that his phone be immediately changed to an unlisted number.

"Emergency? Of course this is an emergency!" he said to the operator. When he refused to accept her statement that "she would put him on a list for service calls at the earliest possible moment," his anger rose again and he began to rage at her. When she inquired pleasantly if he would like to speak to her supervisor, he suddenly realized that he was being treated as if he were placing a crank call and hung up, then lifted the receiver from the base.

He sat by the phone, taking satisfaction from the sound of the dial tone. When the warning whine began, he glanced at the pillows on the couch, but did not move.

He sat quietly for a few minutes, then walked over to his record cabinet and searched through his tapes until he found a recording of

Ravel's *Bolero*. He put it into his tape deck and experimented briefly until he found the point where the orchestra was braying in full volume, just before the final shrieking cacophony.

He took the handpiece and phone base and placed them on the record cabinet, the whine still sounding, and placed his bass speaker next to the phone, so that the speech aperture was only an inch away from the speaker; then he depressed the connector buttons of the phone, holding his fingers on them until the phone rang.

He said, "Yes?" put the phone down, started the tape with his left hand and turned the sound control to full volume with his right. When the music ended, he depressed the phone buttons.

He repeated the process for the next four calls, then switched the stereo amplifier to "microphone," searched through a drawer for a small mike, plugged its jack into the set, and placed it an inch from the speaking portion of the phone. The next two callers were assaulted with the sounds of their own voices, greatly amplified and distorted by the crashing feedback.

Pleased with himself, he shut off the stereo set, put the handpiece on its side once again, brushed his teeth, had a glass of orange juice; then he put on a track suit, drove to a nearby park, and jogged for a half hour.

When he returned, he showered, dressed, and left the house, taking the morning paper with him, and paying no attention to the phone. He ate a leisurely breakfast at the hotel restaurant, reading the paper slowly. From time to time he stopped reading and stared at the linen tablecloth; his earlier exhilaration had departed, and a small headache had begun to throb.

He went to his office; his secretary had not yet arrived, and Dieter sat at her desk and called the phone company, asking for his home phone to be changed to an unlisted number at the earliest possible moment.

When his secretary came in, Dieter was at his desk making a list of people he would have to notify as soon as he was informed of his new number. After he was finished, he carefully organized the work ahead of him for the remainder of the week so as to keep the time required in the office at a minimum.

When the office calls started two days later, this time in the afternoon, he called in his secretary and told her she was not to answer the phone for the rest of the day. When she asked why, he said, "Please sit down, Mrs. Reynolds, I wish to tell you a story. When I was young, very young, I worked in my father's inn, long hard hours, carrying suitcases, fetching newspapers, shining shoes, and all that sort of thing. I learned to speak several languages, but I also learned that the world basically contains those who give orders and those who simply say, *'Ja, mein Herr,' 'Oui, m'sieu,'* 'Yessir.'

"The same is true of the world of business. Those who give orders pay a price for that privilege, wages. Those who take orders are paid for taking them, again, wages. They are also paid, in part, to spare those who give the orders from having to listen to unnecessary questions. Is that clear?"

Mrs. Reynolds lowered her face; when she raised it, she looked at a spot about a foot to the right of his ear and said, "No questions."

But I have questions, he thought. I am surrounded by them coming at me from all directions, pressing me, pushing me. Where to? Perhaps no place. Perhaps all they mean is to push me, to make me jump when they say jump. But why?

He realized that the outer office was unusually quiet. He opened his door and looked; Mrs. Reynolds had emptied the drawers of her desk and had piled their contents into two stacks. When she saw Dieter, she said, "It is also possible, Mr. Holzer, to refuse the pay, as you can see."

"Please, Mrs. Reynolds," he said, "I spoke more harshly than was warranted. You are an excellent secretary and we have come to understand each other's ways. I ask you please not to decide now. I do not wish to offend you further by speaking of money now, but if at some point you would wish to discuss your salary, you will find me sympathetic."

"I don't know," said Mrs. Reynolds, but she sat down.

When he left his office at the end of the day, he went to a bar catering to businessmen like himself. As his eyes adjusted to the shadows, he saw an acquaintance sitting at the bar, turned around, and left. I do not need idle talk, he thought, just quiet, anonymity, peace.

He walked back to the garage, got into his car, and drove south across Market to Harrison, until he found a bar serving the local warehouse trade. He sat at a table and drank steadily for almost two hours, speaking to no one.

I think we're getting to him," said Selig.

"I hope so," said Aryeh. "I hope so."

"It's more than hope. I couldn't resist and called him. I drove Sylvia out of her mind, walking around the house, practicing what I would say, mumbling to myself, and once she even made the children leave the room. But I upset her for nothing. I called the second morning of the second round; a recorded voice cut in, saying that the number I had called was out of service."

"Temporarily?"

"No. I waited until the operator came on, and she said she had no further information. That means he's gone to an unlisted number, although that's not going to do him any good if we decide we need it. I know somebody who knows somebody, and so on."

"There is no use in that," said Jean-Pierre. "I, too, have a progress report, which is to say, we are not making progress. I called him and almost punctured an eardrum. When he answered, that is to say, when he picked up his phone, there was a horrible blast of sound, music, I don't know what, something modern. He must have been sitting by his phone, waiting."

Simon nodded. "He's beginning to fight. Well, it was bound to happen. Perhaps we should ease off a bit."

He stood with his back pressed to the one unencumbered bit of wall in his apartment. Selig and Martine sat on a couch at one end of the room, the Kid was stretched out on his back on a rug near them, Aryeh sat on a straight-back chair at the kitchen entrance, and Jean-Pierre sat erect on a wicker hassock near Simon.

When no one responded to Simon, Jean-Pierre snorted and said, "There are always two problems for me in English. One is jokes and puns, and the other is cursing. You do not understand French, and I cannot curse well enough in English. But believe me, I am cursing."

"About what?" asked Selig.

"Because you understand so little," answered Jean-Pierre. "It is exactly now that we must increase pressure on him, not decrease it, if we wish to make him feel helpless. If he fights back, he is angry. If he is angry, he owns himself. If he owns himself, he is not a victim. We must make him capitulate, accept, acknowledge that he is helpless."

"I have another interpretation of what he did," said Martine. "What he did on the phone was lash out at the nearest available target. Those who called him were nothing more than tools, and he must have known that by the second round of calls. He must understand by this time that there is some guiding intelligence in these haphazard events, even though he probably doesn't recognize the pattern. I don't think he's attacking an enemy. He's protesting his own helplessness. If he had a wife, I'd be feeling very sorry for her."

"If he's protesting, he's nowhere near being helpless," said Aryeh.

The Kid lifted his legs over his head, did a forward flip, and stood up. "Jean-Pierre's right. We've got a long way to go, seven more plagues. I think we should step up the pace and put on more pressure."

"Much more," said Jean-Pierre. "And the road is so clear that if I were a mystic and believed in omens, this would be an omen, the fourth plague. Listen, *Pour tuer avec l'épée, par la famine, par la mort, et par les bêtes sauvages de la terre,* 'to kill with the sword, with hunger, with death . . .' " He paused, looked at the others, each in turn, and added, " '. . . and the wild beasts of the earth.' That is from the Apocalypse. And the fourth plague is also wild beasts. An omen, yes?"

"Flies, not wild beasts," said Martine.

"She's right," said Selig.

"No, I'll show you," said Simon. He pushed himself away from the wall and rummaged through a heap of music and folders lying on a library table. "Here," he said to Martine. "This is the Passover service." He pointed. "Wild beasts."

She glanced at it and passed it to Selig.

"Well, what do we do?" he asked.

"Let me tell you what I would like to do," said Jean-Pierre. "I would like to act without going through all these discussions and arguments. I have had an idea about wild beasts for Dieter, and I am reluctant to let it go.

"So far we have given to him a taste of the unexpected, a humiliation, and revulsion. Now, I propose to give to him what so far has been missing. Fear. A touch of fear. Not harm, but fear. And I would propose to do it myself, except I need another."

"I'm it, whatever it is," said the Kid.

"Jean-Pierre, supposing I were to say no," asked Simon, his voice soft.

"Then I would still do what is to be done," answered Jean-Pierre. "There would be disappointment, but I would do it. And if not with the Kid, with someone else."

"With the Kid. Simon doesn't speak for me or tell me what to do."

"Hold it," said Aryeh. "Let's retrace. Either we're the Commando as we laid it out originally, or we're not. The moment we go our separate ways, it's all over. For me, that would be a betrayal of what we started to do. We don't have to approve or disapprove of what he does, merely accept it."

"I would agree," said Jean-Pierre, "but first I must remind you that nobody 'lets' me do what I want to do."

114

"It's impossible for me to stop," said Selig. "If we do, what we've done so far becomes almost meaningless. Dieter is left with a puzzle, but nothing more. No marks, no changes. I hope we agree to go ahead."

He stopped and grinned happily. "Besides, the Bible does say flies, and I've been developing a lovely idea using them. I'd like to do both versions of it—I mean I'd like the Commando to do both. I can work out my idea myself."

"No explanations?" asked Martine.

"Just that it's like Jean-Pierre's—a touch of fear, nothing more."

"Shall we vote?" asked Aryeh.

"No," said Simon after a pause. "Even a majority vote would mean an end to the Commando. I'll stick with it."

"I don't know," said Martine.

"I promise you, I really promise, that nothing will happen to him," said Selig. "But it's time that Dieter comes to public attention and doesn't simply lick his wounds in private."

Martine turned to look at Aryeh, who nodded his head, then at Simon, who smiled briefly, but said nothing.

Martine looked down and studied the back of her hand, sighed, shrugged, and said "Yes."

10

Jean-Pierre sat in a borrowed gray VW Bug across the street and a half block from Dieter's house. When Dieter backed out of the alleyway and turned in the direction of the city's financial district, Jean-Pierre waited until the car disappeared around a corner, made a rapid U-turn, and followed.

Fifteen minutes later, Dieter signaled a left turn into his parking garage, with Jean-Pierre three cars behind him. As Dieter slowed for the turn, Jean-Pierre braked instead of swiveling past him, ignoring the irritated honkings behind him. As soon as he saw Dieter being waved up to the second floor, he turned into the garage, took a ticket from the parking attendant, and shot up the ramp.

He cruised slowly on the upper floor until he saw Dieter walking away from his car, and pulled into a slot four cars away. As he turned his ignition off, Dieter was disappearing behind the elevator doors.

Jean-Pierre got out of his car; he was wearing a pair of white coveralls with lettering on the back that read "Foreign Car Specialists, Inc." He leaned into the back of the VW and took out a pin-pry bar, a small tote box, and a mechanic's rag.

He walked to Dieter's car and looked around the garage. A car was parking at the end of the garage opposite him, but otherwise there was no movement. He had the passenger door open within twenty seconds. He tilted the seat forward, arranged his equipment quickly on the carpeting behind it, tilted the seat back, and locked the door. As he picked up the tote box and walked away, a car drove by, but its driver paid no attention to him.

When the car was out of sight, he quickly took off the coveralls and stowed them and the tote box in the back of his car, locked it, and walked to the elevator. Outside, he looked around for a coffee shop. He found one less than a block away; he sat in it for forty-five minutes, drinking coffee and talking to its two waitresses. Satisfied that he had been away long enough not to call attention to himself at the garage, he returned and retrieved his car, whistling softly at the cost of having left it.

At 3 P.M. he called the Kid.

"All goes well?"

"Beautiful. It couldn't be sweeter. I ran two more checks and it works perfectly. I've got it marked to a tenth of a second; the only thing is we should be within a hundred yards of him, and preferably on level ground."

"There are several places like that on the route. Pick me up at the corner of Bush and Grant at 4. He leaves his office usually at 4:30. The van has commercial plates, yes? Then we can park in a yellow zone until we see him leave, if we can find one. Otherwise, we circle the block."

When they met, Jean-Pierre got into the car, shook hands gravely with the Kid, and settled into his seat without saying anything. They drove down Bush, turned left on Sansome, turned once more, and pulled into a yellow space just vacated by a telephone truck.

Jean-Pierre sat quietly as they waited, but the Kid lit a cigarette, put it out, moved around in his seat, and finally crawled over the transmission housing into the back of the van. When he returned, Jean-Pierre asked, "Are you nervous?"

"There's nothing to be nervous about, not really. It's just the waiting."

"My friends in Le Havre told me that this is the way you feel at the beginning. Later, you come to accept the fact that there is more waiting than any other single thing."

"Were you actually in it—I mean, well, you know what I mean."

"No, said Jean-Pierre. "I never took part. I am not that much older than you, less than half a generation perhaps. But I have memories—of my people, of the way others talked about them, and what it was like for those who lived in those days."

"It must really have left a mark," said the Kid.

"It is why in a special way I am closer to your parents than to you. It left something festering . . . enough. There goes Dieter."

The Kid got out of the driver's side and ran around to the passenger side of the van. Jean-Pierre moved over to the driver's seat and started the car. By the time Dieter had insinuated himself into the traffic flow, they were beginning to angle away from the curb.

Jean-Pierre followed behind Dieter's car in a parallel lane, keeping several cars between them. He followed him up Pine, then swung behind him when Dieter turned into Larkin. When the two cars made a left turn into Pacific, Jean-Pierre said, "I think it is now time for you to be ready."

The Kid crawled into the back of the van. After a minute he said, "All you have to do is say 'Now!'"

"D'accord," said Jean-Pierre. "I mean OK."

As their car crossed Gough, Dieter's was approaching Laguna; when he had crossed, and Jean-Pierre could see that the light was with them, he said "Now."

Earlier that afternoon Dieter had called his secretary into his office and asked, "The Montizambert papers—how far have you progressed?"

"I still have an hour's work; you told me you wanted them tomorrow."

"I know," he said. "But finish them, and then you may leave for the day."

"Is something . . . have I done something wrong?"

"Not at all. Your work is entirely satisfactory. Remember, as soon as you finish, you may leave."

He had not expected any more phone calls, but began to relax only when more than two weeks passed without a repetition. At first, when they had stopped, he kept warning himself that something more could happen, would happen, that he must remain alert and on guard.

Within a few days, he realized that the drain on his energies was taking a greater toll than he had anticipated. He found himself turning to watch strangers whose eyes lingered on him for more than a second; he jumped at unexpected sounds, and once, he started to criticize Mrs. Reynolds for a meaningless error, then saw the look on her face and retreated.

His best protection, he told himself, was to be open to anything which might serve as a clue to what was being done to him, and by whom, but beyond that, to live a normal life.

When the thought occurred to him, he smiled without humor. A normal life. He had carefully built a new life for himself after leaving Germany, putting the past behind, creating a haven for himself, letting himself sink into a culture at first strange to him but that he had finally come to accept, and then to embrace. A normal life. Would it ever be again?

Mrs. Reynolds had already left when he walked out of his office. He thought of having a drink, decided against it, and drove into the growing swell of homeward-bound traffic. Once out of the financial district canyon, he pressed the button preset for his favorite FM classical station. The undemanding murmur of baroque music soon became nothing more for him than a pleasant background hum.

He had begun to consider the problem of Mrs. Zorn once again as he reached Van Ness. As he crossed Laguna, the drift of his thoughts was interrupted by the voice of the announcer stating that for the next sixty seconds a practice disaster alert signal would sound, and he reached out to silence the instrument.

As he was about to touch the button, he froze: the deep snarling roar of some wild animal filled the car, the sound seeming to come from somewhere behind him.

His body was already reacting frantically as he tried to look into the rearview mirror to see what was in the back of the car. The movement to his right caused his hand to turn the wheel slightly to the left; simultaneously his right foot jumped to the brake pedal and slammed it to the floor.

The rear of Dieter's car swerved toward the sidewalk, and the rear fender hit the front fender of a parked vehicle. At the same time, the driver behind him, desperately trying to avoid a rear-end collision, hit Dieter's left front fender as he tried to swing around, sending the front of the car to the right. Dieter's car grazed still another parked car before coming to a full stop.

In spite of the low speed at which he had been moving, Dieter was flung about like a rag doll; at one point he pitched forward with sufficient force to hit his head against the top edge of the steering wheel. When the car finally came to a halt, he sat there, almost dazed, but with sufficient awareness of what had happened to reach and turn off his ignition key. After turning the key, his hand completed the action his brain had ordered earlier: he reached out and pushed the button that shut off his car radio.

Traffic behind him began piling up, and cars coming from the opposite direction slowed as curious drivers leaned out to see what was happening. A police car coming down Laguna sounded its siren and moved rapidly into the middle of the intersection. The driver jumped out into the middle of the street, waving his arms furiously as he tried to unsnarl the developing traffic jam, while his partner ran to Dieter's car and looked inside.

When the policeman found the door locked and slapped the side of the car, Dieter, who was unsnapping his seat belt, looked at him uncomprehendingly, then recovered and unlocked the door.

"You all right?" asked the officer.

"I . . . I think so," answered Dieter. "Nothing feels broken."

"Can you get out OK? Try it, but if anything begins to hurt, stop moving."

Dieter began to slide out from under the wheel gingerly, shifting his body more quickly as he gained assurance. His knees buckled slightly when he stood erect, but he brushed the officer's hand away.

"What the hell happened?" asked the officer. "Did you get rear-ended?"

"This son of a bitch plowed to a dead stop in the middle of the street for no goddam reason," said an angry voice, "and I couldn't get around him in time."

"A wild animal," said Dieter.

"What?"

"A wild animal," he repeated. "A tiger, maybe."

"What are you talking about?"

"I said a wild animal. I heard the sound of a wild animal in the car, in the back, right behind me."

The officer looked through the side window of Dieter's car and turned back to him.

"Let me smell your breath," he said. "I think I'm going to have to give you a sobriety check."

"I am not drunk," said Dieter urgently. "I have not had a drink since lunch and then it was only wine. I tell you, I heard the sound of a wild animal in the car. Are you afraid to look, even with a gun?"

The policeman took a step closer to Dieter, his face set in angry lines and said, "Mister, until we find out otherwise, you're in big trouble. You could lose your license for this, and I sure as hell hope for your sake that you've got one hell of a lot of insurance. Now step aside."

He moved past Dieter, not quite touching him, but giving the impression he had brushed Dieter aside. He leaned into the car, extending his arm over the back of the front seat and pulled the button latch of the rear door. The fender had been pushed in and was pressing against the door frame, and the door refused to give for a moment.

He pulled it wide, one hand on his holster, looked inside, looked at Dieter in disgust, looked at the crowd of bystanders and said, "Now, if you'd said pink elephants . . ."

". . . There's something on the back floor," a man standing in the front rank of the crowd said.

The officer turned to look at him, mimicked disgust, and turned back to Dieter. The onlooker walked up to the car, leaned into the rear compartment, lifted the carpet, and said, "Look."

The officer went to the car, looked down, crouched, and said, "I'll take over."

He pulled at the carpeting and exposed a tiny plastic device attached to a length of aerial wire that ran along the back edge of the seat and around to one side.

"I'll be damned," said the officer. "It's a chip speaker."

"What is that?" asked Dieter.

"It's the smallest speaker they make, and. . . ." He stopped, pushed gently at those crowding around him, and said, "Look, the show's over. The only ones I want to see here are the ones whose cars were damaged."

As the crowd began to drift away, he turned back to Dieter. "If somebody wanted to broadcast the sound of a tiger, like maybe from a record or tape, directly into your car, this is the kind of thing they'd use. I won't say I'm convinced, but maybe if you can tell me more about this, you'll be off the hook, although it's my guess your insurance company is going to be awfully unhappy with you."

Down the block, a green van with two men in the front seat pulled away from the driveway it had been blocking. The car slowed as it passed the group of damaged cars, now huddled together like sheep in a rainstorm. The man in the passenger seat pulled his window down as the van moved slowly past, and stared at the scene, his face impassive.

The policeman had become almost protective toward Dieter. He called for a tow truck and a cab, first removing the speaker and its wire. "Whoever broadcast into your car is long gone, and this stuff is hard to trace, but we'll try," he said.

The driver who had hit Dieter's car protested vigorously when the officer informed him that he was likely to be held responsible for the damage to Dieter's car, no matter how quickly Dieter had stopped. Dieter paid no attention to the argument, limiting himself to giving and receiving information about insurance coverage, and accepting the officer's offer to trace the owners of the parked cars and give them Dieter's name and address. Dieter thanked him politely, but his manner was so strained that the officer asked, "You sure your head didn't get hit? Maybe you should see a doctor."

Dieter tried to smile but failed. "It is not a doctor I need."

He refused to let himself think on the brief ride to his house, looking out at the people and houses as if he were traveling through a strange land through which he would never pass again. At home, he had two drinks in quick succession, then took a long hot shower, ate sparingly, had another drink, took a sleeping pill, and went to bed.

When he woke, his first thought was that he should have seen a doctor, that there was a chance of concussion. But he had slept well and felt no pain, and dismissed the thought. When he got out of bed, he moved about gingerly; with increasing confidence he tried a few simple exercises and felt no adverse reaction.

He prepared eggs for breakfast and began to eat; at one point, as he put the fork into his mouth, he realized that he had let them get cold and that his thoughts had carried him back into that hellish region of uncertainty—no, anxiety. As he began contemplating a life full of bizarre occurrences like those that had already taken place, his eyes misted over; he wiped them immediately and angrily.

He debated briefly about going to work, then called a cab. He nodded approvingly when the driver went over the crest of the hill down to Bush and made a left turn; the man was making no attempt to lengthen the trip at Dieter's expense. The driver maneuvered smoothly through traffic to take full advantage of the staggered light system, but began slowing down two blocks before the turn to Dieter's office, and finally came to a halt, the motor still running.

"Why are you stopping?" asked Dieter.

"There's some kind of mess up ahead. It must have been a pretty nasty accident; I can see lots of flashing lights and police barricades. No fire engines though."

"I will get out here," said Dieter, paid the driver and walked down the street. Both the sidewalks and the roadway leading to his office building were blocked off, and uniformed police were shunting curiosity seekers away.

"My office is in that building," said Dieter, pointing. "I must go through."

"That's the last building I'd let you in," said the policeman. "The bomb squad is taking a bomb out of it right now. They ought to be out in a couple of minutes and then we'll take all this junk down."

As Dieter stared past him, two men in bulky protective clothing came out of the building carrying a large box suspended from heavy handles. Someone in the second-story office leaned out and applauded; a plainclothesman down on the street, well out of range, yelled, "Get back inside, dummy!"

The two men put the box into a large cumbersome van parked in the street and moved off, a patrol car in front and one in back, red lights flashing and sirens screaming.

The patrolman began removing the barricades, waving pedestrians through. By the time Dieter walked into the lobby of his building, vehicular traffic had started up again. The lobby was empty as he entered, but suddenly filled with people talking excitedly.

It's not possible, said Dieter to himself as he rode up in the elevator, it's not possible, but nodded in resignation when the elevator stopped at his floor and someone behind him said, "This is where they found it."

He turned a corner in the corridor and saw that the door to his suite had been opened all the way back to the wall. He began running toward it, then slowed down, still walking rapidly. The outer office was empty, but the door leading to his own office was still locked. He examined the room rapidly, but saw nothing out of place or otherwise disturbed.

As he unlocked the door to his office, his secretary came in from the corridor. "Mr. Holzer, I'm so glad to see you. It's been a terribly frightening experience."

"They say there was a bomb. Was it in this office?"

"Oh, yes! I was the one who called the police."

"I wish to hear about it, Mrs. Reynolds."

"Well, I came in promptly at 9, and went to work on some filing I had to do. About 9:20 a delivery boy came in with a package addressed to you."

"What kind of package?"

"Quite ordinary, I'd say. It was a kind of very low-key gift wrapping, with a ribbon tied around it, a very plain bow, and a small address sticker with no return address on it, typed. It could have been a birthday present, although of course I knew it wasn't since it isn't your birthday."

"Didn't it seem a bit odd?"

"Yes, it did. Then it occurred to me it might be from an admirer of yours, and I was rather charmed with the idea. I signed for it, and put it next to my desk so I could give it to you as soon as you came in."

"What made you call the police?"

"It was the phone call. About a quarter of an hour after the package

124

was delivered, somebody called. It was a kind of muffled voice, the way it sounds in movies when somebody puts a handkerchief over the phone to disguise his voice. And he asked whether a package had been delivered for you. And then, when I said yes, he asked, 'Did you hear the ticking inside of it?' "

"And so you called the police?"

"Frankly, Mr. Holzer, it took me a minute to understand what he'd said. I guess I just didn't want to believe it. Then I picked up the package, and sure enough, I could hear a ticking inside. Well, there have been a lot of bomb scares around, and even though for the life of me I couldn't think why one should come to you, I decided to take no chances; so I called the police, and they said they'd be right here and to notify the building manager and have the building cleared, and I did, and then I began running around on this floor to warn people."

"What did you do with the package?"

"I did the only thing I could think of. I put a wastepaper basket over it and pushed it under my desk. It was a kind of silly thing to do; I guess I was thinking that maybe that would help keep the blast down when it happened."

He had stared at her desk the entire time he had questioned her. Without raising his eyes he said in a quiet voice, "You did very well, Mrs. Reynolds. Very well indeed. Now let us get back to work."

He unlocked the door to his office, stepped in, then came back, and still not looking at her, he asked, "What kind of questions did the police ask?"

"They wanted to know if I knew of any enemies you might have, and I told them you were a man of excellent reputation and as far as I knew that you never had any trouble with anybody. They said they would investigate further, and if they find out anything, they would be in touch with you."

"Yes," he said. "I'll be in my office all morning. I want no phone calls, no interruptions whatsoever." Without waiting for an answer, he marched into his office, closed the door and leaned against it, taking very deep breaths. After a few moments, he went to a small stand behind his desk, brushed several magazines from its surface, lifted it high in the air, and then smashed it to the floor.

He barely heard Mrs. Reynolds call out and could not have testified as to his answer. He stood staring at the splintered pieces, his lips pressed tightly together; then his face lost all expression and his body slumped. He sank to his knees and carefully gathered the broken and splintered pieces, bundling them together almost tenderly, and placing them next to the wastepaper basket.

He sat down at his desk and opened a folder he had left on it the night before, but closed it when the letters and figures began to blur. He swiveled his chair to look out of the window. Seeing two men on a rooftop across the street, one of them pointing in his direction, he leaped up and hastily closed the drapes, then stood breathing in long, shallow draughts.

His phone buzzed. He stood looking at it as anger began to stir in him, but he did nothing. It buzzed twice more, then stopped. After a short interval, he heard a cautious knocking on his door.

"I want no interruption, Mrs. Reynolds," he called. "None." His voice rose in pitch as he spoke. "Now let me have some peace."

"I'm sorry, Mr. Holzer," she said, "but there are some police officers here, and they say if you refuse to talk to them they'll come back with a warrant for your arrest for obstructing justice."

"Just a moment, please," he called. He went to his private lavatory, put a little water on his face, wiped it, adjusted his tie, looked at his hair, and stepped back, looking at the face in the mirror as if it were the first time he had seen it.

Then he opened the door and said to the three men standing in the outer office, "Come in, gentlemen."

Without looking at Dieter, a tall, very thin man in a three-piece business suit marched past him and came to a halt in front of the desk with a precision that suggested familiarity with parade grounds.

The other two men followed him into the office; both were in uniform and one carried a small package. When Dieter came back to his desk, the tall man said, "I'm Captain Stonehouse and I'd like to know what's going on here."

"People are trying to kill me," said Dieter. "There are people who have been doing very strange things to me, and now they are trying to kill me."

"How?" asked the Captain. "With this?"

Without turning around, he snapped his fingers and extended his hands. When the policeman holding the package placed it in them, the Captain held it above Dieter's desk and turned it upside down. A stream of dead flies poured out, and a cheap alarm clock hit the desk and bounced onto the floor.

"With that?"

"I don't understand," said Dieter.

"Neither do we," said the Captain, "but we intend finding out. This little morning's work cost the city and county of San Francisco well over three thousand dollars and kept some policemen from more important duties, just to find out that what was supposed to be a bomb was full of dead flies. I ask you again, what's going on?"

"I know no more of this than you do," said Dieter, "except that somebody tried to kill me, and might have killed my secretary."

"You're not listening, Mr. Holzer. Nobody tried to kill you. Somebody apparently wanted to frighten you, but not kill you. I think you're supposed to know what all this means, and if you decide you do, you're to get in touch with me immediately."

"Yes," said Dieter. "Yes, Captain."

Part III

And there was blood throughout the land of Egypt. But the magicians did the same by their secret arts.

Exodus 8:21

————————— 1

Less than a mile from Dieter's office, a group of men sat in an aluminum trailer converted into a semipermanent installation. The corner on which the trailer had established residence gave evidence of being a mating ground for buses—dozens of them sat side by side, nose to rear, and in other combinations.

The lot housing them marked the end and the beginning of a suburban transportation system that fed thousands of commuters into the city of San Francisco during morning hours, and spewed them out to the suburbs in the afternoon and evening.

The group was composed of drivers for the system; the trailer housed the dispatcher's office, records, and places for the drivers to sit and talk to each other, or to rest in exhausted silence waiting for the next run.

A week after the roar of a tiger in Dieter's car had caused it to attempt to couple with cars nearby, the drivers sat discussing their passengers, employing adjectives normally used by zoo keepers discussing their charges.

"I swear she works the line," one of them said. "Five times now I've seen her sit with a different guy, and each time, by the time she gets off, she's given him a little slip of paper. Trouble is, I don't get the same freaks on the return run, so I can't tell whether the guys stay over in the city, but three gets you five they do."

"What he means, the trouble is she never gives him a piece of paper," one of the men said.

The laughter and the jeering had barely died down when another driver said, "I got one, comes in from Terra Linda every day of the week, and no matter what the weather is, he's got this light tan coat he wears, like a raincoat, buttoned all the way down. I pick him up in the rear mirror every once in a while, and he's got this glazed look on his face, and maybe a little sweat, but his hands are right out in the open. I got passengers who meditate on the way home, but what this guy's doing I don't know and I don't want to know."

The talk slowly shifted to the variety of objects that passengers tend to leave on buses, the drivers trying to outdo each other with stories of bizarre packages, then shifted again to a general discussion of the madness of the human race, and back to the problems of bus drivers.

"We got it good compared to the Muni drivers," one of the men said. "Some of them could tell you stories that'd grow a beard on a mushroom."

"That's nothing," another said. "You want to hear stories that knock you right out of your skull, you talk to cops. My cousin, he's on the force, he tells stories you wouldn't believe. Any of you guys see the story that time about those frogs hopping all over the opera house?"

When several of the drivers nodded and made comments, he said, "I can tell you the inside story of that one, and if you want to know what's weird, that's weird."

"They got the guy that did it?"

"No, but it's only part of what's been going on with one of the people in the box. My cousin, he got it from a sergeant who covers his precinct. It seems that this guy, the one in the box, is being hassled, and nobody can make sense out of it. Some crazies keep doing stuff to him that nobody can figure."

"Like what?"

"There's this one morning, he walks out of his house, and he opens the door of his car, and they rigged up a deal where what looks like blood, but ain't, comes pouring all over his clothes and everything.

"And last week, he's driving down Pacific, and he hits his brake like there's a little kid right in front of him, and the guy behind him plows into him, and he bounces off and hits a car that's parked. And when the patrol car comes up, he swears that some kind of animal gave a bellow right in his ear. They think he's drunk, but just to make sure, they look, and sure enough there's a chip speaker, you know, one them little things, in the back seat.

"And there's still another thing. That bomb scare where there was no bomb, just flies in a box? And you know who that happens to? You got it."

After a few comments, shakings of heads, another horror story, and more small talk, the group disintegrated into its individual components. One of the drivers remained at the table, drinking a second cup of coffee, and idly making designs on a piece of paper.

He wrote "blood" and filled in all the enclosed spaces, then drew droplets falling from the word, filling in their spaces as well. He wrote "frogs" and drew a series of little downward curved semicircles, each over a pair of parallel wavy lines. He wrote "wild animal" and surrounded the words with teethlike jagged lines, and suddenly stopped and said, "son of a bitch." He looked again at what he had drawn, and went off to look for the driver whose cousin was a cop.

2

In less than twenty-four hours his excited comments had become the bottom rung of a ladder that successively led to the cousin's wife, the cousin, the cousin's sergeant friend, the precinct commander, a detective sergeant, and finally Dieter.

Dieter's secretary looked surprised when the man who entered the office identified himself as a police officer and asked to see Dieter; his appearance offered no clue to his occupation, but he had the look of embarrassment that she associated with newly recruited volunteers raising money for charities.

She excused herself, picked up the phone, and asked Dieter if she could come into his office. "I wanted to let you know before you saw him that it was a detective sergeant who wants to see you, I mean after the way they came in last time."

When Dieter saw the uneasy look on the man's face, he said immediately, "I have no further information to give you."

The officer said, "It's not that. It's that maybe we've got something."

Dieter asked eagerly, "You know who they are?"

"No, sir, it's not quite that either. It's . . ." He paused, and gave a remarkable impersonation of a man about to dive off a melting iceberg into the Arctic.

"We were wondering, that is the Department, that is, if you have any enemies that are, I mean, do you have any enemies that are Jewish?"

Dieter stared at him in shock and finally blurted, "Jewish? Jewish enemies? What are you talking about?"

"Look, I didn't mean anything, and the Captain told me to be sure to explain to you that it has nothing to do with your name or the way you . . . or your being German or anything, but it's just that we've come across something that could just make some kind of sense out of what's been going on."

Without describing how he had come by the information, he repeated the briefing he had been given about the first four plagues and the Children of Israel.

"Like in that old spiritual, you know, 'Way down in Egypt land.' It could just be coincidence, but so far it's the only thing we've got. If it is the same thing, we figure they used flies instead of vermin. Anyway, what we'd like is for you to think about somebody you might know who might be some kind of Jewish terrorist or something like that, if you know the kind I mean."

"No, I don't," Dieter said sharply, then recovering, said, "I'll think about it."

After the policeman left, he sat at his desk, listing questions on a sheet of ruled paper, but always coming back to the first line: Who?

The obscene happenings must be the plagues. "They" must be Jews, that followed logically. The one discrepancy was in the plague of vermin, as the policeman had described it; but his dictionary also defined vermin as "noxious human beings," and that they had been.

He knew little of the professional Nazi hunters, but it could not be them, he decided, not for several reasons. Long ago he had let himself consider whether what had taken place that day had been evil. He had indeed ordered men to be killed, but he had only been carrying out orders, his captain sitting in the command car all the while. And the men killed had not been simple civilians. They called themselves partisans but had been more like scavenger dogs yapping and biting at the heels of strangers, except that these carried weapons and used them.

In any event, it was a far less questionable act than had been committed by men now in responsible and respected posts, in the United States, as well as in Germany. And finally, from what he knew of the Nazi hunters, they were not given to petty revenges in private; theirs were public occasions, announcements, trials.

Unlike others, he had never hidden or slunk away into some dark corner or changed his name. He never denied his origins when confronted directly, but when some mistook him for a Swiss, he never corrected them. When he came into the country, his papers had been in order; he was a citizen of the United States, equal to any other.

He considered his life since coming to the United States. He had done nothing to mark him as different from other men. He belonged

135

to organizations, none of them political, and had no ties to any part of the organized German community. If occasionally he felt curiosity about the "new" Germany, it had withered before blossoming into a desire to return.

He pushed the pad away from him, stood up, and began pacing the room. He had built a life for himself, and he felt a moral rage, a furious anger, as he considered what they had done to him in these past weeks, not only the barbarities themselves but the consequences to his being.

He had always been careful with his body, indulging appetites, but always within a reasonable range, balancing excesses with exercise and rigid self-control. And yet now he became impotent on occasion. He knew it was not a medical matter; nothing was wrong with his body. It was, instead, a result of what "they" were doing to him.

That was bad enough, but there had been worse. He woke one night with sweat covering his body, the bottom sheet uncomfortably moist against him. He went to the bathroom, wiped himself dry, and crawled back into bed, slipping between the top sheet and the blanket. When he woke in the morning and looked at the turned-back covers, he realized with disgust what had happened: he had wet himself. He could not remember the last time he had done so, but had a sudden vivid flash of memory, his father standing over him yelling, with a leather strap in his hand.

At least, now, those pressures were behind him. There might be more plagues, if they were not stopped, but no more would he have to live in a world from which reason and order had fled. And they had to be stopped, but how? The police were useless, he told himself. They asked questions, gave promises, but accomplished nothing; consider how long it had taken them to decipher the meaning of this obscene puzzle.

He sat down again and looked at the pad. That miserable question: Who? If not Nazi hunters, could they be Jews of a different stripe, perhaps some he had unwittingly offended? And if so, when? He had barely formulated the words of the question when memory provided a possibility: the night in the bar when he had talked too much, carried away by the desire to impress that dark-eyed beauty of a schoolteacher.

He knew it was a desperately slim lead, but he began to spend more time than usual at the bar, dropping in night after night, studying those around him, looking for a sign, a mark, any kind of revelation of his enemies.

One night, while sitting at the bar and staring at the drink in front of him, he immersed himself so deeply in thought that when he raised his eyes and looked into the bar mirror, his own image was that of a stranger. As he realized that the face at which he stared was his own, he had a vague sense of being watched. The glance slid past without engaging him, but it seemed to Dieter that it had lingered on his face. There was something more; the man's face was only vaguely familiar, probably that of another of the regulars of the bar, but on it was a trace of an expression he recognized, one he had seen elsewhere but whose meaning he could not translate.

The watcher was leaving; on an impulse, Dieter slid off his stool, left a couple of dollar bills on the counter, and followed the man out of the bar. He was getting into a car that resembled his own; when its backup lights went on, Dieter studied the license plate. The impulse to follow had been based on the thinnest of speculation, but once back inside the bar, he wrote the number on a piece of paper and put it into his wallet, forgetting it almost immediately.

Three days later, when he had to take a business trip to Eureka, several hundred miles up the California coast, he decided to drive, feeling that the trip might settle his mind and perhaps even act as a stimulus to some new line of thought.

On the last leg of his trip he rounded a curve and found a long line of traffic stretching up the steep hill ahead. He put his head out of the window and looked up the hill, but could see no reason for the delay. In disgust, he pulled out into the opposite lane, assuming that if he had to squeeze back into line, some obliging motorist would make room for him. Several drivers hit their horns as he passed, but he paid little attention to them except for a sardonic wave of his hand.

He had gained only about two hundred feet when he heard a horn beeping frantically, and mingled with this sound, the shriek of a police siren. He looked up the hill and saw a logging rig barreling down in his direction at a speed that indicated its brakes had gone.

He could see no opening in the line of cars on his right, and there was no usable shoulder on his left. He reacted immediately. He braked to a screaming stop, threw the car into reverse, and backed down the hill as fast as he dared, until he came to a small turnout. He backed into it only a few seconds before the truck roared by, its horn still sounding, a blurred white face, its mouth open, staring at him from the cab.

A highway patrol cruiser screeched to a stop beside him, and its driver called out, "You stay here until I get back, you goddam idiot, or I'll have your ass!" and roared off again.

Dieter sat for a moment, the car's engine still running, then shut the ignition off. He understood that he might have been killed because of the chance he took, and that someone with slower reflexes or lesser driving skill probably would have been. But that reflection was quickly displaced by anger at the highway patrolman and his insulting tone. And, dear God, he thought, still another policeman.

He considered leaving, but decided to do so would be foolish. The line of cars was already moving up the hill, but moving slowly; even if he somehow joined it, the patrol car would soon catch up, and if not, his car was too conspicuous to escape a network of radio alerts.

A car horn sounded behind him. He turned to look and realized that he was blocking the entrance to the pullout. He backed further into it and managed to turn his car so that he faced the south exit without blocking it.

When the highway patrolman returned, less than ten minutes later, he was still angry. As the officer approached, Dieter said, "Look, you have no right . . ."

The officer leaned into the open window, put his face close to Dieter's, and said in precisely articulated anger, "If you've got a remnant of brains in your head, you'll shut up and hand me your driver's license, if you have one. You're getting a ticket for driving on the wrong side of the road, and another one for reckless driving. One word out of you and you'll get something a damn sight worse. And if you fight the tickets, I'll gladly give up a day's pay for the pleasure of standing in front of a judge and describing exactly what you just did!"

The two men stared at each other for a moment, then Dieter pulled out his wallet, extracted his driver's license, and handed it to the patrolman.

A few minutes later, after examining the car registration as well, the officer wrote two tickets. Then stopping for a moment as he walked away, he called out, "Don't try making a U-turn on this hill or you'll get another ticket," then got in his car, made a U-turn, and drove away.

Dieter went south for a half mile before he found a side road that permitted him to turn around and continue on to Eureka. The surface levels of his consciousness guided his hands and feet in a variety of small adjustments as he drove, but he wandered too close to the yellow divider, and a passing driver hit his horn in warning. He suddenly realized that he had driven several miles with no memory of the countryside or even that he had been driving.

A sign indicated a rest area two miles ahead; he drove to it, parked, and lit a cigarette. The episode with the truck had all but vanished from his mind; he was engrossed in fantasies of what he might have said to the officer, the statements he could have made in a courtroom about the officer's arrogance, and above all, the punishments he would have liked to inflict upon him.

As he sat and smoked, a wartime episode came pushing out of the recesses of his memory. His regiment had been stationed in an area once largely pacified, but in which increasing amounts of guerilla activity were taking place. He was at the regimental command post when a detail brought in a man suspected of being one of the leaders.

"Come along, Holzer," a major had said, pronouncing his name with an amused smile, "this is part of your education."

The interrogation officer, a translator, and several enlisted men were in a barren room with the prisoner, who sat stripped naked on a hard chair, while a series of questions were hurled at him. He sat as if already dead, saying nothing.

Shortly after the beating started, Dieter left the room, aware of the derisive look on the major's face. Dieter was young, younger than all the other officers, and took mental notes on the conduct of the officers he most admired. He did not concern himself with the prisoner, although he was uncomfortable with the beating and what was to come. Still, he already had the soldier's distaste for those without uniforms who fought and ran and hid and fought again.

His principal interest had been in the conduct of the officers in the room. Except for the interrogator, no one had said a word, or shown either pleasure or distaste in the proceedings. But their faces all reflected the same curious expression and he slowly deciphered its meaning: however the prisoner responded, whether he gave them information or not, he was going to die, and they were watching to see what his reactions would be when he realized this, watching as if he were an interesting specimen on a microscope slide, and they were scientists.

He sat up with a start; his cigarette had burned down far enough so that his fingers had felt the heat. He put it out and lit another one, the memory already drifting away.

He took a few puffs, put out the cigarette, decided he was ready to continue the trip, and started the motor. He looked into the rearview mirror and then into the side mirror, started to back out, and then stopped so suddenly that he was thrown backward. Two memories had suddenly fused: that man in the bar watching him—now he understood the meaning of the expression on his face.

He completed his business in Eureka and drove back to San Francisco more relaxed than he had been in months. The puzzle had been solved, and its originator identified, of that he was certain. He decided against wasting time on further speculation, since professional help could be purchased easily.

He made inquiries after he returned to the city; two mornings later he was sitting in the office of an investigator who, he had been assured, specialized in "very confidential" cases.

"I want all the information you can procure concerning the owner of this car," Dieter said, handing him the slip of paper on which he had copied Aryeh's license plate number. "Personal information."

"What does that include? How personal?"

"How does he make his living? Where does he work? Where does he live? What organizations does he belong to? What are his politics? I am . . . eager . . . to know who his close friends are, and most especially whether there is a special group he has been seeing regularly for the past few months."

"Are you referring, shall I say, to his sexual habits?"

"I do not care whether he prefers men, women, or dogs, but I do want to know the identity of his intimates. Beyond that. . . ." He made a face and waved his hand in dismissal of the thought.

After discussing cost and other technical matters, Dieter paused, then said, "There is one more thing about his friends, those that he meets with regularly, if there are such. If you should identify such a group, I would then discuss with you similar profiles."

He looked at the ceiling and said carefully, "I understand that you are reputable and that of course you obey all laws. I would not think of asking you to perform an illegal act, as for example, putting a microphone in somebody's apartment or perhaps using some more contemporary device for the same purpose.

"But I desire very much the information I have asked you to procure, and quickly, and should you include in your fee an item designated, shall we say, 'unallocated expenses' or 'unforeseen expenses,' I would not hesitate to pay."

"I see," said the investigator, and penciled a note on his pad.

"Finally, I should like to reiterate that it is not the subject of the conversations in which I am most interested, but rather the identity of those speaking."

"Yes," said the investigator, and made a final note.

After, when Dieter sat at his table waiting for his lunch to be served, no small lines of tension touched his face, and he might have been a man sitting for a portrait to be labeled "Composure." While waiting for his *omelette aux fines herbes,* he sipped a glass of wine, his fingers gently caressing the wineglass, his fingers moving from the stem to the curve and back again.

Soon "they" would come out of the shadows, no longer lurking menaces, half seen in a dream; they would be people, like the man in the bar, individuals with identifiable faces, occupations, histories, residences—and vulnerabilities.

He filled his glass to the brim, letting light glint off its surface, staring into it as if he saw nothing but glowing promises, tipping it slightly from side to side, unaware that drops of wine were dripping onto the white tablecloth.

He was roused out of a dream without shape, a beguiling fantasy without detail or end, by the waiter, "M'sieu! M'sieu!"

When he looked up the waiter pointed and said, "M'sieu, the cloth!"

Dieter looked at the stains on the tablecloth, and still not fully emerged from his revery, said, "Do not worry, they will pay," and then seeing the expression on the waiter's face, caught himself and said, "I will pay."

The waiter's face cleared, and he said politely, "No, m'sieu, there is no need of that. If you permit." And without waiting for an answer, he carefully spilled salt over the spots and placed a napkin over them.

Twice in the days that followed he had picked up the phone to call the investigator, but had changed his mind each time; the man was a professional who knew his job, he reminded himself, and pressuring him might produce delay rather than speed. And the man had performed the first part of his assignment commendably.

Now the work was done. He stood at his desk, looking down at a row of photographs, placed with such scrupulous care that they might have been resting on an invisible line. Below them he had arranged another row, this of plastic binders, each with a single name written on it.

He stood with his hands clasped behind his back, studying each photograph in turn, as if he were savoring a prize collection of butterflies, each impaled on a pin. Dieter no longer needed to memorize them; he had looked at them so many times since bringing them home from his office that that they were firmly implanted in his memory. He appraised them in the professional manner of a street caricaturist studying a subject's face for salient characteristics. Interest flared briefly in his face as he studied Martine's photo, but vanished quickly; his face hardened when he looked once again at Aryeh.

After a few minutes he turned and faced the wall; an observer would have thought him to be deeply interested in an engraving of a nineteenth-century balloonist about to make an ascension. A number of lords and ladies strolled on the grounds of a French estate watching the preparations; he ran his forefinger up and down each little figure.

He put the photos of Aryeh and Jean-Pierre to one side, turned around and sat down, and looked again at the others. "Children," he muttered, "little children, nasty little children," seeing them lying on a rug, feet drumming, fists banging, mouths open, shouting like infants seized with frustration. That he could deal with, that he would deal with.

He put the four photographs in a neat pile, gathered the folders, put the photos on top of them, and placed them in a desk drawer. He picked up the photos of Aryeh and Jean-Pierre and put them in the exact geometrical center of the desk. A photographer had caught Aryeh in mid-stride just after he had left an apartment building. Aryeh looked grave, serious, a man contemplating important and troubling problems.

A child in an adult's body, thought Dieter. I could have fathered them all, and he amused himself with a vision of five children with grown-up faces, bent over the back of a bench in a neat row, naked bottoms exposed to Dieter's strap.

"But not him," he said aloud to Jean-Pierre's photograph. He looked at the broad, almost peasant face, simultaneously seventeenth century and contemporary because of the sweep of hair, curved down over the forehead to the corner of his right eye, then falling down to the chin, the other side falling straight, past the ear, both sides curling very slightly at the ends.

"You, you know," he said to the photograph, although he could not have explained what he meant. He put the two photographs with the others, locked the drawer, put out the light, and went into his living room.

He placed his favorite armchair so that it sat directly between his stereo speakers and put a bottle of Courvoisier and a small glass on the rosewood table next to it. After switching on his amplifier he stood looking at a row of cassettes on the shelf above; he pulled one out, returned it, fingered another, and then crouched to look at the row of records on the bottom shelf of his stereo cabinet.

Mozart, of course, he thought, but the darker Mozart, the mystical Mozart. *The Magic Flute,* certainly, but not Pamino and Pamina with their charming little songs; it would have to be The Queen of the Night.

"It was while listening to her sing her aria that inspiration came," he told Mrs. Zorn.

"I sat there, reading my family Bible, a fine old leatherbound volume, one of the few of our possessions to survive those terrible bombings.

"According to the Bible, it was not the famous Moses who brought down the first plagues, but his brother Aaron, whose descendants became the High Priests of the Israelites. And I discovered further, that after he performed the plagues of blood and frogs, the Pharaoh's priests used their magic to reenact them as well."

"Priests, magic, plagues," murmured Mrs. Zorn. "This is all positively Jungian." Her face was alive with interest, and she leaned closer to him as she spoke. Dieter looked at her with pleasure; she sat on the couch in a garment somewhere between the lounging pyjamas of the 1930s and a contemporary jump suit. A small opal-set medallion hung from a gold chain around her neck, and he let her see him looking at it. "Stop looking at me like that, Dieter," she said. "Remember your Ecclesiastes, 'a season for all things' . . ."

He was pleased with her, and himself. Ever since that night of the frogs, when he had become so angry in public, she had begun a retreat. The pace had changed, and the pleasures of deliberately prolonged expectations, small shifts, and brief hesitations had vanished. Instead, the chase had taken on the quality of watchful waiting between two commanders, neither wishing to risk defeat for a dubious advantage, and he sensed that given the alternative she was prepared to accept disengagement rather than combat.

"Yes," said Dieter. "While listening to the opera and all its mystic trappings, I began thinking of the Pharaoh. I could almost see him and his retinue and court magicians on one side of the river and Aaron and his staff on the other, and I began then to think of myself as . . ."

". . . the court magician."

"Yes," said Dieter. "Exactly."

He stood and walked to the window; beyond the small balcony of her apartment, he could see the lights of North Beach and beyond them, Coit Tower; to his left he could see the outline of the Embarcadero, and beyond, the Bay.

"Perhaps not the magician," he said reflectively. "Look out there, at the darkness and all the mystery and magic it hides. Perhaps I shall become King of the Night."

He could see her reflection in the window; she was still sitting on the couch, her eyes intent on him. He walked to a glass étagère placed against one wall and fingered her collection of netsukes, moving them around as if they were pawns in a chess game. After restoring them to their original positions, he turned to face her and said, "Whatever I call myself is of little importance. What is important is that this game be brought to an end, and not by them, but by me."

"What do you propose to do?" she asked. "If I know you, Dieter, it will be something devilish."

He considered her, framing his response carefully. When he had first told her the story, he had left out mention of the episode of the bar and Aryeh, ascribing actions of the group to some vague knowledge of his having been in the Wehrmacht, and condemning him out of hand.

She had said, "But how Old Testament, 'an eye for an eye' "; and he had looked at her suspiciously, then realized that she was condemning them, not him.

"I must admit," he said, "that I was greatly tempted to mirror their actions, but as in a dark mirror, a mirror made of black marble, perhaps. But I am above them, and I will not get down on all fours and frolic with them.

"No, I will find some way to let them know that I am aware of their childish games, something that will tell them that it is all over, perhaps something with a small discomfort in it, something to help them grow up."

She rose from the couch and stood near him. "You are a wicked, wicked man, Dieter—Prince of Darkness. I would not want to be those little children of yours," she said, and pretended to shiver.

He said nothing, and they stood looking at each other. He saw her face change; she lowered her eyes almost shyly, then raised her face, her eyes opened wide, and said suddenly, "Oh sir! Please sir! Do not punish me! I promise I shall be good, sir," and with hands clasped at her breast in mock supplication, slowly retreated as he moved nearer to her.

5

Aryeh sat at his desk in the small office he shared with another instructor, behind a barricade of books, manuals, and theme papers perpetually on the point of collapse. His metal desk abutted another; each had a swivel chair behind it and a straight back alongside. On the entrance wall, next to the door, a large metal-frame bookcase held books and stacks of file folders.

The wall behind him carried a theater lobby poster in French, displaying Brigitte Bardot and Jeanne Moreau in the strip sequence from *Viva Maria!* Aryeh sat leaning back, bracing himself against the desk with his knees, his head against Bardot's thighs, talking to a student.

"Your paper is a nice piece of work, and I'm going to give you an "A" on it, but I'd like to caution you about something. You get somewhat carried away with symbols. Things are themselves first, and then symbols, and if they don't work on the first level, it's all a bullshit intellectual exercise. If you have a mind that's crazy enough, you can make a construct of anything. It might be fun, it might be interesting, but the question you have to keep in mind, always, is whether the construct comes from you or from the work you're examining."

"Well," said the student, "I think most of it is bullshit too, but I thought that's what you wanted. It's the way you talk, isn't it? I mean, like in the *Seven Samurai,* you pointed out that all the samurai who die get killed by a gun, and that's Kurosawa's point, about the old order being replaced by the new, that time had passed those men by."

"I did say that. I think it's true," said Aryeh, "but it even may be that Kurosawa didn't have that in mind. But the point I'm making is even if you never saw that, it's a hell of a story. If it weren't, nobody would talk about it or go to see it or bother with symbols, except college teachers and critics. Right?"

After the student left, he sat thinking about a film series for the following year: the American Western, but from a different approach. There had to be a way to show the early Peckinpah *Ride the High Country*. Theme: the dignity of death? It was there in that beautiful final scene, but he could hear the derisive comments of his students and his colleagues when he used it in the same sentence with Peckinpah's name.

But the major preoccupation of the film could not be denied: men who had outlived their time. It ran through most of his work, and other films as well—Henry King's *The Gunfighter* and that film with Kirk Douglas. Yes, he thought, I can work it all into a metaphor for an America longing to return to a past it never had.

He was consulting several catalogs of 16-mm films and scribbling on a ruled yellow pad when a student messenger brought him a parcel. "It came parcel post and there's no place to put it, so they sent me over," she said, extending it to him with both hands and adding "that paper is weird."

He had almost given up deciphering the language being created by the generation in the wake of his own; but however she means it, he thought, she's right. The package, about a foot square and almost as high, was very heavy; the paper wrapping was covered with pyramids, sphinxes, and humanoid figures with cat heads. The label carried no return address.

As he began to open it, he realized that the messenger was watching with interest. "Thank you," he said.

"Oh, that's OK," she said.

"Thank you," he said, glancing at the door.

She turned to look in the direction of his glance, said, "Oh, sure," and left.

He pulled the paper away and uncovered a plain corrugated carton in which shredded newspaper surrounded a plastic mixing bowl, filled with poker chips. Except for a single blue chip on the surface layer, all those he could see were white.

As he sat starting at the chips, another instructor put his head in the door and asked, "How about a cup of coffee before class?"

Aryeh quickly put the lid back on the bowl, then waved him away without saying anything. He lifted the lid again and looked at the chips. Suddenly, as their significance penetrated, he felt as if his face had caught fire and every blood vessel in his body had become distended and was pressing outward against his skin.

Once in his childhood, he had stolen money from his father's bedroom drawer, lied about it, and was caught in the lie. His father, with unusual gentleness, had said, "This time, nothing, as a gift from me when I was a child and did the same thing. Next time . . ." The episode had faded away, but he felt himself burning with the same kind of shame he had felt when the lie was exposed.

Shame was followed by anger, anger at himself for feeling shame. This was no childish misdeed in which he had been caught; he knew what he was doing, he would continue doing it, he owed no apologies to anyone, and sought no forgiveness. Briefly, he cursed Dieter for the indignity that Dieter had inflicted on him, for making him feel, if only for a moment, as if he had committed a loathsome act.

He found some Scotch tape in his desk drawer, rewrapped the parcel, and put it under his desk. He stood looking down at it for a moment, picked up his notes for the morning lecture, and walked slowly across campus, no longer conscious of his feelings but considering the basic meaning of the bowl and its contents.

Number one, he told himself, Dieter knows. He knows what's being done to him; that's the meaning of the Egyptian paper. Number two, he knows that I'm involved, which is why he sent it to me. Number three, he remembers that night in the bar, and that power game. And the blue chip?

He put the thought aside when he found himself in front of his classroom. Luckily today is film, he thought, I can sit in the darkness and think.

"Today we're going to see Buster Keaton's *The General.* Just before class I talked with one of you about symbolism and the need to be cautious about laying it on something that's not there. I suppose I could do it with Keaton, but I love him far too much to reduce him to symbolism.

"One of the reasons we're going to see this film is that you've had a heavy diet all term, and it's time for a little relaxed enjoyment. But we'll talk about an aspect of the film later, one that validates my showing it to you and saves me from being charged with self-indulgence. Keaton saw himself in a world where objects were hostile, where he was buffeted about by powerful forces—contrivances, machines, life itself—and his reactions lift his comedy to the level of greatness. I may even use the words existentialist or absurdist if somebody provokes me enough. Let's go."

It always comes back to power, he thought as he took his seat in the darkened auditorium. Life, films, children's games, chips. And now Dieter informs me that he has power over me. Because of his knowledge? Then he became caught up in the film, and with the rest of the class, found himself laughing as Keaton, in exquisite frustration, threw a stick of firewood at a howitzer that he had primed to fire at the enemy and that had, almost of its own volition, turned and aimed itself at him instead.

"I still like Chaplin," said a student after class, "but the thing that gets me about Keaton, he doesn't ask you to pity or admire or sympathize with him. It's like he's always kind of looking over his shoulder winking at the audience and saying, 'See how silly life is.' "

"Yes, indeed," said Aryeh.

I would have said absurd, but silly will do. In my situation, too; I wonder how they would react if they knew what I have on my mind. I'd better call Simon, he thought. Talking about it might help relieve the pressure.

Simon was sitting at his piano, playing a transcription of the orchestral part of Haydn's *D Minor Cello Concerto* and simultaneously listening to his student play the solo part. He stopped and said to the student, "Look, maybe it'll help if we talk about Haydn a little bit. You've got to remember that what you're trying to do is something like loving somebody. You bring everything you are to the other person, for their sake, not yours. You're trying to intensify them, in a way.

"Forget all about that "Papa" Haydn business, and listen to him as he really was, in the music. Papas are not supposed to be wild, and yet he is, right here," he said, pointing to the passage the student had been playing.

"There's something here, something he's trying to let out. Maybe it comes from a Gypsy tradition, maybe it was the only way he could let loose in his time, and he's doing something he couldn't do any other way. Let yourself . . ."

The phone rang; he excused himself and went to answer it. After Aryeh finished talking, Simon asked, "Are you sure about the chips?"

"I am, Simon. I can still hear that woman saying, 'and the white chips have to take orders from everybody.' "

"So Dieter knows what's up."

"More than that. He knows who I am and what I do. Why else send the chips to me at school? It's a warning to stop."

"It could be more."

"How?"

"If you go back to Exodus and the commentaries, not the Haggadah, you'll see that Jehovah warned the Pharaoh before each of the plagues. But there's something else; when Aaron brought down the first two plagues, the Pharaoh's priests used their magic to duplicate them."

"That's why the Egyptian paper?"

"It's possible. Watch yourself, yes?"

"You mean stand aside when I open my car door and don't go to the opera and don't answer my phone? I promise."

"I hope it's that simple. Keep in touch," said Simon, and hung up.

After his student finished the hour of instruction and left, Simon wandered the apartment, flexing his fingers and thinking. It seemed so simple at first, he thought, but maybe there's a detour sign up ahead. Whatever we had in mind, at the beginning, any of us, now it's different.

He took a small watering can made of brass, with a plunger for controlling the fine spray, filled it, and made a circuit of his apartment, watering the plants that needed daily injections of fluid and thinking, not for the first time, they own me, not me them.

I wonder whether Aryeh has told Martine about the latest, he thought. Perhaps I should call her. He found his phone book, propped it up on the music stand, and turned to the page where her number was listed. No. That's for Aryeh, he told himself; then, with the phone book still on the stand, he took his cello and played the passage his student had been practicing, accentuating its wildness beyond permissible limits.

 7

Simon's warning troubled Aryeh more than he cared to admit to himself, but as the days passed and nothing happened, he forgot his concern and began trying to decide what the Commando should do next, if it were indeed going to do anything. He found no idea to cling to, and when he tried to clear his mind of Dieter and allow his unconscious to go to work, nothing emerged.

Demonic possession, that's what it is, he told himself, driving across the Bay Bridge three days after he had received the parcel. All this time I've welcomed thoughts about Dieter and what to do to him, and now, when I want some respite, he won't go away. People take memory courses; why aren't there forgetting courses?

The rest of the way home he paid minimal attention to his driving, using the rest of his mind to design a sixty-second film: Medium shot of an industrial building displaying a sign: "Opening Soon! The Forgettery Factory!" followed by a tracking shot to a small sign to one side of the building's entrance: "We Forget For You," below which would appear a rate schedule:

Words	10¢
Names	50¢
Politicians	$1.00
Emotional traumas	$2.00
Broken love affairs	$5.00
Dieters	$100.00

The last shot of the film came to him as he pulled into a parking space near his apartment house: Aryeh, Prop., standing in front of the building, unable to open the doors because he had forgotten the keys.

Amused at the idea, and himself, he loped down the block and ran up the steps to his building. He stopped in the lobby, opened his mailbox, and rifled though his letters with the faintest touch of expectation, but found nothing of immediate interest. He pushed them into the pocket of his jacket; as he reached for the inside door, his key extended to unlock it, the door swung open against him, and he jumped out of the way.

His next-door neighbor came out, saw him, and said, "Aryeh, I would like to speak with you."

"Certainly," Aryeh said.

"Since we've been neighbors, I've never complained to you or about you, right?"

"Right."

"I've never said a word about the harem you seem to keep in there, right?"

"Right."

"I never complained about the music, or laughed in your face the day you informed me that rock is to today like Beethoven was to his day, right?"

"Right."

"I never complained about the smell of you-know-what, right?"

"Right."

"Well, whatever it is you have in mind with your front door, I don't like it. Interesting, but I don't like it. It's messy, and smells, and don't tell me it's conceptual art."

"Believe me," Aryeh said, "I left my apartment this morning before 7:30, and I didn't leave anything on my front door. What is it?"

"Go look. If it wasn't you, you certainly have some weirdos among your friends."

Aryeh ignored the elevator and ran up the two flights of steps to his floor. He could see his doorway as soon as he came out of the stairway exit. Hanging from the doorknob of his apartment door was a large turnip, its long leafy top still attached, a blue ribbon wrapped around its mid-section holding it suspended from the doorknob. A large sticky red pool was on the floor immediately below it, and drops of the same substance had splashed on the door and the hallway rug.

He looked at it uncomprehendingly for a moment, then crouched on one knee and touched a finger to the substance on the floor. It was blood.

8

Jean-Pierre woke up slowly, then stretched himself as if he were on the rack and got out of bed. He dressed and washed quickly after rubbing his face and deciding he could postpone the indignity of shaving another day. Before leaving, he went to the stern and stretched the World War II camouflage netting over the dozen plants growing in pots near the rail. The county had relaxed its vigilance, but there clearly was no point in taking unnecessary chances.

He made his way carefully along the rotting pier leading to the parking lot where he left his pickup truck. He stopped briefly to look at the Bay; an unusually high plus-tide lapped at the edges of the houseboats and derelict barges. The sun had just appeared over the Tiburon hills to the east and patterned the water in patches of purple and gold.

He thought of the people he had grown up with in France and what they would have thought of the life he had carved out for himself. "You have found a nice refuge for yourself, Jean-Pierre," he could hear them saying, "but what are you doing with your life? Tell us." He saw them, not as they probably were, balding, fat, gray, but as they had been, listening as he told them of the Commando and its pinpricks, all of them laughing.

Still, one rides with history and does what one does, he thought, and climbed into the truck and drove to the morning restaurant. He had almost finished his breakfast when an acquaintance who was building a concrete boat down the road from his shop stopped at his table and asked, "What are you up to?"

"Up to? The usual. Work".

"No, I mean in that place of yours; it stinks."

Jean-Pierre shifted in his chair and asked, "Can this be the same man who argued so passionately last year that we had a right to keep our boats as we pleased as long as they hurt no one? Has there been an outbreak of aesthetic flu?"

"I'm not talking about your boat, Jean-Pierre. I mean your shop, and I mean it stinks, really stinks. What have you got in there?"

Jean-Pierre studied him for a moment to see if he were serious, found no clue, shrugged, and went back to his coffee. He finished reading the paper, signaled the waitress for another half cup, and sat thinking about the Commando. They were all good people, but they knew so little of what the world was really like.

He paid, climbed into his truck, and drove down the hill to his shop. The morning chill was abating, and he opened his window as he approached; even before parking the truck, he understood that the comment about the shop was meant to be serious.

A stench hung in the air, and its center seemed to be his shop. He reached for the key to the padlock on the front door and stopped; the lock was still in its hasp, but there was a freshly made deep gouge below the hasp, and it did not rest tightly against the doorjamb. He put his hand on the hasp and pulled; it came away in his hand, and the two hidden screws that held it in place came with it.

He pushed the door open with his left hand, at the same time reaching around with his right hand to switch on the light and stood there, revolted. The stripped bodies of frogs in varying stages of decomposition littered the floor and covered his worktable.

9

Aryeh had three hours to fill before the Commando would meet at his flat, and he faced them as though they were a black hole in space. He had made no dinner preparations, found himself ravenous, and ate steadily: a slab of Gruyère, two apples, several slices of cold roast beef, and a container of raspberry yoghurt.

After eating, he sprawled full length on his couch and watched TV; Captain Kirk of the *Enterprise* was being forced to face a Western marshal in a surrealist showdown. He shut the set off as soon as he fathomed the resolution of the story, tried reading, failed, and then prowled his apartment, pacing north to south, east to west, as if he were a newly committed prisoner trying to ascertain the limits of his confinement.

He had completed his fourth passage and started on his fifth when he looked at his watch and calculated; fifteen minutes to the bar, fifteen minutes back, leaving well over an hour for Dieter-watching; if Dieter were not there, a chess game would clear his mind, if not his spirit.

He put on a down jacket and went to his car. When he reached the bar, he circled two blocks before finding a parking space; there were empty spaces in the bar's parking lot, but he wanted an observation post, not a meeting with Dieter, not even an accidental one.

He hesitated as he put his hand on the ornate brass door latch; he knew he was being childish, but he shrugged off the thought and went in. The after-work contingent that used the bar as a decompression chamber prior to suburban reentry had left, but had not yet been replaced by the nighttime hunters and prey of both sexes. The "restless hour," he thought, for people like himself, and looked about for a chess partner.

A burst of laughter came from one of the few occupied tables near the rear entrance of the bar: the occupants were Dieter, a somewhat younger man and two women, both of them young. One of the women leaned against Dieter; he saw her face in quarter profile and recognized her. She was a sometime performer in porno films of local manufacture, and when not busy in the arts, had developed an enthusiastic clientele for other services. He regarded the scene with satisfaction; Dieter probably did not know it yet, but he was going to have to pay for it, like it or not.

A waitress came over to him, put a white coaster on the small table in front of him, and took his order. She stopped at Dieter's table on her way back to the service end of the bar. When Dieter turned to speak to her, he saw Aryeh, but his face did not change, and he continued speaking without apparent interruption.

A few minutes later the waitress brought Aryeh his drink, after stopping at Dieter's table. Aryeh sipped his drink, at times looking casually in Dieter's direction. The bar remained unusually empty and quiet. Just as Aryeh had begun to think of leaving, Dieter stood up and strolled to the front end of the bar. He examined the bar's bulletin board, then turned; as he passed Aryeh's table, he squatted, back erect, and reached down to the floor. When he stood up, he placed an unused white coaster on Aryeh's table and said politely, "This belongs to you, I believe," and strolled back to his table.

Aryeh stared at the coaster, anger forcing bile up into his mouth. He looked at Dieter, who stood talking to the woman in the chair next to his. Aryeh mentally pinned a target on Dieter's back, took a deep breath, and letting some of the air out of his lungs, slowly pressed a nonexistent trigger, waiting for the moment of release, nurturing the realization that if he had had a real gun, he might have used it at that moment.

The taped music which filled the bar paused for a moment, and he could hear Dieter's voice. Althought he could not make out the individual words, the tone he once described to himself as "Walter Slezak charming" could be heard. My God, that was an intuitive leap I made that night, he thought; not charming, but the Walter Slezak bit was apt. In Hitchcock's *Lifeboat,* Slezak had played the part of the indomitable Nazi, sneering at the others for their weaknesses (Tallulah Bankhead? John Hodiak?). Dieter was sneering at him in the same way; a muttered sentence "I have power over you" could not have been clearer in intent.

But like Slezak's character, the statement had been false. Slezak's Nazi had secreted a supply of water to sustain himself; Dieter had his assurance, and nothing else. Aryeh stood up and walked to the back of the bar as if he were going to the restroom; as he passed Dieter, he pretended to stumble and heard a glass fall over.

"Sorry," he mumbled without looking, and kept moving. He heard small sounds behind him and walked into the restroom grinning, but his pleasure with himself had disappeared even before he heard the door close behind him. That would have been a nice trick if you were sixteen years old, he told himself. Yes, Aryeh, you certainly struck a great blow for humanity.

When he passed Dieter's table going back to his own, he looked straight ahead. No one spoke as he passed, but when he was ten feet away, he heard Dieter say, "It is hard to believe that they were once reputed to be graceful desert warriors."

Aryeh stopped at his table, put some money on it, and walked out into the night. He drove home with precision, his hands at ten and two o'clock, his eyes straight ahead, concentrating on his driving; he returned ten minutes before the time for the meeting, but Martine, Simon, and the Kid had already arrived.

Martine and Simon sat on the apartment house steps, Simon with his elbows planted on the step against which his back rested, Martine facing him, talking; the Kid leaned against the handrail listening to them. They waved when they saw him approaching and went to him.

"Are you all right?" asked Martine, putting her hand on his arm.

"Do you want the fifteen-minute guided tour or a one-word answer?"

"One."

"God knows."

"That's good enough," said Simon. "We were afraid you were going to tell us you were fine, just fine."

"If we're going to stay on the sidewalk, let's play jacks, otherwise let's go inside and wait for the others," said Aryeh and walked up the stairs.

Inside the apartment he said abruptly, "I have something to tell you, something that happened tonight."

"What about Selig and Jean-Pierre?" asked Simon.

"Well," said Aryeh, "I guess I'd better wait for Selig. Jean-Pierre will be here, but late. When I told him about the meeting, he muttered something about wild frogs not being able to keep him away."

"Strange," said the Kid.

Aryeh shrugged. "It's a strange world," he said.

He stood looking out of the window, paying no attention to the others. When the doorbell rang, he said to Simon, "You get it, I want to bring out the exhibits."

He took Dieter's package from a kitchen cupboard and placed it on the living room coffee table, then returned to the refrigerator for the turnip, bits of dried blood on its surface still visible through the plastic sheeting in which it was wrapped. "Exhibits A and B," he said. "For those of you who have forgotten, or perhaps never heard that part of the story, I'll explain again," and described the pecking order the colors represented.

When none of them spoke, he unwrapped the turnip. "Exhibit B, minus the blood. He's been studying his Bible. He's one of Pharaoh's priests, performing the impossible."

Martine said, "My father used a German expression that comes to the same thing, 'You can't put your hands in a naked man's pockets.' "

"We do have to grant him a degree of wit," observed Simon.

"Yes," said Aryeh turning to face him. "Yes, indeed. And I can see you examining one of Ilse Koch's lampshades and saying judiciously, 'One must admit the craftsmanship is impeccable.' Simon, you're the perfect intellectual, you know that?"

Selig, still standing in the living-room archway, said, "Aryeh, it's clear you're hurting beyond that stuff on the table. Has something else happened?"

"Nothing, nothing at all, except I made a damn fool of myself tonight, and Simon's witty Nazi presented me with another calling card," and he described the episode at the bar.

Jean-Pierre came in during the recital in time to hear about the white coaster.

"Have you gone there before, to observe him?" he asked.

"Several times," said Aryeh. "Too many."

Jean-Pierre nodded. "Then that perhaps explains how he came to learn about you, but it does not explain his knowledge of me."

When he finished telling about his discovery of the frogs, the Kid said, "That's revolting."

"What do you think happened to the frogs we let loose?" asked Simon. "Do you think they were put tenderly into a lily pond somewhere?"

"Damn it, Simon," Aryeh said, his voice becoming hoarse, "you're doing it again."

"Stop it, both of you," said Selig. "We can't let ourselves get diverted from the question we have to face. What do we do now that he knows?"

"Continue, of course," Jean-Pierre said immediately. "Only now we strike the blows more fiercely. Why is there any question of that?"

"I don't know," said Aryeh. "I don't know. I don't know where we are, what we should do. Everything's changed. Let me sit and listen to the rest of you."

"That's the point, of course, Aryeh," said Simon. "Everything's changed. The one thing we can't do any more is what we agreed we wanted to do in the beginning: to make him feel what its like to be a victim in a world where he's powerless.

"We can still do things to him. We can finish the plagues, but now that he clearly knows their significance, he's no longer a resident of a world without shape, and he can resist. He has already."

"No, goddamnit," said Aryeh. "I'm confused, but not that confused. The idea that he lifts his little finger and we run like frightened children is unacceptable."

"But Aryeh, I'm not saying that. I'm not saying that we let it rest here."

"Excellent," said Jean-Pierre, and turned to Martine.

"Simon has made me see that you are the only one of us truly risking yourself in this, so I wish to make it clear to you that you are not particularly in my mind when I ask whether anyone here thinks we should let it rest here?"

"What risk?" asked the Kid.

"I'm sorry," Simon said to Martine. "I hadn't expected Jean-Pierre to repeat what I told him."

"It's not the repetition I mind," she said. "It's not knowing what you're talking about, either."

"As I understood it, you're reading the law in an attorney's office, and when you finish, you take the bar. When you pass, you still have to be approved by a Bar Ethics Committee. If any of this comes to them, you'd stand a serious chance of being rejected."

"Nobody here has done anything criminal," objected the Kid. "Certainly not felony level."

Simon shook his head. "It's beyond that, in another area. From their point of view, what we're involved in is fundamentally against the whole concept of law. We've elected to be judge, jury, prosecutor, executioner. Breaking the law is not the point; ignoring it is."

"If you're saying we're the Clantons and he's Wyatt Earp, you're out of your head," said Aryeh.

"Simon, you're talking as if this is Nuremberg, and it isn't anything like that at all," said Martine. "There's a level where what we've been doing is indefensible, but don't inflate it."

"The question before us is one we're all trying to avoid, but nevertheless, it remains," said Jean-Pierre. "What is it you want, Simon?"

"I want us to stop," he said. "But not yet. It seems to me that we have to do one more plague. Then we stop."

"Why should we stop, anywhere?" asked Selig.

"No," said Jean-Pierre. "Excuse me, Selig, but the more interesting question is why Simon wishes to continue for even one more plague."

"It's very simple. Too damn simple, but I'm stuck with it, we all are. It's that we can't let him put the final double bar on the score. In the beginning, the whole concept had a kind of adolescent appeal. You said 'symmetry in the universe,' Aryeh, and it sounded as if we were meting out cosmic justice. But we were like children saying that life isn't fair, as if we sat in Martine's balance scale, waiting for justice to put weight on our side and even helping it along. Now . . ."

He stood up and walked over to the window and slapped the palms of his hands on the sill, then examined them as if he expected to see stigmata. "In the beginning, he was a kind of symbol. Now, we're all symbols. Us for us and him for them. I don't want them to finish it."

"And what do you suggest?"

"That we take the responsibility for ending it. Now. Five instead of ten."

"Murrain," said Aryeh. "A disease of cattle. What do you propose to do, Simon? Will you grow fungus on his Beef Wellington?"

"And what do you write on your students' papers when they resort to cheap sarcasm, Aryeh? Would you have put it that way if nothing had happened and we were moving forward unimpeded? It also means blight, and God help me, I know how."

"For me, I will agree on one condition only," said Jean-Pierre. "If Dieter agrees, that is to say, if he does nothing more after the fifth plague, it is over. But I tell you openly, I am very comfortable with that condition, because he will not agree. Do you expect him to fold his hands and bow his head and accept whatever Simon will do, no matter how small? Never."

"I see it the same way," Selig said, and the Kid nodded vigorously. Martine and Simon looked at each other and then at Aryeh.

"I won't argue," said Aryeh. "If nothing more happens after Simon uses his magic rod, it is all over." He spoke with a questioning inflection, but no one said anything further.

As they left, Martine said to Simon, "If you'd like help, or company, I'll go along."

"Me, too," said the Kid.

Simon put his arm around the Kid's shoulders and said, "Two are enough."

Aryeh, walking to the elevator with them, looked back at Simon and then at Martine. She came up to him and asked, "Are you sure you're going to be all right, Aryeh?"

He shrugged. "Yes, mother."

"I'm concerned for you," she said.

"I'm concerned for myself," he said, touched her cheek with the back of his hand, and walked back to the apartment. He started to open the door, but felt something wrong, paused, and realized he had not heard the sound of closing doors. He looked back; the three of them stood at the elevator, watching him.

If I hadn't gone to the bar before, he thought, I'd go again, then pulled out an imaginary red pencil and printed in block letters: LOGICAL INCONSISTENCY! If you hadn't gone before, you could not go again!

He stood in the living room with his car keys hanging from his index finger and twirled them, faster and faster. As he bent to pick up a glass from the floor, the keys flew from his finger, and moving in a shallow trajectory, hit the brass-wire sculpture. He bent over it, straightening and smoothing individual wires, then began cleaning the room.

He stretched the work out as long as he could, moving with deliberate inefficiency, making as many trips as possible, then resumed pacing the apartment. When he realized he was playing with his keys again, he said aloud, "I hear you," put on his down jacket, and walked out of the apartment.

The night fog had not yet formed; the air was soft and the sky sharp and clear. He drove over to Geary, up to Twenty-fifth Avenue, across to Sea Cliff, and through the Presidio to the Golden Gate. His objective was the view site to the west of the bridge, but it was crowded and he turned back into the Presidio proper, following the road that led him to another view area on the eastern side of the

Presidio. The lot was empty; he pulled in and parked parallel to its guardrail, and sat looking out toward the Bay, brooding.

I could just as well not have been there tonight, he thought. I was just another warm body in that room. For that matter, it's been like that since the beginning. Not that I was ever elected leader of the Commando. Perhaps we never really were a Commando. And maybe it's really all over. Simon said he knew what he was going to do and not one of us asked what it was.

Another car pulled into the parking area and came to a halt a few feet behind him. The sound of its motor died away, but the subdued gleam of the car's orange parking lights glanced off his windshield.

I wish, he thought, I wish ... I don't know what I wish. It's all become vague; the only constant is Dieter.

He had been sitting with his elbows spread wide, his hands clasped behind his head. He let them drop into his lap and slid down into the seat as if a movie were about to start on a screen in front of him. A car door opened and closed behind him; a moment later a young voice asked. "Sir? Are you all right, sir?"

He sat up and lowered his window. A young man stood there; he was about seventeen, casually but neatly dressed, and his hair was long enough to be fashionable but without making a statement. Prep school, Aryeh decided.

"We saw you sitting there, my friends and myself, and we thought from the way you were sitting that perhaps you were in trouble or something."

Aryeh smiled at him. "I'm fine," he said. "Just fine. No problems; just enjoying the view."

"Well, sir, in that case, I hope you'll forgive us for disturbing you," he said and walked back to his car.

Nothing to forgive, thought Aryeh, cranking up the window of his car. My God, this is the self-involved generation? The children of Holden Caulfield? He sat erect, smiling to himself, thinking that there were occasions when life produced the precisely needed gesture.

The headlights of the car behind him suddenly blazed; Aryeh raised his hand without turning around and waved it in thanks and farewell. He heard no motor sound and admired the car's tuning, then realized that the car had not moved. He lowered his window again and listened; their motor was not running. They'll kill their battery like that, he thought, and turned his attention back to the problem of the Commando.

The car light continued to reflect off his windshield, and he began to feel like a prisoner outlined in an interrogation light, his questioners sitting in the darkness beyond. He turned around to look at the other car; the lights seemed to be aimed directly at his eyes, and he covered them with one hand and waved once more with the other. He could see nothing, and the lights continued to fix him in their glare.

Perhaps they were unconvinced by what he had said, he speculated, and were telling him so with their headlights. Whatever; it was time to leave. He started his motor, turned his headlights on, and curved the car toward the Arguello Extension.

His lights illuminated the great mass of eucalyptus trees on the other side of the road, their trunks breaking the light into fingers that probed the darkness beyond. He admired the effect briefly, then realized that the other car had moved quietly behind him, once more bathing him in the glow of its headlights. He pulled away, turning left onto the Arguello Extension, to the entrance into the Presidio from the south. The other continued its pace, a few feet behind him.

In the short distance from the parking lot to the exit, his mood changed from pleasure to growing unease, with no foundation in reason. The car behind him had begun to change from hovering concern to . . . what? . . . he asked himself, and made a sudden sharp left turn into West Pacific, a kind of mews which paralleled the Presidio border. The other car followed.

The surface of the roadway was interrupted with asphalt bumps designed to act as a safety measure to protect children who might be playing on it. When he slowed to a crawl, the other car slowed; when he quickened his pace, the other car followed suit so smoothly that an invisible rope might have joined the two cars.

He came to a full halt at the stop sign on Presidio Avenue, then shifted into neutral, set his hand brake viciously, and got out of the car. As he walked toward the other car, it backed up, matching its pace to his, stopping when he did. When he walked back to his own car in disgust, thinking he had let himself be trapped into some childish game, it moved forward again, then waited.

He got back into his car, engaged the clutch, and made a quick turn onto Presidio. When he came to the corner of Pacific only a few feet ahead, he ignored its stop sign and shot down the next block, prepared to do the same at the corner of Clay, but the lights of an approaching car were already dangerously close, and he braked to a quick halt.

As he made a right turn onto Clay behind the passing car, he realized that the lights behind him had disappeared. He slowed down as the next corner approached, telling himself that the paranoid strain in him had momentarily taken the upper hand, and that his trembling was for nothing. A blur in his rear-vision mirror caused him to look into it; the other car had turned off its lights and sat quietly behind him.

He drove as quickly as he could down Clay; when he realized that he had returned to Arguello, the Presidio entrance to his right, he turned left and drove down the small hill. Ahead of him he saw the Lake Street synagogue, its great tiled dome touched by light from the half-moon. Moved by an impulse whose source he could not define, he slid to the extreme right of the street and pulled to a complete halt in front of the synagogue's main entrance, shutting off the car's ignition and turning the lights off as the car stopped.

The other car had continued its pursuit, its pace slowing as he stopped. It pulled alongside of him, a few feet away, and blinked its lights on and off several times, and then drove away. He thought he heard the sound of laughter, but could not be sure.

He could feel the action of a pulse in his neck, and felt his heart beating heavily. Naive little Selig, he said to himself, did I actually call him that? It's naive little Aryeh, always ready to embrace the idea that good does exist in the world.

Caring, considerate, sweet-faced, vicious little children, playing an amusing game. The next step is lighting fires under sleeping old men in Golden Gate Park. Dieter would like them, he thought, and sudden knowledge pushed its way out of the protective layers of his self-doubts: I want him to pick up the gauntlet.

Part IV
דשבא

1

Simon called Martine and asked, "Can you take a weekday off? We're going to Dieter's place in Inverness; it's a fairly long trip, and it's too risky to do on a weekend."

"Is the plague that involved, I mean time-consuming?" she asked.

"No. The plague itself is the smallest part of it all," he answered. "Two feet square."

"Each day that passes, I value Selig more," she said. "He's the only one of all of us who speaks simply. Wait. I'll check."

Simon leaned his head against the side of the phone booth while he waited, watching a man and a woman at odds with each other. She spoke fiercely, he placatingly; he reached for her hand, and she jerked it away. He began circling; she turned her head away. He talked steadily, and Simon could see her lips forming "but," whereupon the man began talking rapidly, touching her hand, her arm, her shoulder, and finally her cheek. She raised her face to his, looking at him almost supplicatingly; he put his hands on her waist, and she let herself be drawn to him. He kissed her, and arm in arm they walked down the street. The picture of felicity, Simon thought; I'll give him three blocks.

"Yes," said Martine.

"Yes, what?" asked Simon, his eyes still following the couple.

"Yes, sir?" she asked tentatively, then laughed. "Yes, I can take a weekday off."

"Fine," he said. "Thursday? 9:30?"

"Yes. I live at . . ."

"I know the address," he said.

"Fine," she said and hung up.

He left the phone booth and strolled to the corner; on the way he passed the man he had been watching, now alone and looking angry.

Thursday, as they crossed the Golden Gate Bridge, he said, "It's probably shorter to go up 101 and over on Sir Francis Drake Boulevard until we hit the coast, but the coast road is much prettier, and there's less traffic. If you have the time, I'd prefer that route."

"I have the time," she said.

Small bursts of conversation were punctuated with longer silences that bordered on the uncomfortable. Once, when she glanced at him after a long period of quiet, his face was outlined against the ocean to the west, and he looked tense and unhappy. With that olive complexion and that fierce nose, she thought, you could put a desert robe on him and he'd make a perfect Arab chieftain.

Once, he asked in a tone so deliberately casual that she felt her face flush, "Have you known Aryeh long?"

"Years; he introduced me to my ex-husband, but we're still friends anyway. In spite of . . . of anything else . . . I mean whatever else . . . we've always been primarily friends."

He nodded, and said nothing.

"His mind is very interesting, you know," she said. "He treats ideas like soap bubbles and gives them an iridescent sheen, and sometimes I imagine I can hear Indian clubs clicking as he juggles concepts. But . . ."

". . . it's wearing?"

"No, although sometimes I find myself wishing he would say things more directly. It's more than that; no, it's something else. Metaphors can be lovely and poetic, but . . ."

She paused and looked at him and away again, looking straight ahead as she spoke. "Once, when I was wondering whether something could truly develop between us, we were walking along Richardson Bay, on a windy day. Up ahead of us, on the shore, there was a . . . flock? . . . of coots, mud hens, searching for grubs or worms on the shore. I guess we startled them, and they flew up suddenly, all together, and landed in the water about ten feet out. They're not awfully graceful, but that sudden movement, and those plump little bodies with a touch of white at the tail . . . the feeling of spontaneous life was marvelous.

"Aryeh said 'Marvelous!' and I remember thinking to myself, maybe, if we both react to things like that with the same wonder, and then he said, 'Beautiful! A perfect metaphor for people who think they can totally control their own lives.'

'What do you mean?' I asked him, and he said, 'Look at them. Each picked its own landing site, some on the crest of a wavelet, some in a trough. No two landed at the same moment—all out of sync with each other—and yet there they are, all of them, facing at precisely the same angle into the wind.' "

"Be gentle with him." Simon said. "The other feeling might have been there as well."

He paused and his manner became tentative, as if he were offering a gift and did not know how it would be received. "The other night, when Aryeh accused me of being an intellectual, I had a sudden impulse to put up my arms protectively, like this," and he let go of the wheel for a moment, putting both arms in front of his face, "and call out, 'I feel! I feel!' "

He was smiling slightly when he finished, and she thought, whatever problems you have, that isn't one of them. She looked at his profile again and suddenly felt as if she were in her Friday night gymnastics class, hanging from the high bar, swinging back and forth until she became a giant pendulum, her body moving in an ever-increasing arc until she reached the apex of the swing, suspended for an infinitesimal moment above the bar, the magic moment when the world stood still and everything was possible.

She turned away from him suddenly, so that he could not see the flush of discovery on her face; he felt the movement and asked, "Is something the matter?"

"No, nothing," she said. Her voice as calm as she could make it, she asked, "Do we have far to go?"

"We'll be there soon. Afterward, we can stop for a bite to eat, if you'd like."

"That would be nice," she said.

They skirted the end of Tomales Bay after leaving Point Reyes Station; he pointed and said, "Over there, where you can't see it, is the Pacific. His place is up in the hills to our left."

A few minutes later he slowed the car, looking for some landmark of which she was unaware, then turned sharply to the left and followed a paved road up into the hills. After following the road for a half mile, he turned again onto a graveled road, moved along it for several hundred yards, and turned into a road that was hardly more than a dirt track.

Twenty feet farther their way was barred by a weathered redwood gate made of a rectangle of braced two-by-fours, and fastened to a post by heavy rusted hinges. At the opposite end, the gate was fastened to another post with chains and a massive padlock. Neatly centered on the top crosspiece was the kind of sign that is a staple of small-town hardware stores: "No Trespassing. This Means You." Flanking it were other signs, usually sold by stores featuring hand-buzzers and small pillows that emit obscene noises when sat upon: "Guard Dogs On Duty! Survivors Will Be Shot!" and "Trespassers Will Be Violated!"

"I would have expected better of him," said Simon as he pulled to one side and parked.

"My father collects signs like that," Martine said. "He thinks they're funny."

Simon looked at her so oddly that she thought she had offended him in some mysterious fashion, then realized that he was looking through her at some undefined thought.

174

"Martine," he said, "it's not that I'm trying to protect you," he paused, and started again. "I really don't care very much for what I'm about to do, and I think it may offend you, so if you really don't mind, I'd rather go off and do it myself."

"Be careful," she said.

"I don't expect that there's anyone here, but I'll take a look," and he climbed over the gate.

Martine watched him walk rapidly up the road on the other side; it continued for about fifty feet, then curved into an open space in front of a rustic redwood cabin whose covered porch and railing gave it an East Coast look. He disappeared around a side of the cabin, and returned almost immediately.

He waved at her, climbed back over the fence, and went to the back of the car. She heard the trunk being opened; Simon reappeared carrying a corrugated carton from which a wisp of steam escaped. He put the box at the base of the gate, pushed it through, climbed over, and picked the box up. He held it away from his chest and went back along the road.

When he returned he held the empty carton by its lid, threw it over the gate, and climbed over. He put the box back into the trunk, slammed it shut, and got back into the car, his face flushed and strained.

"Do you want to tell me about it now?" she asked.

"Later," he said, and stretched his arm along the back of the seat; she thought he was about to touch her, but his eyes were fixed on his side mirror as he rotated the wheel. He turned and backed twice, then drove out the dirt road and into the town of Inverness without saying anything.

When they sat at an outdoor table in a small coffee shop, Martine said, "Of all of us, you're the one I don't quite understand, myself excepted. I thought I caught a glimpse when you suggested The Conscience Collective, but it's not much more than a glimpse. You seem to keep pulling away, but you stay on."

"I don't understand myself clearly, either, but it might help if you think of me as the wicked brother."

She repeated the phrase aloud, and said, "That sounds as if it should be in italics or at least in capital letters."

"It should be. During the Passover ceremony, there's a passage about four sons and how they should be taught the story of Passover. One of them is described as the wicked son, the one who asks the wrong questions. He asks, 'What does this holiday mean to you?' and there's an exposition as to how by using the word 'you' he separates himself from the others, making himself an outsider. The answer he's given is that if he had been there, during the Exodus, he himself would not have been saved because of that."

His eyes were on hers as he talked, although once he looked down at her hand and touched it with the tip of a finger.

When she said nothing, he added, "For a religion so permeated with love, it made barbaric demands on those in the group."

"Perhaps," she said softly, "that was the only road to survival."

"Perhaps, but sometimes I wonder if survival is enough." He pushed himself out of the angled redwood deck chair in which he sat and walked over to the border of plants between the coffee shop's patio and a side road. He plucked a small section of one plant and brought it back to her.

"This is a succulent," he said. "Sometimes it's called an ice plant. It's largely a desert plant, adaptive to conditions of drought. It stores water in its leaves or stems; that's why it often has a bulbous look to it. When there's no water, it survives even when plants nearby wither, because of what it has stored."

"That's almost admirable," she said.

"Perhaps, but it's not a plant I've ever cared for. Do you know the lodgepole pine?" he asked, and went on without waiting for an answer.

"The tree has a slim, straight trunk, and you can see why it got its name from the Indian use of it. It's a first-growth tree and has a small exceptionally hard cone that it drops in profusion. When a fire sweeps the forest, the heat opens the cone, and the nutrients added to the soil in the fire's wake help the forest reseed and perpetuate itself." He smiled at her. "Beauty, utility, endurance, patience. That's my choice."

"You sound like you're describing your ideal woman," she said.

"Perhaps," he replied, reaching into his pocket for his wallet as he stood up. "Anyway, it's time to go."

They drove back along the same route, more silent than they had been earlier. As they neared the Bolinas lagoon, she touched his arm and said, "Simon, you really didn't answer my question back there. You defined your role in the group, but you really haven't told me why you're in the Commando."

"See," he said. "You're a wicked daughter, you said 'you.' No. I'll tell you the best I can.

"Do you know Resphigi's *Pines of Rome?* In musical form he describes various stands of pines, as they were in ancient Rome.

"The fourth variation describes a stand of pines near the Catacombs, and he uses something like a Gregorian chant. The sound is deep, rumbling, mysterious, and every time I hear that particular passage, something in me growls and turns around. In a different way, the same thing happens to me when I think of Dieter and his kind."

A few minutes later he pulled over on the shoulder, shut off the motor, and turned to face her. "I better tell you what I did back there. Dieter has an extensive garden of succulents, one that Selig's report says he's very proud of. It contains not only the usual varieties you find around here but some exotic varieties from Africa and Korea. I found one whose looks I especially disliked and spread dry ice over a section of it, two feet square.

"Succulents can't stand that kind of cold, and die. When Dieter sees it again, that one small patch will be brown instead of green."

"I'm glad you spared me. And still I want to know whether he'll understand."

"He'll understand when he sees it, I made sure of that. And just in case he hasn't been coming out here, I'll drop him a line."

He started the car, and then switched the ignition off again. "I'll tell you something else, then I'll shut up. In the Passover ceremony, after all the ritual and the feasting, songs are sung. It's one of the loveliest parts of the whole celebration. But even earlier, there's a kind of recitation or chant, *Dayenu*. It means 'it would have been enough,' and it's used in a kind of 'this is the house that Jack built' form, something like this:

"'If Jehovah had let us go from Pharaoh's power and not opened up the waters of the Red Sea, *Dayenu*.'

"'If he had opened up the waters of the Red Sea and not destroyed the Pharaoh's warriors, *Dayenu*.'

"'If he had destroyed the Pharaoh's warriors and not led us safely into the desert, *Dayenu*.'"

He stopped and grasped the rim of the steering wheel so firmly that white patches showed at his knuckles. "Do you know what I almost did back there? He's got an underground sprinkling system; I don't know why, succulents would do well enough from the fog alone. I almost turned it on, the faintest trickle, unnoticeable on the surface.

"Do you know what would have happened? The plants would have gotten too much water, and he wouldn't have known it. The roots of the plants throughout the garden would have started to rot. The plants would have continued to look healthy, until they fell over dead. And I actually considered doing it.

"*Dayenu.* If we had done the blood and not the frogs, *Dayenu*. If we had done the frogs and not the vermin, *Dayenu. Dayenu, Dayenu, Dayenu!*"

When they arrived back at her house, he parked his car across the street. She asked, "Would you like a cup of coffee, or a glass of wine, or something?"

"I think maybe . . . No, thank you," he said, "but I'll walk you across the street."

He walked up the outside flight of steps with her, waited until she took out her key, shook hands with her and said goodbye. She went in; as she came to the foot of the stairs, she looked back. He was still standing on the outside landing, his back to her.

Once inside the apartment she went to the window and looked down, and saw him crossing the street to his car. She watched as he opened the door, paused, partially closed it, and then leaned forward with his arms on top of the car, his chin resting on them. He stood in that position for half a minute, then closed the car door, locked it, and came back across the street to her building.

She ran around the room, straightened a picture that was already perfectly plumb, moved her rocker one degree toward Mecca, glanced at herself in a mirror and began to push a tendril of hair into place, then muttered "Oh hell," and flicked it back again. She paused when the downstairs buzzer sounded and then pressed the button that released the front door catch.

When Simon knocked on her door, she was sitting in an armchair, staring at a copy of the *California Law Review* that she had finished three weeks earlier. She waited for him to knock a second time, then calmly, sedately, walked to the door and opened it.

Simon was leaning against the doorjamb in much the same position she had seen him in at his car, his face hidden by his arms. His face still concealed, he said, "I wanted to explain to you about jelly beans."

"I beg your pardon?" she said, cursing herself for her inanity.

He stood up and faced her, his countenance expressionless. "You see," he said, "it is not commonly known that there are two kinds of jelly beans. There's the ordinary sugar kind, and there's another, smaller kind, made with pectin, and having a slight tartness under the sweetness. We don't talk about jelly eggs, of course."

"I don't believe you're telling me this," she said, but her legs were beginning to tremble, and she put a hand on the doorknob for support.

"Our conversation today was serious, and almost somber," he answered, "and I realized that it was very important to me for you to know that sometimes I have a craving for jelly beans, marshmallow peanuts, candy corn, and even Rachmaninoff."

She stared at him and said, "I can count up to two in Hindustani."

"I know who wrote *The Charge of the Heavy Brigade,*" he said.

"I know the difference between palisander and coriander," she said.

"I know . . ." he started, but she put her hand on his lips and said, "A pox on metaphors. There's a time to talk and a time not to talk. Get in here."

2

Please, Dieter," said Mrs. Zorn. "The road. It's in front of you, not where I'm sitting."

The route they were taking north from San Francisco was an uneasy compromise between the shifting contours of the hills to their right and the coastline of the Pacific to their left; curves were frequent, and cars moving southward appeared with little warning.

Dieter kept watching Mrs. Zorn with pleasure. He found her charming, with the special tone he had noted in women who thought they were still considering whether to have an affair but had already made a decision. The signs were all there for him: she sat relaxed on the seat, one hand trailing out of the window as if the air were tropical water, the other stretched out on the back of the seat, her body turned toward him, laughing at even the feeblest witticism, and using his name in every other sentence.

He was bemused and knew it; the seducer seduced, he thought. When he had seen her that morning in her loose white dress and wide-brimmed hat, looking as if she had just stepped out of the frame of a Renoir painting, two thoughts came together in his mind for the first time without recoiling: Mrs. Zorn and marriage.

They stopped for lunch in Bolinas, in a restaurant housed in a converted Victorian dwelling. The waiter who took their order wore sandals, a thin white blouse that swooped to his midriff, and a Star of

David on a threadlike gold chain around his neck. He greeted them pleasantly, took their order, and moved away; as he left the table, Dieter turned around to watch him go.

"Attractive, don't you think?" asked Mrs. Zorn drily.

"No," said Dieter stiffly, then said, "As a matter of fact, he is, but that is not what caught my attention. It's just that I had not associated the one thing with the other."

Over the coffee, he spoke of the Commando again. "I must admit, I find myself surprised at my own restraint. In fact, I find myself almost regretting that it is all over, now that I know the meaning of the pattern. It would have made for an interesting challenge."

"And as I told you, while I do admire the way you have handled that man Aryeh, and the wit with which you became a magician, the subject tires me. Now, enough of that; show me your hideaway."

When they came to the gate she smiled as she read the signs, but made no comment. Inside the cabin, she looked around and said, "You do believe in living well, Dieter. I had expected Spartan simplicity, I think, but instead you have all these charming furnishings."

"If I tell you that there is only one truly charming thing here, you will probably accuse me of flattery. So I will content myself with saying that the second most charming thing here is the garden. Come, I will show it to you; there are plants from Africa and Madagascar and all kinds of romantic places."

A winding path led up a slope from the rear of the house; it was made of railroad timbers acting as buttresses and steps, the sections in between filled with multicolored small stones from the Pacific shore. The path curved for twenty-five feet through low shrubs and trees; when Mrs. Zorn stopped to look at a flame-colored leaf, Dieter cautioned her not to touch it.

"Outside of the flowering plum, that is one of the few red leaves in this part of the country, but unfortunately, it is poison oak. After I bought this property I fought it for two years before bringing it under control; but its roots go very deep, and it continues to surface."

The path ended at a flat, open expanse crisscrossed by small paths and patterned plantings. Mrs. Zorn said over her shoulder as she examined it, "This is fascinating, Dieter. You will have to explain it all to me. Is that your favorite plant over there, where you have a blue flag?"

"Blue flag?" He looked over her shoulder. "I left no blue flag here. Excuse me."

He moved past her and walked rapidly along the path and stopped in front of a small rough square of decaying plants, some of them already sun dried. In the center of the patch a piece of half-inch dowel had been set in the ground; at its top hung a small, unmarked piece of blue cloth, cut into the shape of a pennant.

"Goddamn them!" said Dieter. "Goddamn them! May their souls fry in eternal fire!"

"What is it, Dieter? Vandals?"

"Vandals? Vandals are mindless. This was done by calculation. By them. Do you not see the blue flag?"

"Yes, Dieter. I called it to your attention."

"Of course, I . . ." He stopped and took her hand.

"Please forgive me. This, this"—he motioned to the dead plants—"this is the worst they have done so far. It is not that the plant is rare; it is, but I can get others to replace them. But they have destroyed a kind of life. It is ugly."

"I agree, of course. But how do you know it is the Commando? The blue flag? Are there things you haven't told me?"

He hesitated. "Some minor details. But I assure you, it is unquestionably them."

He walked a pace or two along the path, looking down at the plants. "I see things like this and feel as if perhaps I do not know myself. The rage that builds in me when I think of these . . ." He paused and looked up at the tops of the hills and said, almost to himself, *"Untermensch."*

"Under people?" asked Mrs. Zorn. "Do I have that right?"

Still looking up at the hills, his eyes studying them as if their shapes and colors bore a message, he said, "When I was a small child, a very small child, I heard my parents use that term, and I took it to mean as you said, under people, people who lived in the ground under our feet, moving upside down, their feet pressed against ours, matching our steps so that we wouldn't know they were there. Sometimes, when I walked, I would pause in mid-step, trying to catch them out."

He laughed without humor. "Once, in the forest, looking for mushrooms with my father and my younger brother, I saw a deep hole in the ground, perhaps made by a mole, and crouched down trying to look into it. When my father asked me what I thought I was doing there, I told him I was trying to see an Untermensch." He folded his hands in front of him, almost in a praying position, and looked at his thumbnails. "They teased me about it for years. The only time I came home on leave, when I was already an officer, there was a little party for me, blood sausage and beer, that kind of thing."

Mrs. Zorn laughed. "Blood sausage? Really, Dieter?"

"It was all we had," he answered and regarded her briefly. "You and I had more at lunch than all of us had that day. It was wartime, and we were never well off."

"Yes," said Mrs. Zorn. "Finish your story."

"During the meal, my father pounded on the table, instructed the younger children to be quiet, and said, 'Dieter, I have an important question to ask you. You have been in the war now over two years and you have seen many strange things and strange places. Tell me, have you found any Untermensch crouching in holes?' and he laughed and laughed."

"What does the word really mean?" she asked.

He hesitated, then said, "It's something that belonged to those times. It meant people who were . . . inferior . . . something like that. You know."

"I'm not sure I do, but I think I grasp the sense. And you still think of them in those terms?"

She spoke pleasantly, but without her earlier warmth, her tone carrying no more than polite interest.

"No, of course not," he said, "and if I ever did, it was without serious thought; I had not even been to college in those days. Rational men do not apply such concepts to whole peoples. But these men—and the woman, too—subhuman, that is a better word for them."

He bent down, keeping his knees from contact with the ground, and began pulling the plants, hurling them into the low growth beyond the garden border.

"A woman," she asked. "The same as the others?"

"No," he said. "She is German." He was still on his knees as he spoke and did not see the expression on her face as she looked at him; it was similar to the one worn by Aryeh the night he had seen him in the bar's mirror.

He stood up and said, "We will go back to the cabin. I need to wash my hands."

"And then we will return to the city," Mrs. Zorn said. "I feel the beginning of a headache."

"But," he said, "but you talked about how good the air felt, how exhilarated you were by the freshness of the ocean breeze."

"That was earlier. I feel differently now."

"No," he said, "that is not it. You are reacting to something . . . something that is perhaps better left as it is. We are both civilized people, and we both know that certain conventions are very useful. Shall we go?"

During the ride home he tried to restore her earlier mood by using his charm as if it were a soothing balm. His manner, as he drove, was quiet and relaxed, and when he spoke, calling attention to aspects of plant life or curious configurations of the coast, every phrase was carefully planned.

At the bottom of a plunging hairpin turn, just before the road shot upward, he pointed to a small stand of tall plants with thick but delicate foliage shaped like green feathers.

"Fennel," he said as they drove by, "a most beautiful and unusual plant. I would drive by here in winter and see ugly, dry, brown stalks standing there, and then suddenly months later, these, in full bloom, but nothing on the ground in between, no signs of what had happened to the old stalks. Then once, at just the right moment in spring, I saw the answer to the riddle; the new growth was growing up the stalk of the old, filling it until a new plant emerged."

"So, in a sense, nothing changes," she said.

"It can, of course, be read that way," he said. "But what I saw was new life arising from decay," and turned his attention to the road. She made no response.

A few miles later, as they reached a narrow deep valley between two scrub-covered hills, he said, "You see that field out there, with the Pacific just beyond? It is worth coming to see in the spring for itself alone. Wild mustard covers that field, so that there is a mass of glowing yellow color against the blue of the ocean beyond. They say that wild mustard"—he stopped, muttered "Uncle Max," then continued—"it once covered the entire state of California."

"You said 'Uncle Max.'"

"Yes, I know. Odd, but I had a sudden vision of his face as I spoke," he said.

At her apartment house he got out of the car and opened her door. "I'll call you," he said, "and I hope you feel better quickly."

She shook hands and said, "Thank you for an interesting day." As she walked away he realized that she had not addressed him by name on the entire trip homeward.

He sat and watched her walk up the steps. The lobby doors opened as she approached, and she walked through, away from the sunlight into the shadow beyond. She might have turned once and acknowledged my presence, he thought, and sat staring at the darkness beyond the doors.

His mind drifted from thoughts of Mrs. Zorn to the succulents, to the Commando, touching and again flitting away without resolution, like dragonflies skittering aimlessly on the surface of a still pond. When the doors opened again, and a uniformed doorman came up to the car, relief flamed in him.

He opened the window on the passenger side for Mrs. Zorn's

message, possibly an invitation to join her in her apartment. The doorman said, "Sir, I'm afraid you cannot park here, but we do have spaces for guests in our garage."

Dieter stared at him, noting the rich color of his skin and the faint tinge of an Oxonian accent. "And how do you know that I am not waiting for Mrs. Zorn?" he asked, in the tones of one speaking to a willfully backward child.

"In that case, sir, I would ask you to park up ahead, to allow others to use this space for disembarking."

"And should I not, what then?"

"Sir, I should call Mrs. Zorn and ask her to explain to you the rules we have developed for the safety and convenience of our tenants."

"And if Mrs. Zorn instructed you to allow me to stay here?"

"Oh, sir," the doorman said, "Mrs. Zorn never instructs, merely requests, sir."

Nothing in his tone, facial expression, or posture gave the slightest evidence of anything but deference. Dieter looked at him for a moment, nodded, said "Touché," and drove away.

He shot out of the driveway into the street and made a sharp left turn, narrowly missing a car coming up the hill; when its driver honked at him angrily, he honked back, thinking, I will show them. But the picture that remained in his mind was that of Mrs. Zorn walking calmly, unconcernedly, up the steps and out of his life.

He drove without pattern, first in the direction of the financial district, some vague notion of going to his office in mind, but the late afternoon sun no longer penetrated the gaps between the steep buildings, and the absence of pedestrians gave the area the look of a city whose inhabitants had fled.

He drove down to the Embarcadero, past the great sheds and wharfs with glimpses of the Bay beyond, all the while weaving satisfying little fantasies in which Mrs. Zorn was the chief figure: either she was calling him, supplication in her voice, apologizing for her coldness, for the thin line of contempt which underlined her silences, or he was being introduced to her again at some dinner party or other, and acknowledging her existence with the faintest of nods.

Slowly the thoughts dissolved and disappeared into the source of the day's angers and disappointments: that patch of lifeless earth, those pitiful little clumps that like himself had been uprooted, then after taking root in a strange land had been attacked by evil.

This day had been destroyed; he had made no plans and could think of nothing of interest to do. He went to see a film that he forgot a block away from the theater, ate a light supper without enjoyment, and returned home.

When time came for bed he had difficulty falling asleep and tried a trick he had learned in the army; he stretched out with his hands behind his head, body relaxed, but instead of inviting sleep, he fought it off, willing himself to stay awake, fighting the onset of drowsiness until raising his eyelids one time more became an intolerable burden. As he drifted off, he muttered "Uncle Max."

Sitting at breakfast, the thought of his uncle recurred. He pushed his coffee cup away, closed his eyes, and leaning his chin on his hands, tried to reconstruct the moment when he had seen the face that he had not thought of in years.

He visualized the scene: the drive down from the ridge, high above the ocean, the curving hill to the valley floor, the horses grazing peacefully on the hill opposite, the meadow that stretched out to the Pacific, the conversation with Mrs. Zorn, then suddenly, Uncle Max. But nothing came to him except the remembrance of Mrs. Zorn's comment about nothing changing, and he understood into what mold she had cast him.

He drove to his office with thoughts of Mrs. Zorn and of his uncle drifting in and out of his mind like the first wisps of fog over the Pacific at the end of a warm day. Then, at a Japanese restaurant, he warned his lunch companion about the potency of the *wasabe,* "One asks for it as mustard, Japanese mustard, but it's more like a delayed-action bomb. Be careful."

Suddenly, the connection was there. Uncle Max, sitting at his favorite table, the *Stammtisch,* with his cronies, telling interminable

187

tales of the war, the Great War, not the war of machines but his war, fought hand to hand by real men – Uncle Max, decorated, wounded . . . and gassed. Gassed, gassed, gassed. Gas. Wild mustard. Mustard gas.

What a marvel the unconscious is, he reflected as he realized what had been revealed to him. Not merely the connection of thoughts, which had been little more than a momentarily intriguing puzzle, but the suggestion that crouched behind it. He could almost hear his uncle, "We set off the canisters, but with bad luck, of which I have had my share; a breeze came from no place, and one of our squads was caught in the gas. And can you guess who was in that squad, young Dieter? Your Uncle Max. When we began to cough they sent us to the hospital; and then, the boils . . ."

Boils. Yes, boils. The plague, the next plague, the sixth plague, his plague. If he continued the game.

Without his uncle, he might not have known how to produce boils at will, that is, if it was a real possibility. Telling himself that it was but passing curiosity, he told Mrs. Reynolds that he would be gone for an hour, and took a cab to the main branch of the San Francisco Public Library.

"World War I?" the librarian asked, and without hesitation said, "You'll find it in History. Turn right as you go in, go to the end of the reading room, and turn right again. You'll see the stacks facing you; you'll find your material on the upper level."

He climbed the stairs to the upper level and walked down the aisle, looking at the overhead numbers that identified the cross aisles. As he approached the one he sought, he found his way barred by a man sitting on a window ledge, writing. His hair was gray and greasy and hung in little ropy strands, and he held a huge sheaf of paper on his lap, writing furiously in letters so large that no more than two dozen covered a page. He wrote steadily, mumbling to himself, but stopped when he saw Dieter approaching, gave him a knowing wink and said, "We'll have to hurry. They'll be coming soon."

Dieter walked around him; he looked back once, feeling both revulsion and fascination, but the man had gone back to his writing.

When Dieter found the section he was looking for, he thumbed through a half-dozen books before he found a description of mustard gas, "Yperite," and its effects on its victims.

At least that once, he reflected, Uncle Max was telling the simple truth, and mentally saluted the old man, dead by now. As he left the cross aisle, he peered down the passageway, and walked out, relieved that the insane babbler had left.

Mustard gas. Would it be possible to find a chemist who could make a very small amount, in no way lethal, diluted in its active ingredient, its effect temporary? Then, feeling as though he had burrowed into a stranger's brain, he shrank away from himself. Had they really brought him to this, that he could consider, even for a moment, doing such a thing? They are making an animal out of me, he thought, an animal like each of them is.

When he returned to his office, Mrs. Reynolds had a look of controlled excitement on her face, almost as if she had bad news to tell him. He took a deep breath and waited.

"The police called, and they'd like you to call Captain Stonehouse's office, when you get a chance."

He nodded and said, "Get them on the phone, please."

When he identified himself, the voice at the other end said, "Yes, Mr. Holzer. This is Sergeant Owens. The Captain asked me to call you to tell you that we haven't been able to trace anything but that we did find something, one fingerprint. But we're afraid it's no use, we've run it through, and nothing. The Captain asked me to request you let us know immediately if something like this happens again, and be careful of handling anything in case there are more prints."

"I see," said Dieter, tempted for a moment to tell the Sergeant where he might find the other nine fingers, and to whom they might be attached. "That is all?"

"Well, there is something queer about that one print, according to the lab. It's on the top of the clock at a funny angle, not the way somebody would handle a clock like that, and there's no matching print on the bottom the way there would normally be. It's almost like somebody put it there deliberately, but it's probably just an accident that they left it."

"I see," said Dieter. "Thank you."

Cunning, very cunning, leaving it like a delayed time bomb, to tell me that they know I can do nothing to them, he thought, then realized that it was no more than a taunt, that they had not expected him to discover their identity.

He knew that it would be easy enough to find some way to provide the police with complete sets of prints, letting them know who was connected to the bomb scare. They could do little with but one fingerprint to go on, but they would poke around, ask questions, and the Commando would know it had been exposed. And if he sent the print anonymously, he would have to say nothing, declare nothing, expose nothing of himself to the police.

But in a way, if he did that, the Commando would have won. They would smile among themselves at the picture of Dieter needing help from the police, unable to triumph by himself. But if he stopped, if he did not carry out the sixth plague, they would think the same thing, that he was fearful of them, that they had succeeded in cowing him.

He could see them, sitting wherever they sat, gloating, rubbing their hands, laughing at him, exulting in what they thought to be their superiority. And yet, he considered, there was another kind of superiority; if he refrained, letting them think what they pleased, if he could be comfortable in the knowledge of his moral superiority, did it matter what anyone thought? Moral superiority; Dieter, he told himself, you are becoming banal. But still, it was worth more thought.

3

Several days later, as he sifted through his personal mail, he found a postcard showing Tomales Bay and Inverness. A tiny blue arrow had been pasted to the front of the card, pointing roughly at the location of his cabin. The message portion bore only a blue pennant.

He looked at it for several minutes, ignoring the rest of his mail, squinting to read the name below the unfamiliar face on the stamp, and reading the description of "beautiful Tomales Bay" as if he were a tourist planning a trip. He studied the photograph on its face, noting a familiar beach, the town, a winding trail he had once walked to the ocean, all the while keeping his mind blank.

Slowly, he began to smile, a small smile of pleasure growing larger and larger. He made a small sound: recorded in outline on' an oscilloscope, it would have resembled the wave forms made by a dog's bark; heard, it would have transmitted the same information as his smile.

It is all changed now, he thought; they could not let it rest, and so they have made a decision for me. It is no longer a question of Germans, Jews, police, sentimentality, or morality. They are the barbarians at the gates, cloaking themselves in imagined righteousness, but in the end what is the difference between the vandalism of vandals and the vandalism of zealots? Yes, he decided, it is now on their heads. They wish to continue? I shall oblige.

He spent the rest of the evening prowling his apartment, weighing ideas: adding one, discarding another, never quite satisfied that he had achieved a balance. On the one hand, he rejected the thought of the boils produced by mustard gas; on the other, whatever he produced must be in accordance with the sixth plague. On the one hand, he did not wish to defile himself by doing what they had done; on the other, it must carry at least the same intimation of their vulnerability.

He stayed awake long past his usual bedtime, but finally found an answer that satisfied him, an equation with equal sides. On one side, their most vulnerable point; on the other, an irritant no more than two inches square, as against their two feet, yet within the description of the plague.

He awoke at the usual time the following morning, but dressed casually, putting a heavy sweater over a thin wool shirt, and drove to Inverness, stopping for breakfast on the way. He ate slowly, still reconsidering his plan. When he got into the car outside the restaurant in Stinson Beach, he hesitated after he started his car, but continued northward.

At his cabin he went to the shed where he kept his gardening equipment, put on a pair of canvas gloves, and picked up a shallow wicker basket and a pair of brush shears with curved blades and 18-inch handles. He headed up the path to the garden but stopped several feet before it opened up into the planted area, and went to work.

As he began to cut he saw that he had exposed several inches of skin at his wrists. He stopped work and went back to the shed, where he discarded the gloves and put on another pair with leather palms and long, flaring wrist extensions. When the basket was filled with cuttings, he brought it back to the shed and used a small shears to remove the leaves from the stems.

He found an old aluminum pot, filled it half full of water, added the leaves, and brought the pot into the cabin. He put it on his stove, lit a match, and turned on the gas, carefully adjusting the flame to a simmer. After cooking the mixture on the stove for over an hour, he shut off the flame and put the pot to one side. Then he drove down to Inverness, called his secretary, and had a cup of coffee. He returned to the cabin, completed the process, and drove back to the city, letting his thoughts drift, and occasionally reaching out to pat a small jar wedged into the back of the passenger seat, its top tightly screwed on and wrapped in aluminum foil.

The following morning he left his office shortly before noon, went to a stationery store down the block, then took his car from the garage and drove to Martine's house.

4

The day seemed unusually long to Martine; the policeman had framed his answers with great care, but she had dug out the information she needed and felt satisfied. Content with her weariness, she put the tape recorder in her shoulder bag, collected her papers, and went home.

As she explored her mailbox, her downstairs neighbor opened the front door and said, "Wow, Martine, is that some uncle of yours! Older men have never turned me on, but I could make an exception for him."

"My uncle?" asked Martine. "I don't . . ."

"He said it was a surprise. You know, he's not all that great looking, but that accent of his. . . . Is he ever charming!"

"Accent?" asked Martine softly.

"You know, kind of Swiss or Austrian, but I guessed you being German, that was it. But anyway, he came by and asked if he could leave a surprise package for you, and I gave him the extra key you left with me for emergencies."

Martine stared at her. "You mean you let a perfect stranger into the house, with all that's going on in S.F.?"

"Oh, don't be silly, Martine. He asked for you by name, and he knew where you worked and all. You know, you're acting funny. If it was me, I'd be running upstairs to see what's in that fancy white package."

"I forgot something I have to do," said Martine abruptly and ran down the steps; her neighbor staring after her. She went two blocks before finding a public phone, and called Simon, fiercely willing him to be home as she listened to the phone ring.

When he answered, she said, "Simon, Dieter was in my apartment today, and according to my downstairs neighbor, he left a surprise package for me, a white package, and I can't bring myself to go in."

"I'll be in front of your place in twelve minutes," he said. "Hang in."

They walked up the stairs together silently. Simon took the key from her and opened the door cautiously, standing to one side and pushing it with his foot. As the door swung to a ninety-degree angle with the wall, a large white package came into view. It rested on the table next to her rocking chair, wrapped in ornate white paper and tied with a wide white ribbon ending in complex swirls.

Simon walked to the table and stood looking down at the package, a hand resting on Martine's shoulder. "The question is," he said, "what is he up to? Is this the second plague, is he picking up where we left off, or simply making a statement?"

"Happy, happy, happy," said Martine. "Frogs or boils. Do I have a choice?"

"Let's see," he said and put his hands on the side of the package. He looked at Martine, shrugged, and lifted it a few inches, then put it back on the table.

"Not frogs. Whatever it is, it's awfully light."

"I'm all right now," Martine said. "Let's take it outside and find out what Pharaoh's priests have sent." She unlocked the sliding glass door which led to a small deck and moved it to one side. Simon picked up the package, and holding it level, carried it to a round metal table.

"Here goes," he said and reached for the ribbon.

"No, wait," said Martine. "I can handle it from here. It's my surprise, after all."

She pulled at the swirls; they came away easily and fell to the table, exposing a small piece of cellophane tape that held the triangular ends of the wrapping paper. She sighed once, gave Simon a tiny smile, and pulled at the tape. The folded ends of the paper rose slightly; she carefully undid the taped triangles, then pulled the paper away from the top of the package, exposing a box with an embossed white covering.

She pushed the paper away from the package and stood looking at the cover of the box, held in place by four more strips of tape. Simon took a small penknife from his pocket, opened the tiny blade, and extended it to her.

She rested her hand on the cover as she cut through three of the tapes, drew a deep breath, cut the fourth, and stepped back quickly as she removed her hand.

194

"Nothing," said Simon and bent down, his ear close to the box. Once again he said, "Nothing." He moved around to the other side of the table and said, "Start lifting the cover, but tilt it up at the same time so I can look inside."

As she began lifting, he motioned her to increase the angle of tilt, shook his head, then picked up the box and showed it to her. "Nothing. There's nothing in there."

"I don't believe it," said Martine, looking into the exposed interior. "Not even a chip."

"There must be something here that escapes us, unless his getting into the apartment is supposed to be a warning in itself, and the package is merely an accent mark."

"He's already accomplished more than that. He's dirtied me, just by having been here."

"Yes," said Simon and put his arms around her. She rested against him, sighed, and said, "We're going to have to search the apartment." Ten minutes later, she sighed again and said, "Nothing seems to be out of the ordinary."

"Martine," he said, "I have a thing over in Oakland in a little while. I can come back after it's over, or if it's important to you, I could probably dig up a sub."

"No. I'm in good shape. Besides, it's my Wednesday night, and even for you . . ."

". . . I know. Anyway, it's rather nice knowing my only rival is a god." She tilted her head and looked up at him. "Woden," he said.

She put her chain lock in place after he left and suddenly felt both hungry and sleepy. She sprawled out on her bed, trying to push out thought, but after a few minutes she said *"Dayenu"* and went to her refrigerator to see whether there was sufficient food for her dinner. Sustenance, she thought as she peered into it, but not pleasure, then decided angrily that Dieter was not going to interfere further with her life and its normal course and went shopping.

She ate dinner before her usual bath; then instead of dressing she put on a nightgown and robe, watched television until all the voices seemed to be saying the same words, and went to bed. She fell asleep quickly.

The following morning she went to the office, discussed the depositions with a legal secretary, then went with her supervising attorney to the Federal Office Building to listen to his oral argument in a case she had been following. The hearing had been set for 10:30, but the previous case was still under argument.

They sat on a rear bench; after a few moments he looked up from the papers he had been studying and said, "Christ, you're restless; keep it up much longer and you'll have His Honor looking at us."

"It's not restlessness. My shoulder blades itch."

"Then go out in the corridor and have yourself a good scratch," he whispered, one eye on the bench. "There's still plenty of time."

"I'd better. It's getting worse by the minute."

She stood in the corridor, arms crossed over her shoulders, scratching with a pleasure that bordered on sexual ecstasy, then stood for a moment enjoying the cessation of irritation and headed back to the courtroom. Several feet before she reached the door the itching began again, and suddenly changed into tiny volcanoes erupting from beneath her skin, sending out droplets of corrosive acid. She groaned involuntarily and put a hand to the wall to keep herself from sinking to her knees.

In near panic, paying no attention to others in the corridor, she unbuttoned the top two buttons of her blouse and reached her right hand over her left shoulder. She could feel a series of protrusions, like tiny boils, as far as she could reach. She pulled her hand away, buttoned her blouse, then wiped away the beads of perspiration on her forehead, neck, and shoulders, and yielding to panic, raced to the nearest lavatory.

She removed her blouse and stood looking in shock at her reflection in the mirror. A wide rough band of tiny reddish pustules ran across her back from shoulder to shoulder, and she could see droplets of blood where she had scratched. She groaned again; the burning sensation had subsided, but the itching continued unabated. She

196

ripped several paper towels from the container, soaked them in cold water, and applied them to her shoulders. She knew the relief they gave her was only temporary, but even the tiny respite seemed a gift from paradise.

She put her blouse on again, trying to keep it from clinging to her body, but wherever it touched the inflamed area, it acted as if it were coarse-grit sandpaper, and she knew she needed professional help as quickly as she could find it.

She found an elevator about to descend and pried its doors open. In the lobby, she started for the main entrance, realized in time that traffic would be going in the wrong direction, and dashed to the Turk Street entrance so quickly that a passerby had to do a jig to maintain his balance. A taxi pulled up at the curb as she ran out the door; she pushed aside the man about to get in, without saying anything.

He was about to protest, then looked at her face and said, "Whatever it is, you need it worse than I do."

"Kaiser Hospital on Geary, the emergency entrance," she told the driver. "There's a five in it for you if you make it fast, and I'll pay any traffic tickets."

"You got it," he said.

He drifted in and out of traffic lanes, keeping just ahead of changing traffic lights, but just beyond Fillmore, a siren sounded behind them.

"Goddamn," he said.

"Please. Keep going," she said.

"Lady, I could lose my license if I don't stop."

She had the door open even before the cab came to a complete halt, and ran to the police car, unbuttoning her blouse as she ran. "Look," she said to the driver, "I've got to get to Kaiser."

He glanced at her shoulder, started the siren again, and said, "Take off. I'll clear the way."

At the emergency room of the hospital an intern took one look at her back, said "Poison oak," and sprayed it with cortisone. Relief was almost immediate; as the itching subsided she murmured "Dear God" and decided that if he had extended it, she would have licked the hand that applied the spray.

Under a nurse's instruction, she washed herself with a medicated soap, trying to cover every portion of her body she had touched after she first felt the rash.

"I'm not very hopeful about this," the intern said. "The stuff goes subcutaneous almost immediately. I'll give you lotion to apply everywhere it crops up, but I better warn you, if it erupts on your face, you're going to look like the entire cast of *The Night of the Living Dead.*"

"How long before . . ."

". . . before you feel human again? That's hard to say. I've never seen a case as bad as this; I'd say you're also having an allergic reaction to the poison oak. Perhaps a week. Certainly not less."

She moaned softly, "Damn, damn, damn."

"Have you any idea where you got it?"

"I have an idea," she said, "and I wish it would go away."

I think what Holzer did was to rub some poison oak on something in the apartment," said Simon. "The gift box was simply misdirection, the bastard."

As Jean-Pierre listened he decided that the meal had been a poor idea; sometime, when this was all over, the three of them might enjoy having dinner together, but not until then. Simon spoke rarely, spending most of his time pushing food from one side of his plate to the other. And look at Aryeh, Jean-Pierre thought; our Commando leader plays games with the waitress, a man on the prowl, no care in the world.

They moved in silence to Jean-Pierre's houseboat after leaving the restaurant. Simon walked with his hands in his pockets, looking down; an Indian scout could not have examined the ground more intently for signs of hostile tribes. Aryeh whistled a simple melody over and over, but his face had lost the liveliness it had when he was talking to the waitress. "My God," he said, pointing. "What the hell is that?"

Walking down the road were a group of men and women carrying shovels over their shoulders, in loose formation behind two figures in black costumes on which white skeletons had been painted, each carrying a scythe.

"Fighters to the last ditch," said Jean-Pierre. "I mean that exactly, literally. They wish to prevent a ditch from being filled in to make way for a parking lot. They say it is a live creek that should be preserved, others call it a sewer outlet, and some say it is no more than an effluent from the Bay."

Simon nodded to the marchers as they passed. "What do you call the group?"

Jean-Pierre shrugged. "It does not matter. It is a lost and meaning-less fight. They are a small group, few supporters, no power."

"But they fight," said Aryeh.

Seated in the houseboat, Simon and Aryeh watched Jean-Pierre as he went to a cupboard and opened its double doors. Facing him at eye level was a three foot length of twine, stretched taut between two hooks at either side of the cabinet. A number of plants hung sus-pended by their roots from the twine. Two of the plants seemed dried out; Jean-Pierre tested the leaves of one with his fingers, then moved to the other. The leaves crumbled slightly between his fingers, and he took a Swiss Army knife out of his pocket and cut a stem and several leaves from the plant, laying them on a piece of waxed paper.

"No," said Simon. "This is not a social occasion. Another time." Aryeh nodded agreement. Jean-Pierre picked up a wooden milk-bottle case, upended it, and sat facing them.

"You were right, Jean-Pierre," said Simon, "and I was wrong. I didn't understand people like him. But I do now, and it's our turn. I want Holzer to suffer."

"The succulents, and what you did to them, you think that failed?"

Simon shrugged and said, "It was not much worse than pouring salt on garden slugs."

"There is a possibility that what he did to Martine in reprisal turned out worse than he expected. He couldn't have anticipated Martine's allergic reaction," said Aryeh.

"Aryeh," Simon said, "I could remind you of your remark about intellectuals, but it would be beside the point. Before, I might have agreed with you, but the moment he walked through her door, even before that, he accepted all the possibilities, and that makes him responsible for what happened. Anyway, that no longer concerns me. It's our turn, and I want to get to him."

"How do we make it hail? And hard enough to hurt," said Aryeh. "That's the important part."

"That dry-ice trick of yours," said Jean-Pierre. "Perhaps we could somehow use that for hail."

"No," said Simon. "I want something different. I've been repeating that line from Exodus over and over in my mind 'And fire ran along the ground,' but nothing comes."

"His car, perhaps?"

"I don't want it to be a simple act of destruction, like setting fire to his car. Nothing like that, but something that fits the plagues and cuts deep at the same time. You have ideas, Jean-Pierre. Everybody's agreed, and we can act when you come up with something. Whatever it is, Aryeh and I will come into it."

"Happily," said Aryeh. "With a great deal of dedication. I brought her into this."

"You both understand that he will retaliate, do you not?" asked Jean-Pierre. "And in kind?"

Simon and Aryeh looked back at him without speaking, and he noted that the expressions on their faces were remarkably similar. Is that the way men looked when they were waiting for a train full of Nazi soldiers to explode? he wondered. Or did they wear no expression at all?

As they walked back to the parking lot, Aryeh in front, Jean-Pierre asked Simon, "You and Martine? Something?"

"Very something."

"And him?"

"He knew without my saying anything. The friendship remains."

As Simon got into Aryeh's car, he said, "There's no hurry. In fact, I would enjoy letting him think we've abandoned the campaign. When we move, it'll be that much more devastating."

Jean-Pierre shook hands through the open window and walked back to his boat. On board, he went to the counter where he had left the cutting and removed all the leaves from the stem, crumbling them in his fingers. He took a cigarette paper from its container, put some of the crumblings on it, and crimped one end. He put the remainder into a small plastic jar that he sealed tightly, put it into the cabinet, and stretched out on his bunk.

After the first deep drag, he propped himself against a pillow and turned on one side so he could watch a huge fogbank slowly rolling over the Sausalito hills from the west, then lay back and let his thoughts wander away. Once he laughed with pleasure at the sight of Dieter's head bobbing up and down against the rafters, like a balloon filled with enough helium to float, but not enough to escape the bonds of gravity.

6

Dieter's housekeeper looked carefully at the parquet oak floor of the living room and hallway, searching for traces of unpolished paste wax, saw none, and put the cleaning supplies away. All that remained was the collection of sheets and towels for the French laundry and a final inspection. She was in the bedroom when she heard the knocking on the front door.

When she opened it, two men stood there in the familiar brown and orange uniforms provided its employees by the Pacific Gas and Electric Company. One man, the nearer, held a clipboard with a sheaf of papers; the other, standing slightly behind him, held a small toolbox.

"Good afternoon," said the man with the clipboard. "We're trying to trace down a minor gas leak somewhere on your feeder line. It's nothing dangerous, but you know how it is these days, any energy waste is important. Can we look at your stove?"

"It's electric," she said.

He turned to the second man and said, "Typical." His companion nodded and said, "Stupid, stupid, but what can you do?" The first man crossed out a line on his clipboard paper and said, "Then it's going to be very easy. We'd like to look at your hot water heater, please. Have you smelled any gas around it recently?"

"I wouldn't know," she said. "It's in a closet and I never go there."

"Well, there's probably nothing there, or you would have smelled something, but we'll look anyway."

She looked past them at the PG & E pickup parked in the alley entrance and said, "This way, but please make it fast; I'm almost finished here and I want to go."

Both men nodded and followed her down the hallway. She pointed to a door; the man in the lead opened it, dropped to one knee, and said to the other, "Put on the light."

The housekeeper said, "There's no light here."

"There should be," the man said severely, turned to the other, and said, "Get the long flashlight from the truck."

The second man disappeared; when he was out of sight of the housekeeper, he went into the living room, opened the catch of a double-hung window that gave access to the alleyway, returned to the hallway, ran outside, and returned with a flashlight.

A few minutes later the man with the clipboard said, "Nothing here. You're in good shape. Thank you."

She walked with them to the door, watched them climb the steps to the next house, and returned to her work. Ten minutes later she left the house, carefully locking it before she went.

Fifteen minutes after she had gone, a truck with a tank and generator on its flatbed and three-inch-wide hoses in coils pulled into the alleyway. On the rear and sides of the tank appeared the words: "Holistic Home Insulation, Inc."

The man sitting in the passenger seat of the truck climbed down, walked over to a window, and pushed up against its frame. When it resisted his pushing, he took a large paint scraper out of his pocket and inserted its edge into the crack between the window molding and the casing around it. When he had broken the paint seal along the window sides and bottom, he put the scraper in his back pocket and pushed against the window; it slid up easily.

The driver of the truck had already removed the lid from a threaded intake fitting near the base of the tank where it lay in a treadle; he attached the hose to it and carried the nozzle end to the other man. While he was returning to the truck, his companion pushed the end of the hose through the window so that a foot of its length was inside, and pulled the window down until it touched the hose. The man at the truck waited until a sheet of plastic had been fitted around the window opening, then started the generator, and after a moment, opened the valve at the tank opening.

A quiet humming began, followed after a brief interval by tiny rattling sounds from inside the house, like that of far-off machine guns.

7

Dieter moved carefully into the kitchen, intent on not making himself an accomplice to destruction. The first presentiment he had that the Commando had once again carried out an operation was the light scraping sound he heard as he opened his front door. He stood still, holding his breath so he could hear better, trying to identify the sound, and waiting to see if it would be repeated. He had pushed the door only a few inches, and there was not enough space for him to reach in and snap on the hall light.

There was no resumption of the sound; he waited, then pushed against the door again, cautiously. He stopped as soon as the sound repeated itself, but the infinitesimal delay between perception and reaction allowed him to move the door enough to reach the switch and flick it up.

The floor of the hallway and living room was covered with what seemed to be small, white, nearly translucent pebbles; every surface, as far as he could see—tables, chairs, cabinets, books—was covered with them. "And hail covered the land of Egypt." He knew this passage by heart, had tried to anticipate some version of it, and yet was almost stunned by what he saw.

The kitchen floor had only a scattering of the pebbles, but he moved in a gait that was almost a shuffle, pushing the bits aside with the sides of his shoes. When he bent down and picked one up, he examined it, then touched it to his lips; it was rock salt, the kind using for the pickling and preserving of meat.

He began sweeping the salt into little mounds, then realized he did not have enough containers to remove it, and confined himself to sweeping pathways through the house so that he could assess the damage.

He discovered the point of entry quickly; a small Victorian table under a living-room window had been scratched by some heavy metal object, but bore only traces of salt. Almost all of the other wood surface had been damaged, but lightly; the greatest damage had been done to the floor which would have to be sanded and refinished.

He walked around sighing deeply several times, then called a hotel and reserved a room for the next several days. Whatever services he required to make the place habitable again were beyond reach by that time of day, and he would not spend the night surrounded by constant reminders of the Commando. He packed a bag, went to his car, and drove to the hotel, then called the housekeeper and asked several questions.

He showered and dressed carefully before going out to dinner, and before putting away the trousers he had worn, he examined the cuffs to make sure no salt had found its way into them. During dinner, and later in his hotel room, he reflected on what had happened with the calm of one who had mastered disaster by fully acknowledging its inevitability.

He had felt shock, he admitted to himself, but not surprise. The nature of what they had done was something he might not have done himself, but it had been well thought out and well executed.

He imagined himself standing on a lecturer's platform at some Army staff school, discussing with the majors and colonels in front of him their reworking of Antietam or Austerlitz or Rostov-on-the-Don. He awarded the Commando an "A" for Planning and Logistics, and another for Tactics. He hesitated when he considered their mode of entry before giving them a "B+" for Intelligence: it was done nicely enough, but what if the housekeeper had asked for ID. No; they would have been prepared. What if she had called PG & E to verify their story? Again no; she would have done that only if she had become suspicious, and they would have had a backup story in any event, or an alternate mode of entry.

He pulled back with amusement at himself for what he had been thinking. After the heavens had opened and decreed that he should be an officer, he had gotten all his training in the field. The lowest rank of all, but still an officer, although that would not have happened, even with his knowledge of languages, if the casualty rate in his unit had not gone above 30 percent.

Briefly, very briefly, for the terrain was dangerous, he let himself speculate on the vagaries of history. If he had been but three years younger, he would have escaped service, exactly like his next younger brother. But then he would have never become an officer, would not for the first time in his life have felt what it was like to give commands instead of receiving them, and he would never have left Germany in the recognition that his rank, while a boon to him in a victorious country, was a liability in that country and because of that particular war.

And if he had been but three years older, he might have fought the entire war, or most of it, and possibly climbed higher. But if so, he might have eventually done something even more . . . He brushed the thought away and returned to the contemplation of his next move.

The pattern of escalation was classic, but it seemed to Dieter that they had leaped a step or two. Why? Eagerness? Hatred? What he had done to the woman? No, it was out of proportion. Were they warning him that they would take control of the sequence, that personal destruction was to come? No; whatever else, they were not madmen. Did they wish him to send out a *parlementaire* with a white flag to discuss surrender, a confession, a capitulation?

What they wanted was not the point; the point was that he recognized that they had made it necessary for him to respond, at a time when the first beginning of a thought had entered his mind: that the time had come for it all to end.

But it was now clear that he must respond, and since they had set the level of response, he would adjust to their terms. But he would spread his reaction over each in turn, first the three who had not yet felt blows, then the others. But first would come a fanfare, a roll of drums, a curtain-raising announcement for their leader.

The world has come full circle, reflected Aryeh; the chair he sat in seemed to have been set precisely where he had been the night it all began. And not too far away sat a woman who might have been an older, more bitter version of the young woman who had told the story.

He thought of one of the favorite devices used by writers of science fiction and poets: the concept of an infinite number of worlds, existing side by side. Suppose he were an inhabitant of another world, where the only differences were that she had not talked about power, or that Dieter had not tried to seduce her with sympathy, what then? Would he have felt more comfortable with himself?

Meanwhile, he was here, and he knew that the bar would soon be nothing more than a memory. When it was all over, he would stop coming here, find a substitute, or perhaps find another way of filling the empty spaces of his life. Meanwhile the bar had become a DMZ, a neutral zone for him and Dieter, where they prowled and skirted each other, looking for signs on each other's faces out of the corners of their eyes.

When the waitress came over to him, he said, "I'm still nursing this one."

"That's OK," she said. "It's that the bartender is going off duty for awhile, and he has a package for you. Do you want it now, or do you want to pick it up when you leave?"

He sighed and said, "Bring it over. I was a Boy Scout once." When she looked blank he said, " 'Be Prepared.' "

She brought him the package and handed it to him carefully, as if she thought he was on something. He looked at the blue wrapping paper and grimaced; we treat colors like a couple of street gangs fighting over a vacant lot as if it were prize territory.

He traced the outline of the package with his fingers, then weighed it: a book, he decided, a novel. Or perhaps a candy box shaped like a book, with "To My Valentine" on its cover and something loathsome inside? Or a letter bomb? No. He sighed and unwrapped the package carefully. The first guess had been correct; there was a book inside, and when he looked at it he told himself he should be amused, but he was not; the book was Nathanael West's *The Day of the Locust.*

He closed his eyes and coùld see the passage in Exodus, on the right-hand side of the right-hand page, the first full paragraph, "For they covered the face of the whole land, so that the land was darkened, and they ate all the plants in the land and all the fruit of the trees which the hail had left; not a green thing remained, neither tree nor plant of the field, throughout the Land of Egypt."

To hell with the eleven continental western states, Simon decided. Eight concerts in fourteen days was excessive; too many strange halls, stranger food, and transportation that was either not on time, broken down, or that rattled. He offered a small prayer of gratitude for northern California as he looked down on the Sierra Nevada, leaning across his cello case in the window seat.

Johann Quantz had the right idea, he decided; after a childhood of carrying a bass viol, he turned his attention to the flute. I'll do that in my next reincarnation, he told himself, and patting the cello case, addressed it mentally with, and I'll stop paying an extra half fare for you, you monster. Still, it gave him privacy, and he wanted it even more than usual.

He had called Martine several times during the two-week tour; each time she assured him that all traces of the attack were gone, mental as well as physical, and each time he heard something behind the affection in her voice, a whisper of something held in reserve, like a composer holding back resolution until the final few bars. She's dissipated the anger that still fills the rest of us, he thought, but she's replaced it with something else, or perhaps she senses something the rest of us don't understand yet.

He looked out of the window again, and for a moment could not make sense of what he saw: a distorted checkerboard of huge red and white squares, then realized that he was looking at the salt-drying beds at the south end of the Bay.

The sky had been clear and sunny over San Jose, but a bank of high fog hung over San Francisco. As the plane banked for its final approach, he could see the southeastern end of the city, the fog curving above it like a huge half-open clamshell; on the water below, a single boat with two white sails sat on the gray water as if permanently anchored. Whatever else, he decided, God is a good stage designer; I couldn't have managed that better myself.

As always, he waited patiently until the other passengers filed past him, then walked down the narrow aisle holding his cello case upright in front of him. Halfway up the inclined passageway leading to the waiting room he saw Martine, her face carrying the same concern with which she had looked at Aryeh the night they had decided to continue.

"What is it?" he asked after they embraced. "What's happened?"

When he tried to disengage himself, she clung to him, and without moving her cheek from his said, "It's him. He got into your flat."

"Not my other cello!"

"No, not that. Not quite. Your plants."

Every third day after Simon left for his tour, Martine came to his house to water the plants. He had a long-term lease on a building in an area once the province of the "flower children" and now struggling to attain an earlier respectability. The building was not quite in the Victorian mode, but was a church-mouse version from the same period. Two flights of outside stairs with a large landing in between served as both fire escape and outside entrance to his flat. Three days earlier she had climbed the stairs, unlocked the door with its outsize key, and found devastation.

Simon's hanging plants were nothing more than green shreds; every cabinet door and drawer in the flat was open, and a parade of ants maintained a continuous march in and out of his kitchen cabinets.

What was left of plant life was infested with aphids.

"I tried," said Martine, "but I couldn't get rid of the bugs. Except for the plants, nothing had been damaged."

"Except for the plants," said Simon.

"There was one other thing," she said.

"Only one?"

"I couldn't decide whether to tell you about it," she said, "since you wouldn't have known if I didn't. But then I thought you have a right to know, and besides, you don't need that kind of protection.

"Your practice cello was lying on your music table, out of its case, and one of your slicing knives was balanced on the strings, near the bridge. I couldn't tell whether it was a threat or . . ."

She stopped; he waited, then asked, "Or?"

"After I recovered, I thought about that for a long time, because it bothered me. I tried to put myself in his place and think like him. I thought of myself, with that knife in my hand, ready to cut the strings or gouge the wood or something. And it did occur to me that I might have left it the way it was, that for a man who goes to Mozart operas, that might have been the point where he drew a line for himself."

"We know where his kind draws lines," said Simon.

10

"This is your apartment?" she asked.

"Yes," the Kid said.

She turned the doorknob. "You left the door unlocked," she said.

"I know. I always do."

"How come?"

"My father once told me a story about his father, my grandfather. He had a little clothing store, and the last thing at night, he would take the money out of the cash register and leave the drawer open. So one day my father asked him if it wasn't an invitation to a burglary.

" 'No,' my grandfather says, 'Anybody who's been around knows that it's empty when it's left like that. Somebody else comes in, finds it locked, breaks it open, it would cost me more to replace the register than it would anything they took."

"That was smart of your father to tell you that story," she said, looking around his living room. "You mean it would cost you more to get the front door fixed than to replace anything you've got here."

"Right," he said. "And my father was right about something else."

"Like what?"

"Well, once we were walking down the street behind a girl wearing a body stocking and jeans, and he sighed and said, 'Reuben, your generation doesn't know how lucky it is. A good half of my generation had no idea of what his wife's body was like until his wedding night, unless he was lucky enough to take her swimming first.' "

"Somewhere in there lies buried treasure, like a compliment maybe?"

"Well," said the Kid, "if sex objects ever come back into popularity, they may use you for the first casting."

She stuck her tongue out at him, then did a series of rapid poses: pom-pom girl, a fast bump and grind, ten seconds of belly dance, then walked to the bedroom with a narrow-eyed look that could have signified either incipient lust or myopia. She paused at the door and said in a throaty tone, "If you need anything, whistle," pulled her T-shirt over her head, and twirling it in one hand, went in.

"I need, I need," he called and stopped at her shriek. He recovered and raced into the bedroom; she stood at the bed, pulled-back cover still in her hand, looking at the sheet covered with dozens of tiny little legs and bodies held together by an obscene brown mass.

He stood staring at them, and barely heard her say, "My God, look there! And there! And there!"

He kept staring at the sheet, his face fixed in disgust. He stretched a finger tip toward the brown mass like a man about to touch a stove he expected to be red-hot; he touched, and his face changed. He pressed harder, and the mass crumbled under his finger. He lifted a tiny piece to his nose and smelled.

"It's not all that bad," he said. "It's only chocolate."

"Only? Only? I want out of here."

11

Selig patted his lips with his napkin, pushed his chair back, and walked to the window.

"It's lovely out," he said. "With luck, it's going to be a perfect day for your ferry ride over to Marin."

"Yes," Sylvia said.

He recognized the tone; it had run through every recent conversation, like slubbed thread in an otherwise smoothly woven fabric. Behind its surface reserve he could hear anger. Another debt Holzer owes me, he thought.

"You're doing it again," she said.

"What?"

"Your fingernails. You keep picking at them."

"It must be some kind of infection," he said. "I'll talk to the doctor."

"It's nice that you'll talk to somebody about yourself," she said.

He pulled a rush-topped stool to the window ledge and put his face to the eyepiece of the telescope. He turned the focus knob and a large white blur resolved into a passenger ship nearing the Gate.

He sighed. "That ship looks so beautiful. We might consider taking it one of these days to Vancouver or even Alaska."

"That's nice," she said. "I mean that you'd actually consider leaving whatever it is that holds you here," and a pulse beat later, "I'm sorry, Selig."

212

Her voice had softened and he tensed. He could hold out against her anger, he told himself, that was the price he paid for what he had undertaken. But he could not hold out much longer against the pain behind the anger.

"Did you put the package in the car?" he asked. "I'm leaving shortly."

He heard her chair scrape and the sound of her sandals slapping against the slate floor. Blessed silence, he thought, peering through the telescope again, then heard a choking sound.

He turned around. She stood in the doorway, her face white, her eyes wide, pointing with short stabbing motions to the door that led from the kitchen to the garage.

He ran to the open door, put a foot on the top step just beyond it, and stopped almost in mid-stride. Facing him was the passenger side of the Mercedes, its interior now possessed by grasshoppers—dozens of them, crawling, hopping, dormant. What he could see of the upholstery bore tiny rents and tobacco-brown spittle.

"My God! My God! My God!" whispered Sylvia behind him.

12

On Sunday, dressed like a San Franciscan out for a day's sailing on the Bay, his clothes clearly proclaiming his purpose, Dieter parked his car on one of the lots bordering the basin in which Jean-Pierre's houseboat was berthed. He walked out on one of the docks and stood with a pair of binoculars to his eyes, looking first down Richardson Bay to the city, then across to Tiburon, up the slopes of Mt. Tamalpais, and then down to the houseboats clumped along the western side of Richardson Bay.

He found Jean-Pierre's boat easily and grunted with satisfaction;

near the stern, he could make out a group of clay pots underneath netting of some kind. After a minute of casual wandering, he went back to his car.

The following evening he dressed in clothes he had brought back from Inverness: paint-stained heavy-duty Levis, work boots, a black sweater with a tear on one side, and a small blue cap with stiff sides and a narrow brim. When he looked in the mirror, he decided that he looked like a North Sea fisherman just in from a herring run, the slight stubble on his face adding to the effect. Satisfied that his appearance would not draw a second glance in the houseboat community in Sausalito, he got into his car, a box of grasshoppers in the trunk.

An unusually heavy fog covered the bridge and a strong wind made driving precarious. The fog thinned after he emerged from the Waldo Grade tunnel but continued to cling to the area.

He drove down the grade and turned off to Bridgeway, then took a left onto the road leading to Jean-Pierre's dock. Potholes and deep ruts had turned the roadbed into a major obstacle course, and he was forced to drive at under five miles an hour. The fog had thickened; his headlights were almost useless, and he could not see the road directly in front of the car.

Fearful of damage to the exhaust system, he shifted into neutral, set the hand brake, and got out of the car to examine the road surface. After mentally marking out a path, he turned to go back to the car, but as he shifted his feet a breeze from the Bay pulled the fog aside, and he saw a group of dark shapes advancing toward him before they were once again shrouded by the fog.

Later, when he recalled the moment, he thought of his initial reaction as a "stab of fear" and was amused to discover that he thought in American clichés; but at the moment itself, it was as if an invisible blade had entered his throat, preventing air from entering his lungs. It's a trap, he thought wildly, and lunged for his car.

He slammed the door shut and locked it. As he released the hand brake he realized that there had been no further movement in the darkness. The fog shifted again, revealing a mass of humanoid figures, frozen in the position he had first seen them. The running engine gave him a sense of security and he waited; when nothing stirred, he turned the car in their direction. His headlights picked out shadowed, immobile, two-dimensional shapes, like tombstones, or curved windows behind which darkness lay, but with human contours. Fear overwhelmed by curiosity, he got out of the car and advanced carefully across the road.

Facing him were about two dozen figures painted on thin sheets of compressed wood fibers, held erect by stakes driven into the ground. Half of them represented women carrying babies, their faces identical, with Picasso noses, and all of them held the babies as if they were Giotto madonnas. The faces of the male figures were more varied, but all were representations of men with short-cropped or no hair, shapeless black garments, and visages set in permanent resignation.

He wandered among the figures until he came to a band of freshly turned earth, slightly sunken below the earth at its borders. Picket signs on long sticks had been implanted in the band: "Let The Creek Flow" and "People's Needs, Not Parking Lots!"

The signs satisfied his curiosity; without knowing details, he could guess at the meaning of the display, and he walked away. The fog had thickened into a faint uncomfortable drizzle, and he brushed away the moisture collecting on his face, then took a last look at one of the male figures and returned to the car.

He sat in it, the engine still running, waiting for warmth to return. He turned on the radio in time to hear the early phrases of the second movement of Mozart's *A Minor Piano Concerto,* and sat listening, waiting for the moment he loved, when the pianist comes to the end of the opening theme, then pauses briefly before dropping into a minor key, somehow suspending time in the interval.

The moment came and went; he sat listening a bit longer, took a last look at the figures, muttered "ridiculous" to himself, and carefully backed up until he found a spot where he could turn to get back on the highway.

When he reached the city, he decided that he needed physical warmth and the comforting bite of alcohol and noise, but not conversation directed at him.

On Union Street he found a bar that catered to tourists looking for the "real San Francisco" and went in. Groups of people were waiting in its entryway; a miniskirted hostess approached him and said, "I'm sorry, but we're full up, and you'll probably have a fifteen-minute wait for a table."

"It's cold and lonely out there," he said, "and I occupy little space. I would take a seat at the bar if you would take pity on me and squeeze me in."

She smiled as if he had offered a solution to one of life's major problems and said, "We'll take care of you," and motioned him to follow her.

He ordered a double Scotch, drank it quickly, and ordered another. He sat sipping the second drink, looking at nothing in particular; once, he stared so fixedly at his image in the mirror behind the bar that it blurred, altering reality and time, revealing a similar but unlined face. I looked like that once, he thought, young, full of the world's possibilities, then thought, no, not you, ever. You worked from the day you could hold a hat or lead the way to a guest's room, hand outstretched, smile at the ready. School, work, youth training, you were nothing but a work animal.

He finished his drink, and although he already felt light-headed, ordered a single, telling himself that it would be his last. He knew he was alternating between sentimentality and self-pity, and worse: he sensed that if he kept drinking he would tell the story again to any stranger willing to listen.

The hostess came by and said, "See, I told you we'd take care of you," and gave him a lingering smile. He smiled back and turned to his drink.

216

She had moved only a few feet when the man seated next to Dieter leaned back from his barstool, examined her legs, and said in a booming voice, "I could show her a couple of ways of taking care of me!" and nudged his companion.

Dieter found the remark, its tone, and the volume with which it was uttered offensive and turned in the direction of the speaker and the man to whom it had been made. Both were men a few years older than himself, typical tourists, he thought, and then realized that the remark had been made in German and that he had been about to respond in kind.

He turned back to his drink again, thinking that the past clung to him like a hump on his back: the Commando, Mrs. Zorn with her "nothing changes." If I told the story to these men, would they turn away, or would they look around, then wink at me and each other, put a hand on my shoulder, and offer to buy me a drink?

He had had enough; he threw some money down on the bar and walked to the door. At the door, he said, "Thank you again" to the hostess. She answered *"Pas du tout,"* looking pleased with herself.

When he looked at her quizzically, she said, "You're French, aren't you? I mean the accent, and all."

He smiled again and left. The fog had thinned and he could see small patches of clear sky, but they became rapidly obscured. He drove home, telling himself that there would be other days for Jean-Pierre and Sausalito. On the way he stopped at a park and released the grasshoppers.

13

On guard? Against what?"

"You can't walk around looking over your shoulder, but be careful."

"It's been three weeks. So far, it's been only Selig, Simon, and the Kid."

"What about the book?"

"A curtain raiser, nothing more."

"Perhaps he's content with what he's done so far."

"Perhaps he's exerting psychological pressure."

"It's been over a month now. It's our turn."

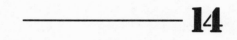

14

They sat in Aryeh's apartment as if in an intercity bus station late at night, each voyager suspicious of the intentions of the next, trying to keep nearby space free of intrusion.

Selig sat in the director's chair, a gold-capped fountain pen in his right hand, taking the cap off and returning it to position, over and over, using only the one hand.

Aryeh sat on the floor, back against the couch, with a highball glass in his hand, moving the melting ice cubes around with his finger, occasionally licking his fingertip.

The Kid stood behind an armchair, resting his elbows on it, his face in his hands, glancing around the room at the others, waiting for someone to speak.

Simon sat with his body inclined, head leaning back, eyes closed, both arms fully extended along the top of the couch, his left hand touching Martine's hair. She sat near him, curled on her side, head pressed against one arm, the other arm resting on Simon's leg.

Jean-Pierre stood with his back to the others at the window, looking into its blackness and the reflection of the room fixed in its depth. He sighed and turned around. If anyone had been speaking, the sound would have gone unheard; it was little more than an intake of breath, but the rest of the Commando turned around to look at him.

He looked back at them and twice made preliminary noises, then turned back to face the window and said, "I think, perhaps, we shall have to consider the possibility of killing him."

Part V

חֵם

1

Jean-Pierre continued to face the window even after the explosion of protest had died away. Only Selig and Martine made no sound. Martine stood up after he spoke and faced him, her rigid body a statement of protest; Selig sat quietly, his face relaxed, but his fingers never stopped their repetitive movements.

When Jean-Pierre turned around again, he addressed Aryeh but looked at Martine directly, as if she were the surrogate for all the others, and her acceptance of his argument would convince them all. He spoke in a low, almost gentle, voice but urgency permeated his words. "It is you, Aryeh, who should be standing here where I am, and explaining the reason for what I have just stated. It is very simple. Arithmetic is on his side."

"I don't understand what arithmetic has to do with anything," said the Kid.

"Now, it has everything to do. All of you know that as well as I do. That is why we sit here and postpone facing what we must face.

"It is we who have the odd numbers, it is he who has the evens, and we all approach the end. We have the ninth plague, darkness. He has the tenth."

"Death of the firstborn," said Selig.

He spoke softly, almost dreamily, looking off beyond those in the room, and Martine shivered. She turned away from him, knelt on the couch, and leaning on Simon, faced Jean-Pierre again.

" 'And the Lord sent out the Angel of Death, and all the firstborn of the Egyptians, even those born of animals in the field, died.' That is how it was," he said.

"No," said Simon. "The Lord sent no messengers, not even the Angel of Death. The Lord of Hosts himself brought death to the land."

"Why are we talking like this?" demanded Aryeh. "Whatever he did once, he wouldn't do anything that barbaric now, not even him."

"We were prepared to," said Selig, his voice as calm as if he were translating lines on a map to help a stranger through unfamiliar territory.

"I never expected it would lead to this," said Martine. "I didn't realize."

Simon put an arm around her shoulders and turned her so that she could see his face.

"Of course you knew," he said. "Whether you realized it or not, the knowledge was behind your reluctance in the first place."

He turned away to look at Aryeh and added, "We all knew, whether or not we were familiar with Exodus, whether or not we could recite the entire list of plagues. The end was inherent in the process. The pressure had to build to the point where something so terrible would happen that the Pharaoh gladly allowed the children of Israel to leave the land of Egypt, even if he changed his mind later."

"But that was then," said Martine, "not now. And not us. We wouldn't have done the tenth plague if it came to that. Never, never."

"Yes," said Selig, "we would have."

When Martine made a tiny sound, he said, "Perhaps not you, perhaps not someone else, but we would have. Not that way, but in some fashion. Think. Why is it we never mentioned the tenth plague when we started, or even when the process was well under way, long before he found out and everything changed? When we began, we didn't say 'nine plagues,' we said 'the plagues.' We never drew a line through the tenth."

"What we did or what we thought is no longer important," said Jean-Pierre. "Let me make the issue clearer. How many of us here in this room are the firstborn of their family, or the only one?"

The Kid said, "Simon," Martine pointed a finger at her chest, and Selig raised his hand.

"Whatever he does," said Simon, "if he does anything, it's very unlikely that he would do it to Martine. The threat was primarily to the Pharaoh's male heirs. And Selig and I can take our chances. Right, Selig?"

"No," Selig said.

He put the cap back on the fountain pen, put the pen into the inside breast pocket of his jacket, and stood up, facing the others, waiting until he was certain they were all looking at him.

"After she was confronted with the grasshoppers in the car, my wife almost went out of her mind. I calmed her down and persuaded her to wait a little longer for an explanation, that I would tell her what had been going on and why I had been acting so strangely. Then after Aryeh called, and she realized that something was still going on, that there would be more, she gave me an ultimatum. What she said is my affair, but I took her seriously." He took the pen out of his pocket and began fingering it again. "So I told her."

He looked down at his hand, watched what his fingers were doing, and took a deep, shuddering breath. "You see, none of you, not even Jean-Pierre, have asked the right question. Not one of you has gone to what is the heart of the matter for me. My wife did, with one word.

"She looked at me with terror when I was finished and said, 'David. Our son David. Our oldest son, David. Our firstborn son, David. You can't let it happen.' And she was right."

"But he wouldn't!" said Martine. "He couldn't!"

Selig shook his head. "There are all kinds of deaths—physical, mental, spiritual, psychological—and none of them are acceptable for David from his hands, not even as a possibility that we will have to live with. I want no more shadows over his life than the world has already put there."

"At least Selig understands," Jean-Pierre said, "and by your faces, I think the rest of you begin to follow. We are back where we began. What will we do?"

"There's only one thing to be done," Simon said. "By now it's obvious. . . . We end it."

"And how do you accomplish that?"

"For one thing, by not doing anything more. He hasn't done anything for over a month now. At first, it seemed as if he were going after all of us for the eighth plague, but for some reason, he seems to have stopped. The reason doesn't matter now. . . . If we do nothing more, neither does he."

"Then it ends that way?" asked Aryeh. "He has the last word again? He takes the shovels back? That was the point of the whole thing, that neither he or anyone like him ever again has the last word."

"And you're willing to sacrifice my ten-year-old son for one of your great concepts?" asked Selig. He raised his hand to point to Aryeh, saw that he was still holding the pen, and threw it to the floor. "Damn you, Aryeh, we're not making a movie out of our lives. We're talking about the future of a ten-year-old, maybe his life. You can't play around with everything in the world until you turn it into a great roaring metaphor!"

"Selig's right," said Simon, but Aryeh turned away, his hands in his pockets.

"Aryeh, please listen," said Martine. "It's true. We're talking about live human beings, not symbols. As much as I despise the man, he isn't a monster."

"I'm willing to go further," said Simon. "If just letting go isn't enough, instead of letting this thing drift along dominating all our lives, all of us jumping at anything unusual, we go to him and identify ourselves, all of us, and tell him it's over. If he's had the last shot, so be it."

"Aryeh, please, what Simon just said makes sense. We did what you wanted to do in the beginning. We really did. And even if we didn't, that's no longer important. Selig's right. What's important now is his son."

"You can say that, Martine, even after what he did to you?" asked Jean-Pierre.

"And even after what we did to him," she replied.

"I will not argue with you, and it is beside the point. What I do say is that this is a man who is capable of anything. He has already proven that."

"And what about us?" asked Simon. "Go back in time. Put yourself in the world as it was five minutes before any of us ever heard of him. Could you have imagined any of us doing the things we have done?"

"That is still not the point," said Jean-Pierre. "Listen to me. We go to him; he listens politely, gives us a charming smile, and then says, 'No.' Nothing more. A simple no. And then we ask what he intends to do. And he gives us another smile and says, 'Wait.' He smiles a last time and says, 'You will find out. If you have given up your plague, that is your decision, but I have not given up mine.' What then?"

"Somebody answer that question for me," said Selig. "Simon? Aryeh? Martine?"

"I don't believe he would say that," said Martine.

"Belief is beyond the point," said Selig. "What if he does indeed say something like that? I have to have an answer to that question."

"We could tell him that we're going to the police and make it clear we're prepared to do it, no matter what lumps we have to take ourselves if we do," Martine said.

"And he would laugh and ask why we have not done that already," Jean-Pierre said.

"More important, what would that do for David?" demanded Selig. "Making that threat conceivably might make him more careful if he sets out to do something, but it doesn't prevent him from trying."

Simon sighed. "Even if he doesn't do something, if we're not convinced it's all over, there could still be damage to David. Selig could become so protective of him that essentially he himself would be the one doing the damage. No. I have to agree with what Selig wants. There has to be certainty, a sure knowledge on both sides, that the whole damn thing is ended for good and all."

"There is no such way," said Jean-Pierre, "except . . ."

He stopped, but no one spoke.

Selig stooped to retrieve his pen, put it back into his pocket and said, "No. Not that. We have to find our way to end it, not his."

Then he looked around the room, his head thrust slightly forward, his lower lip pushing up against the upper one, his face so rigid it might have been carved in stone, and said, "But we have to end it."

Since Selig's attack on him, Aryeh had remained standing with his back to the others, his shoulders slightly hunched over as if he were expecting a physical assault. He turned around, his face alive once again, and said, "The eleventh plague."

"There was none," said the Kid.

"There was none," said Aryeh, "and that's the point. We're stuck in this morass and can't work our way out of it because in the beginning I tied us into the concept of the ten plagues, as if that was the end in itself. The only way to break out is our being prepared to go beyond them, and make him realize that at the same time."

"There's a contradiction in that," said Simon. "How are we going to convince him that we're prepared to go further, if at the same time we tell him that we've stopped, that we're not going to continue with the plagues?"

"That is a good question and it goes directly to the target," said Jean-Pierre. "If you have an answer, tell it to Selig. Convince him and you convince me."

"I can think of an answer, but . . . but I suspect that you'll treat me like the boy who cried wolf. What I mean is, you may think that I'm back on the old track."

"I'll listen seriously," said Selig.

"First of all, I'd propose that we continue and carry out the ninth plague."

"Good," said the Kid.

"No, Reuben, not good. Not the way you mean it, and not the way we've done the other plagues. If we do it, we do it directly, visibly, in front of him, not Commando fashion where we do and run and then watch him out of the corners of our eyes. We do it, and in the doing make clear to him that by exposing ourselves to him, all of us, that we're pledged to ending the situation."

"Make him understand that if there are shovels, we'll be the ones to hand them out?" asked Selig.

Aryeh hesitated and studied his face.

"No," said Selig, "I'm not being sarcastic. I'm listening. Go on."

"I did think seriously about the tenth plague, once. I pictured us knocking on his door some night, very late, and waking him. When he came to open the door, he'd find a real gravestone facing him, with his actual birth date, and a date of death perhaps two or three days after the day we put it there.

"I suggest, now, that we wake him up the same way, but instead of a gravestone he'll find himself facing us, and that we take him someplace appropriate for a suggestion of fear and uncertainty, and that when we get there, we make it clear to him that it's all over. We make the enterprise a kind of earnest of the lengths to which we're prepared to go."

"What are those lengths, Aryeh?" asked Jean-Pierre. "You say that we take him someplace. Splendid. And if he refuses to go with us to this special place, if he resists, what then? Do we use force, do we kidnap him?"

"I don't know," said Aryeh. "Maybe. We'd have to decide that among us."

"Of course we do," said the Kid.

"And if he raises an outcry, if he calls the police?" asked Jean-Pierre. "What then? Do we scatter? Do we run away? No. Aryeh's suggestion is more style than anything. The only way to do it is as if we were real kidnappers and he was our chosen victim—quickly, silently, giving him no chance to call for help."

"No," said Selig.

"No to Jean-Pierre, or no to the whole idea?" asked Aryeh.

"To Jean-Pierre. If we do what Aryeh proposes, doing the whole thing in silence after we first start, a kind of threat hanging over him during the journey to wherever it is . . ."

". . . I know the perfect place," said Simon.

". . . Then it might be convincing. My instinct is that we wouldn't have to face the question of his resisting. His curiosity would make him want to see what we have in mind, and his pride would prevent him from calling for help. He probably feels superior to us, and he will want to maintain that feeling of superiority."

"And that does not bother you?" asked Jean-Pierre.

"If it does, I'll deal with it in my own time and place," said Selig.

"I think we have to do it," said Martine. "All that counts now is getting it over with."

Jean-Pierre walked over to Selig and put his hands on Selig's shoulders. "For the last time, I ask," he said. "I am not arguing, Selig, I ask. What, if then, after we have done all we could, he does not agree? Or, even if he agrees, he leaves a feeling that sometime, someplace, a compulsion will seize him, like it seized the Pharaoh after the Israelites had left? What then?"

"I don't know," Selig said. "I don't know. I would kill him before I would let him harm David, but I cannot believe we have come to that."

Jean-Pierre dropped his arms, studied Selig's face, and walked away. He turned back and looked at the others, one by one, shrugged and said, "I will not pretend I am happy with this, but I can think of a way to make Aryeh's idea work. But not as it is, because it carries a flaw that will defeat it."

He looked around again and said, "I am Dieter, and I stand looking at your faces. What I see is earnestness, determination, conviction, dedication. I also see doubt, self-questioning, a shrinking from physical violence, no matter in what fashion you shape your faces. No matter how fiercely you speak, you do not convince me. I, as Dieter,

230

do not feel fear. And fear is what you must create in him, sufficient fear that if we are to end this matter, the fear will stop him."

"Now it's your turn to answer your own question," Selig said. "How?"

"How is myself. There is only one of us whose face he can look into and know that what is said is what is meant. He knows all there is to know of us, that he has made clear. Then he knows that for me he is no abstraction, that his kind killed my kind, people directly of my blood, that every time I see him I see his feet walking on the graves of people of my own family. If I say these things to him, he will believe."

Martine, in a soft, almost despairing voice, said, "How did we come to this?" then shook her head violently and said to Jean-Pierre, "I think I'm convinced except for one thing. We can't allow this to come down to the two of you, and there's one other who logically should be there with you. Me."

"No!" said Simon. "If balance is needed, then I'm the logical one."

Jean-Pierre shook his head, but before he could speak Martine said, "The two of you, listen. Jean-Pierre, you tried to force me out of this in the beginning; don't try to keep me out of the ending. Simon, it's not a question of balance, it's a question of convincing him. He's not a stupid man, whatever else he may be, and he'll understand that my presence is a symbol of our total determination to end this charade. I'm talking simple sense and you can't deny it."

Simon leaned forward and traced her cheekbone with the tip of a finger. "A character in a play said it for me, 'I have a trembling of the spirit as I hear your words. Fear lays on me like a mantle.' But that was two thousand years ago, and we're not characters in a play. No, I can't deny it."

She pulled his hand against her cheek and said, "It will work, believe me."

"There's still one thing," Aryeh said. "If we do it that way, I mean with Jean-Pierre and Martine as the only ones, and the other four of us, I mean he's going to think . . ."

" . . . You mean that it's as if we were sending messengers to do what the four of us should be doing," Selig said. "Yes. I know how you feel. But it's immaterial now."

"Aryeh, we're all the Chosen People now," said Martine.

Simon clapped his hands together. "We can be there, the rest of us, and it would add to the pressure. We come in another car, but we don't interfere. We don't hide our presence, but we don't proclaim it either. We remain in the background, a kind of dark threat throughout."

"I buy that," said the Kid.

Jean-Pierre shrugged, and Selig nodded.

"If we are agreed, Simon will tell me his 'perfect place' and I will take care of the rest," Jean-Pierre said. "We should act soon."

"The last act, please God," Selig said.

2

Jean-Pierre sat reading at a table made from an abandoned telephone wire spool, its designation marks still legible. A long-neglected cup of coffee sat a few inches beyond the end of the book, small bits of curdled milk clotting its surface. On a shelf beyond, a radio emitted the jovial bleatings of an all-night record program.

When the sound pattern flattened for a moment and a more restrained voice identified the station and announced the time, Jean-Pierre closed the book and tossed it on the bunk. He went to the clothes closet, pulled out a worn Navy pea jacket, and put it on over the heavy black flannel shirt he wore.

Just before leaving the boat, he went to the locked drawer, opened it, and pulled out the blue velvet bag containing the Luger. He took the gun out, examined it carefully, and thrust it into the waistband of his trousers.

When he put the bag back into the drawer, he hesitated briefly and reached into the back of the drawer, pulling out a thin black folder tied with a frayed string. He tugged at the bowknot, opened the folder, and stood looking at one of the two pictures in it, his face showing no change of expression. After looking at the faces in the picture for almost a minute, he tied the folder and put it back into the drawer, then pulled the string of the overhead light and left the boat.

3

Martine and Simon sat on the couch in Martine's flat, her comforter over both of them, listening to the last movement of a Prokofiev violin concerto. The violin, alternately diabolic and lyric, moved restlessly through its song, searching for a resolution that would not come.

When the movement ended, the tone arm continued to move in an endless circuit in the final grooves, sounding rhythmic clicks. Simon stirred, sighed, pulled the comforter to one side. The phone rang as he crossed the room to the record player; but he did not pick up the receiver until he had removed the tone arm from the record and shut off the set.

Then, answering the phone, he listened briefly and said "Yes," listened again and said "We'll be downstairs."

Fifteen minutes later, they walked down to the sidewalk. A horn sounded, and Aryeh waved at them. They walked over to where he, the Kid, and Selig sat in Selig's car, and stood quietly, waiting. A few minutes later Jean-Piere arrived in his pickup.

"My van is around the corner," Martine said. "Wait there and you can park in the space after I pull out."

Jean-Pierre nodded and drove away. Martine and Simon walked to her van; Simon opened his mouth to speak as he faced her, but she put her hand on it, smiled up at him and said, "Do the impossible. Shut up."

She removed her hand, kissed him, and walked around to the driver's side of the van.

Dieter's evening had been pleasant; the food had been well prepared and a touch out of the ordinary, the wine excellent, and the conversation, if not stimulating, had been at least a flight above the threshold of boredom. The evening had almost slipped away before he realized that it was the first time that an entire day had gone by without his thinking of the Commando, for as far back as he was willing to remind himself, and smiled at the thought.

"Something amusing, Dieter?" his host asked.

"I'd say pleasant rather than amusing," Dieter answered. "I was thinking of the taste of the *Schwarzwald Torte* and wishing that I had had the moral courage to accept a second portion."

"There's still time," his host suggested, but Dieter refused and left with the others soon after.

A small turbulence in the air heralded the incoming fog, but it had not yet arrived; he enjoyed the feel of the small currents against his face, thought of a walk in the park near his house, but decided it took something more than moral or physical courage to do so. As he drove away he decided the proper term was something like stupidity.

He found himself thinking of the Commando again as he drove and realized that he had taken a route that brought him only three blocks from the bar. He tempted himself with the idea of a nightcap, then realized that he had not driven in that direction by accident, and that the real lure was the presence or absence of Aryeh.

Not Aryeh himself, he thought. If he went, it would be to see whether Aryeh was there; he himself had been at the bar only twice in the past four weeks, and neither time had he seen Aryeh. And both times the bar seemed a tone shriller than he had remembered, and he had sensed a desperation that he did not want to think about. No, he decided, he was feeling at peace, the thought of Aryeh was an intrusion, and it was time to go home.

He fell asleep quickly, into a soft pleasant dream that seemed to be leading gracefully and uneventfully to the fulfillment of some vaguely desirable goal. As the dream began slipping away he fought to keep it, to continue wrapping himself in its warmth, even as another part of his brain acknowledged an alien sound.

The sound vanished, and Dieter reached out for the dissipating traces of the dream, willing it to return, but it had become formless. At first reluctantly, and then with growing irritation, he heard the sound again and translated its meaning: metal against metal, a knocker against a plate. Someone was at his front door demanding admission.

He turned his right wrist so he could read his watch and pressed the button; computer figures informed him that it was barely past 3 A.M. He blinked rapidly several times, shook his head once, and got out of bed. He walked to the bedroom door, opened it and called out "I'm coming," and went back to get his robe and slippers.

He slowed as he walked down the hallway. He had finally and fully emerged from the dream; all that was left was the memory of having had one, and a question had begun to throb against his consciousness: Who could it be this time of night? As he thought the word "night," other words joined it, unbidden: "darkness" and then "plague" and then "them."

He came to a full stop in front of the entry door, half-turned to look at the living room, glanced at his desk, hesitated once more, then turned back to the door and called out, "Who is it?"

"Martine."

"Yes," he muttered to himself, aware that several feelings were battling for possession of him: anger, resignation, and even a kind of despairing welcome.

He flipped the switch for the outside light and opened the door, leaving the hallway in darkness and standing in its shadows. Martine and Jean-Pierre stood in the alleyway facing him. The pictures he had of them in his desk drawer, next to his revolver, showed each of them in motion, bodies seized by purpose, life in their faces; now, in their physical presences, their faces showing no emotion, they were for a moment less real than the two-dimensional black-and-white shapes in the photographs. He brushed the thought aside and asked, "Yes? What do you want?"

"We want you to come with us," said Jean-Pierre.

"Why? Where?"

Jean-Pierre moved forward a stride. "This is not a social visit. We did not come for conversation. You are to go with us."

"And if I say no? And call for help?"

"Do that," said Jean-Pierre. "Do that. Crawl. I would enjoy the spectacle greatly."

"And if the police come?"

"We have not touched you, yet," said Jean-Pierre. "There will be no police, but if they come, we would tell them what we know of you and what you did and what you have been doing. And after that, you will tell them about what we have been doing to you."

"And when the story reaches the papers, some will think we have been children, and others will think we have been too gentle with you, and still others will envy us. As for you, you'll make the headlines. Rightly or wrongly, you'll forever become 'San Francisco's Nazi Killer,'" said Martine.

While Jean-Pierre spoke, and even after Martine's interruption, Dieter studied his face, then turned to Martine, so quickly that Jean-Pierre moved as if expecting an assault.

"You said 'rightly or wrongly,'" Dieter said. "Does that mean that you . . ."

"It means it's time for you to stop asking questions," said Jean-Pierre. "It's time to go."

"Do you give me your word that no harm will come to me?" asked

236

Dieter. "I ask out of curiosity, not fear."

"Would you actually take our word?" asked Martine.

"We give you nothing, *salaud*," said Jean-Pierre.

"Then, if it is I who offer you my word that I will not call anyone, will you let me get dressed?"

"No," said Jean-Pierre. "Not by yourself. Your word means nothing to us. I will go with you."

Jean-Pierre stood in the doorway of the bedroom watching Dieter dress. When he started to walk to the bathroom, Jean-Pierre said, "No."

"But I have to . . ." said Dieter.

"Fine. That is an unexpected bonus," said Jean-Pierre. "I shall watch with interest as you find a solution."

When Dieter started for the bathroom again, Jean-Pierre said "Look, Holzer," opened his pea jacket, and put his hand on the butt of the Luger. "My friend here says it is time to go, and my friend speaks powerfully. He has already spoken to one of your kind, and is eager to speak again."

Dieter said stiffly, "I do not fear that, or you, or anything you might do."

"Convince me," said Jean-Pierre. "Say it again. I like the sound of the word 'fear' coming from you. Now move!"

With Jean-Pierre close behind, Dieter walked down the hallway, out of the house, and down the alleyway to Martine's van. Jean-Pierre swung the passenger compartment door back and motioned Dieter inside. He climbed in, hesitating a moment when he saw a long-handled shovel lying on the floor near the rear door. Jean-Pierre climbed into the front seat, stationing himself with his body half turned so that he could watch Dieter. As they drove away, another engine sounded nearby, and the rear window of the car was touched with a pair of headlight beams.

Martine drove to Gough Street and followed it over the crest of the hill and down its south slope until she reached the entrance to the southbound lanes of Highway 101. Once on the freeway, she drove at an even 55 miles an hour, carefully signaling every time she changed lanes.

As she guided the car into the turnoff lane leading to the San Francisco airport and San Jose, she glanced into the rearview mirror; Dieter's eyes were reflected in it and caught hers for a moment before she turned her head away. Jean-Pierre saw the movement of her head and turned to look at Dieter; their eyes engaged, but Dieter turned his face away before the eye contact became a battle of wills. Jean-Pierre smiled slightly and turned away.

They drove silently through San Mateo and into Redwood City; when an overhead sign proclaimed Harbor Boulevard as the next exit, Martine shifted into the right lane and clicked on her turn indicator, making sure it continued to signal as she completed her turn. As she neared the Bay, she slowed down; Selig flicked his car lights twice, and she picked up speed again. Dieter saw the flashes of light and tried to look out of the rear window, but Jean-Pierre leaned over and pushed him back into his seat.

A marina came into view, and Martine headed for it. Nighttime fog had clung to the center of the city as they left it, diminishing in intensity as they drove south, but a blanket of it still hung over the lower portion of the Bay. In spite of the fog, small hillocks of some material were visible gleaming dully beyond the marina.

Martine turned the car into a road bordered by industrial and commercial buildings, turning again when she came to a road marked "Private Road—No Public Access."

She drove down the road until she came to a gate whose two wings were held together with a chain and padlock. She braked to a halt, sucked in her breath, and after letting it out slowly said, "Jean-Pierre."

Jean-Pierre turned to look at Dieter, then got out of the car, taking with him a pair of bolt cutters that had been stowed under his seat. He cut through the chain on the first attempt, pulled the gates open and waved his hand. Martine drove through, stopped until Jean-Pierre took his seat again, and drove on.

Large areas of what might have been freshly plowed fields ready for seeding, all foliage uprooted, weeds and flowers alike, bordered the road. But even in the darkness, the fields gave evidence of color: seemingly dark patches turned to white as they passed, and what had seemed to be flat land turned into red pools beyond small dikes.

Martine slowed as they passed a plot that had the same white gleam as the hillocks they had seen earlier, and looked at Jean-Pierre. He nodded, swung out of the car, and said, "Wait." Several hundred feet behind, Selig stopped his car, the engine still running.

Jean-Pierre crossed the road and took a few tentative steps into the patch of white. He stopped, pressed down with his foot, took a few steps more, and returned to the car.

"This will do," he said to Martine.

He waited until she got out, opened the passenger door, and motioned to Dieter to step down. He waited until Dieter was out of the car, then leaned into it and brought out the shovel.

"Here," he said, and extended it to Dieter. "This is for you, *salaud*."

Dieter looked at the outstretched shovel, then at Jean-Pierre and Martine, and put his hands behind his back.

"No," he said.

"Yes," said Jean-Pierre. He pulled the shovel close to his own body, then pushed it against Dieter with such force that he staggered and clutched the handle of the shovel in self-protection.

"Let's go," Jean-Pierre said and began retracing his steps leading to the salt fields, turning to make sure that Dieter followed. Behind them, down the road, Selig's car slowly came to a stop less than a hundred yards away, only its parking lights showing.

Jean-Pierre followed the marks left by his earlier steps, stopped, and motioned Dieter to go a few steps farther. Dieter stood still, but when Jean-Pierre grasped his arm, he twisted away from Jean-Pierre's hand and moved. When he had walked several steps, Jean-Pierre said "Enough."

Dieter turned and faced them, the shovel clasped loosely in his left hand. "Is this the best you can do with your plague?" he asked. "You had taught me to expect better from you."

"We are no longer dealing in plagues. As of this moment, there are no more plagues. It ends here and now, for good."

Dieter nodded but without looking at him, making the action less a response to Jean-Pierre than to some unvoiced thought of his own. Then turning so that he faced the dark waters of the Bay, and leaning his chin on the rounded end of the shovel he asked, "What if I say that it is not finished, that I will not relinquish my turn?"

"One way or another, it ends here," said Jean-Pierre, "no matter what you say."

Dieter turned back and said to Martine, "We could have ended without this. There was a moment if you had come to me . . . But now, threats, a gun, the others sitting back there."

"What gun?" asked Martine.

"It doesn't matter," said Jean-Pierre. "We speak with one voice."

"I see," said Dieter. " 'And the Lord spake with a single voice.' "

"Such words are desecration coming from lips like yours," said Jean-Pierre.

Dieter's face flushed, and his voice rose. "Do you have exclusive rights to God? Is there some heavenly bank where you draw moral interest forever? Is that what gives you the right to do these things, because of what happened thirty-five years ago?"

" 'What happened.' How delicately you put it," said Jean-Pierre. " 'What happened.' It happened. Something happened. Nobody made it happen. Nobody did anything. Nobody was responsible. You compress six million bodies into 'what happened.' "

"Six million," repeated Dieter. "That is what brought us to this? You blame me for it, for all of it? I killed no Jews knowingly. If I killed them, it was not because they were Jews. We were fighting for our very lives. What would you have done?"

He paused, head tilted to one side, as if he were listening to his own words for the first time. "I do not say this as an apology," he added, "because I do not have to apologize to you and your blind morality."

"Jean-Pierre is right," said Martine. "You use words that have no right to be in your mouth. You are fond of saying it was another time and place. We should realize how it was then. We should understand that in the same circumstances we would have acted as you did. We should forgive. And then it will be as if none of it every happened; the corpses will vanish, and we will live inside of a fairy tale."

Jean-Pierre reached down and scooped up a handful of salt, holding it out to Dieter. "Do you see this? Before these ponds are ready for the harvest they take on different colors. But the colors do not matter, it is always salt. Apply it to living tissue and it kills. Like you and yours."

He threw the salt in an upward arc in Dieter's direction. Dieter put an arm up to protect his face, then shook his head to dislodge the pieces that had fallen on it. When he wiped a piece away from his face and rubbed his hands on his trousers, Jean-Pierre said, "Your hands are sweating, *salaud?* Good. They are about to sweat more. Start digging. Go six feet deep."

Dieter stood unmoving. Jean-Pierre pulled his jacket open and pulled the gun out. He pointed it at Dieter and said, "Dig!"

Martine cried, "No!"

Jean-Pierre turned to face her; as he moved, Dieter slid his hand down the handle of the shovel, picked it up, and hurled it in a flat trajectory at Jean-Pierre's gun arm. It missed and hit Martine; the curved edge of the blade struck her neck and she dropped to the ground without a sound.

Jean-Pierre dropped to his knees and bent over her. Even in the darkness, a great bruise surrounded by a thin line of blood was visible on her neck, and she breathed in short, rasping bursts. He cursed, then waved his arm at the others, the gun still clasped in his hand.

Dieter, who had taken a tentative step toward Martine, stopped, pivoted, and ran in the direction of the road. Selig's car had already begun moving, only its parking lights showing. When Selig switched to high beam, the lights of the oncoming car caught Dieter full in the face. He threw an arm up in front of his face, stumbled, fell forward, then still trying to regain his balance, half scuttled, half ran into the darkness beyond.

Even before the car stopped, Aryeh and Simon jumped out and raced to Martine and Jean-Pierre, with Selig and the Kid a short way behind them. The four conferred briefly; the Kid raced to Selig's car and backed it down the road, while the others carried Martine to the van and gently lifted her into it through its back doors.

Jean-Pierre scrambled into the driver's seat, Selig beside him, and started the van. Behind them, Simon cradled Martine's head in his lap, one hand touching her wrist pulse, and Aryeh crouched alongside.

Jean-Pierre turned the van around; as he maneuvered into the final turn, the car now facing the direction from which they had come, he asked, "What do we do about him?"

"We do nothing," Selig answered.

"Nothing?" asked Simon, his eyes fixed on Martine.

"We do nothing," answered Selig. "He's crouching out there where he belongs, in his own *Nacht und Nebel*."

"And that's all?" asked Aryeh.

"No. His papers are stamped Return Is Required. This time, this place, he cannot run away from what he has done. He has to come back out of the darkness."

"And us?" asked Simon.

Aryeh looked out at the water, then turned to look at the spot where Martine had fallen. The marks of their footsteps had become small shadowed pools merging into the night; the only mark of an alien presence was the shovel, a single etched line against the first light of false dawn. He turned again and looked down at Martine's wax-white face and said, "Us? We'll be coming back forever."